TITAN

RISE OF THE KAIJU

WARS

M. G. NORRIS

SEVERED PRESS
HOBART TASMANIA

TITAN WARS: RISE OF THE KAIJU

For Annie, Jill & J.J.
Love always,
Me

Chapter One

Skyler dragged her ruined legs through a lake of blood and champagne. Didn't know where she was going, and didn't matter. Just obeying basic instincts. Instincts that kept her crawling away from what had so briefly been the greatest moment of her life. That moment had passed. So had the lives of all of those people who'd shared in her celebration. All of them were dead. All that remained of Skyler's research team and their project was one bloodstained sack of canisters. She just kept crawling. Kept dragging that burden into the boat's darkest recesses where, she supposed, she would die.

The mutilated thing in front of her was Paul, the project's technical director. It was he who'd first welcomed her aboard the team. Lover of Kansas City jazz music, Italian food, and his dachshund, Peanut, he was now recognizable by his watch, and by the smell of his aftershave. Just another obstacle in her path. Skyler clawed her way over his corpse, and through the shards of a dropped champagne flute.

An empty bottle of the most expensive stuff that a team of government scientists could afford rolled side to side with the boat's rhythmic pitch, clunking dully against the cabin baseboards to the sluice of China's Yellow Sea. Lancet beams of sunlight pierced the scads of bullet holes ripped through the cabin walls. The collective whine of drones was growing louder, as greater numbers of the floating cameras converged on the scene like a swarm of agitated hornets. Every second of the carnage was being recorded, and piped live to the Internet. Their multitudes were grim assurance that Skyler's life was still hanging in jeopardy, and that millions of viewers worldwide were gawping at their screens, straws to their lips, drinking deeply of the last moments of her life with morbid fascination shimmering in their eyes. Cruel memes were probably already popping up all over social media, mocking her fate, her attackers, and prompting endless threads of inane commentary.

Skyler screeched when something slammed against the steel door that she'd bolted shut behind her. They were coming for her. Another impact struck with such force to brighten the room with a flash of sunlight around the seam. Again and again, the cabin strobed with light as the steel door bent around its deadbolt from the blows of what sounded like a swinging axe. They were smashing their way in.

Hitching her way across the cabin floor like a crushed insect, she painted a bright trail of blood wherever she crawled. There was no place to hide where they couldn't track her. Scooting behind a console of scientific instruments, she pulled the sack of freezing cylinders onto her lap, wrapped her arms around the bundle, hugged it tight, and stared at the buckling door. Beyond the crash of steel and humming drones, there was yet another sound that added to the chaos. It was a noise that Skyler couldn't identify, and she hated it. Every deafening roar-grunt was punctuated with the rasp of claws against steel, and what sounded like clattering chains.

"Open the door, little girl. You will live."

Not likely. Not after what she'd just seen happen to an entire crew of unarmed scientists. Popping corks and jubilation were snuffed by the massive shadow that had spilled across their deck, until a rising wall of blackness eclipsed the sun. As though their scientific triumph had disturbed some oceanic horror from its slumbers, the thing emerged from the briny depths until it loomed against the sky. Awestruck, her team stood paralyzed as their boat was dwarfed by the shimmering tonnage that soaked their decks with cascading water that streamed from its back. Once the massive thing became identifiable as a hull of steel, the submarine's portholes swung ajar. Men clambered out, and began dropping like a hatch of spiders from their ratlines. Others racked the bolts of mounted chain guns, and swiveled the huge weapons onto Skyler and her paralyzed crew. Without demands, explanation, or a hint of warning, a thunderous fusillade began hammering the flesh of talented scientists into red mist before spewed jettisons of flame and jingling brass.

A hovering drone eyed Skyler through a bullet hole. The little spy studied her through the punctured steel wall with benign curiosity, before whizzing away. Skyler plunged her hand into the wet sack, and encircled her fingers around one of the twelve frosty cylinders. She could feel the precious liquid sloshing against the container's insulated walls, and her emotions threatened to overwhelm her. This wasn't fair. She didn't deserve to die like this. None of them had. They'd worked so damned hard for so many years, and it was right there in the palm of her hand, the answer to the ultimate scientific question: *are we alone in the universe?*

Another roar-grunt, raking claws against metal. Skyler jammed the canister amidst a rabble of cleaning products, and slid the cabinet door closed. There, her most precious thing of all would hide. Its cooling system contained enough fuel to keep the water sample as cold as the depths of space for another decade, if that's how long it took for it to be discovered. Skyler's last and only hope was that her orphaned canister would one day be recovered by someone honorable, and that she and the others wouldn't have died in vain.

"Oh, God."

A tremendous blow folded the top corner of the cabin door inward, bathing the room in sunlight. A shaved head filled the triangular aperture. Crazed eyes leered from a face that Skyler didn't understand. The lower-half of the man's face was peeled away, showcasing a skeletal grin. The pirate extended his tattooed arm through the opening, fumbled the deadbolt, and flipped it aside. The door exploded inward before a rush of fur and straightening chains, and those roar-grunts escalated to primal screams. Twin beasts, favoring their handler in the skinless aspects of their protruding muzzles, gnashed their bared fangs, and reached for her with splayed claws.

Drones floated into the cabin. The expensive toys of faraway voyeurs jostled one another in their haste to secure positions that would afford the best cinematic angles from which to capture whatever was about to happen to her. Skyler clutched the frigid bundle to her breast, backing into the corner. Nowhere else to go, she could only glower up at the nightmarish face leering over the tussock heads of his leashed baboons.

At this proximity, she could see that the pirate wasn't exactly disfigured. The skinned aspect of his face was in fact owed to a masochistic system of steel wires that radiated from lip piercings to a common anchor point on the backside of his head. It was like a mask—or rather, it was a mechanism by which his face itself was stretched and twisted into a mask.

"What do you want?" she asked, knotting the bag's fabric between her fingers. "I have nothing at all."

It was true. She had no money, and she never wore jewelry. No one aboard this vessel ever carried anything more valuable than a phone or a calculator. Scientists were not wealthy people, and they gave no illusions to the contrary. It seemed a senseless risk and a waste of life for pirates to attack such a boat when the only cargo to be plundered was the treasure of knowledge.

Unable to speak through his facial contraption, the pirate glared down at the bundle in her arms. He hitched his chin, and emitted a throaty bark. The demand was simple enough. He wanted the sack. Whether or not he had any practical use for its contents, it was pretty evident that if she dared to resist him, she would die.

"No," Skyler replied.

This was supposed to be the day of the big payoff. She'd dreamt of this day, and the validation it would bring to her four years of crushing calculations and code to ensure the safe return of an unmanned probe from the depths of outer space. Today, with the whole world watching, Skyler's team had managed to recover the cargo pod containing twelve canisters of water drawn from beneath the icy crust of Europa, Jupiter's frozen ocean moon.

The madman's jaws sprung wide, and he roared at her face. Loosening his grip on the baboons' chains, he allowed the vicious animals another foot of slack. This was her last chance, and she knew it. Violent impulses electrified the demon's eyes.

"I said, no!"

Skyler gritted her teeth, as the thing in the web of wires let chain more links slide through his fingers. Apes lunged at her throat, fangs red and slick with the gore of her fallen teammates, but Skyler refused to relinquish her water samples. She only tightened her embrace. Those canisters were as close to being her children as anyone married to science could ever hope to hold, and if anyone intended to steal them away from her, they would have to pry them from her cold and lifeless hands.

****

Turbines winding down, the Devil Ray settled upon the sea, until the supersonic hovercraft's underbelly was lapped by the waves. Her stealthy profile was reduced to a razor's edge on the horizon. In the distance loomed the black mass of the target. The piratical submarine dwarfed the little patrol boat whose crew of scientists had just been slaughtered. A billowing column of smoke spewed from the crippled vessel. It was an ominous beacon that could be seen as far away as Shanghai.

Collin sucked a deep breath through his nostrils, and exhaled through gritted teeth. This was it. The big day had finally arrived. The Nautical Experimental Weapons Team was going to prove to the Allied Navy, and to the world, that the NEWT program was no laughing matter. If everything went off without a hitch, the military would be forced to recognize their little geek squad as a formidable assault force deserving of some respect, in addition to some continued funding. This test would be pass or fail. Botch the first mission, and they'd be handed one-way tickets right back to their civilian lives.

"Nailed that landing, buddy," Takashi said, as J.J. emerged from the cockpit, and joined the rest of his team in the hovercraft's control room.

"What do you got, Takashi?" J.J. asked. "Any swimmers out there?"

Although their team leader's voice remained steady, the sheen of perspiration on J.J.'s brow betrayed the anxiety gripping his emotions. Collin could relate. He suspected that they were all feeling the same squeeze. Up until now, their program had always seemed like little more than a realistic video game. Not anymore. Things were about to get very real.

"I've got two," Takashi replied, anticipating J.J.'s next question by opening a pair of hologram windows with his fingertips. The pale glow of his ocular implants often widened and narrowed, but those artificial eyes never blinked.

"Which ones you seeing?"

"Disco and Rowdy."

"Alright," J.J. said, clapping twice. He smeared the sweat from his face, and dropped his hands onto his hips. "That's not a bad start. Let's go, Rowdy."

In an instant, tensions throughout the team relaxed by some palpable measure. The first bud of collective confidence began to swell with the assurance that Rowdy was down there somewhere, rocketing toward the scene. Rowdy was the most dominant of their animals, so wherever he went, the others usually followed. Getting them all to a specific location in a short amount of time was the only aspect of a mission that was out of the NEWT's control. Just like human beings, they could be distracted. Something more interesting than the mission could capture their attention, and there were occasionally those days when they'd rather just fool around than go to work. That didn't seem to be the case today. Rowdy's speedy response to the coordinates made it feel as though half the battle had already been won.

"Wait a sec. Here come a couple more." Takashi's fingertips manipulated thin air, conjuring brilliant imagery out of nowhere like some sort of a technical sorcerer. Those bionic eyes of his only added to his wizardly visage. "Looks like we've got Pepper and Moxie."

"Four will work. Let's do this thing. Piece of cake."

"Initiating sync." Jill switched on her laptop controls. "Stand by for the feed."

"Roger." Collin squinted behind the visor of his Mindbender Rift headset, as the choppy video stream began to flicker before his mind's eye. He fought to control his heartrate and breathing before Takashi had a chance to point it out. Nausea passed within a minute or so, but the psychosomatic effects of a deep dive into a host's stream of consciousness could be more serious than a case of vertigo. In Collin's opinion, it was worth enduring a little neurological turbulence for a chance to rocket beneath the waves at fifty kilometers per hour inside the hijacked mind and body of a dolphin.

"Testing streams, one through four," Jill said, as she prepared to switch feeds from one armed dolphin to the next.

Collin relaxed his mind, allowing Jill to hack the implanted network inside his head. It always felt strange being out of control, but he trusted her. Jill knew her way through the whorls of his brain perhaps better than he did. Collin grimaced as she shut down one relay and activated the next, derailing him from one dolphin's sensory stream to another. There was no transition between subjects, just a jarring drop between different bodies. "Check two, Disco. Check three, Moxie …"

"Weapons check, one through four."

Each of the team members had received the same cerebral nanobot implants, the same headset, and the roughly same amount of initial training, as dolphin pilots, but none had taken to the water half as naturally as Collin. As a result, Collin was nominated to be the sheepish star of their show. There didn't appear to be any love lost amongst the others, since each of his teammates had openly expressed their own reasons for relinquishing him the spotlight. J.J. was a physical person, who was more comfortable with the controls of an aircraft in his hands. Jill didn't have the stomach for deep streaming, and Takashi's ocular implants inhibited the visual stream, so he was flying blind.

"You ready to take some pirates to school, Aquaman?"

Collin clicked his tongue, and gave Takashi a thumbs-up. He always maintained a professional level of modesty, but the truth was that whenever Collin was dropped inside the head of a dolphin, the whole experience felt wonderfully natural. He believed that the source of his strength in the streaming seat was his emotional connection to the dolphins. They were more than test subjects to Collin, who enjoyed playing amongst their pod until his hands and feet shriveled into prunes. Being a lifelong introvert, some of the best friends he'd ever made were those dolphins. When a training exercise was over, shutting down the cerebral sync was just the worst. From the point that Jill killed those relays, and yanked the plug on his ocean world, his inglorious return to an awkward human body felt like a small death. There were times when he thought—and he never thought it too loudly—that he might've even been born the wrong species.

"Looks like we've got a couple of inflatable boarding crafts grappled to the bulwarks of the damaged vessel," J.J. said. "We need to take out those chain gunners first, and then focus all our firepower on the inflatables."

"What about the sub?" Takashi asked.

"Looks like a millennial-era model. Double-hulled Russian, if I don't miss my guess."

J.J. never missed his guesses when it came to being a military geek. For having never enlisted in the armed forces, it sometimes seemed incredulous that J.J. should know so much about the military. His expertise occasionally invited teasing from uniformed soldiers and sailors, until they heard the story of his father's sacrifice during the End War, and learned—oftentimes, the hard way—how that particular subject was a can of worms best left unopened.

"I'm saying—can we blow it up?"

"No. No torpedoes. We're authorized to kill pirates, not sink subs."

"Major bummer." Takashi narrowed his bionic eyes to burning slits.

Takashi was just eager. Like the rest of them, he was dying to show the Allied Navy the full power of the NEWT's destructive capability. Their pod of killer dolphins could sink that Russian sub with no more difficulty than if it had been a child's bathtub toy. However, today's mission was a bit of a balancing act. Drones were everywhere, recording everything, and the last thing that any of them wanted was to wind up in some viral video compilation of military fails, right before losing their jobs.

"First target in sight," Collin said.

The NEWTs quieted. All heads swiveled to the monitor that displayed Collin's perspective. Green abysms were rushing by, as Collin maneuvered Rowdy's sleek form alongside the massive submarine. Everyone was surely tingling with the same temptation. Sending that hulking machine to the ocean bottom with one well-placed torpedo would've been just as easy as jabbing a sleeping hog in the butt.

"Oxygen levels?"

"Seventy percent," Jill replied.

The well-being of his dolphin was a top priority, because Collin didn't need to wonder what it felt like to be cerebrally hijacked. Through training simulations, he'd found himself on the receiving end of that transaction more times than he cared to remember. Having your mind commandeered by an outside presence could be a pretty terrifying experience. You had to learn to trust your phantom puppeteer to bring you up whenever you needed a breath, and to release their control whenever the stress levels in your bloodstream indicated that you were having a panic attack. The big difference between dolphin and human hosts was that the dolphins never understood what was happening, or grasped the danger into which they were being thrust.

"Alright," Collin said, "I'm bringing Rowdy up into firing position."

"Permission to fire, when ready," J.J. replied.

Trained dolphin programs in the military were nothing new. Naval forces worldwide had dabbled for more than a century with the notion of transforming the so-called clowns of the sea into living torpedoes. In the end, these earlier programs all fell to the wayside when trained dolphins proved inferior to war machines. Dolphins didn't always follow orders to the letter, and they liked to play around. That was the root of the prejudice that the NEWT program struggled to overcome, despite the fact that their fantastic spin on an old idea was unlike anything that had ever been imagined before.

"Engaging weapon." Collin flipped the left switch on the handgrip. A red circle in the top-left corner of the viewfinder indicated that the dorsal cannons were armed.

"Stand by for shooter mode," Jill said.

The view in his mind's eye was constricted to bobbing crosshairs. Paralyzed beneath the surface, the dolphin's body was being tossed by the waves. That was a situation that could make a pilot become seasick in a hurry.

"Activating stabilizers." Collin closed his eyes, as he flipped a toggle on the handset that closed eight circuits to mercury switches in the lining of the dolphin's vest. Pneumatic valves came to life, and leveled the animal's body with precisely timed jets of seawater. Collin opened his eyes and blinked. Up through the green curtain, atop the black wall of steel, perched a pirate high in a machine gunner's nest. "Locking onto target."

The big difference between the NEWT program and anything preceding it was that the NEWT dolphins weren't trained for combat. Hardly the living torpedoes of the old days, these guys enjoyed the better part of their lives swimming around in the wild, just being dolphins. Their training was limited to responding to coordinates beamed to receptors in the prefrontal lobes of their brains. If they obeyed, and followed a beacon to its destination, they earned some playtime with Collin, and a fish snack. They seemed to genuinely enjoy the human interaction. Highly intelligent creatures, they often towed Collin back to the boat by the little handles on the sides of their vests, as though they understood that boats were where human beings belonged, and not paddling around in the open sea.

Collin twitched when a wet and velvety tongue began lapping at the knuckles of his left hand. Just a little bit distracting because, at the moment, Collin was pretending to be a dolphin. Dolphins didn't have hands, nor did they have pet golden retrievers, beneath the sea. Collin released his controls for a moment to tousle his best buddy's hair. Good dog, but very bad timing. "Could somebody please call the dog?"

"You kidding me?" J.J. was not a fan of their furry mascot. "Hotspot, kennel! Now!"

"Easy, J-man. He's our good luck charm." Collin couldn't see the dog loping away, but he felt the swish of a tail against his arm, and he heard the chuffing breaths and jingling tags fading into the back of the hovercraft, where his kennel and a few favorite toys were stashed. Hotspot didn't have much choice but to obey, because the dog knew that if he ignored an order, his phantom puppeteer would snatch hold of his strings, and override his doggy will. Hotspot was the team's first test subject. The dog was equipped with the same cache of cerebral nanobots as the dolphins, not to mention a few bonus items.

"One day, I'm going to hack into that dog's head and walk him right off a pier," J.J. said.

"Don't do it," Collin replied. "Nobody hacks into Hotspot but me. You'll be very sorry if you try. Trust and believe."

"Fine," J.J. said. "I don't even want to know."

"We've got a problem," Takashi said, swiveling over to the main radar screen.

"What is it?"

"Got a blip coming in hard and fast, six o'clock."

J.J. seized the periscope controls, and swung the topside camera one-hundred-eighty degrees. "Looks like a Mark VII special ops craft," J.J. said. "We've got SEALs on the scene."

"You've got to be joking," Collin said.

"Wish I was."

"What the heck are they doing out here?" Jill slammed her fists against her armrests. "This is our mission!"

"Probably deployed from field command in Shanghai. Someone in the SWCC is losing confidence in us."

"Like they ever had any to begin with."

"We've got no order to abort," J.J. said. "Carry on."

"We must be working cooperatively with the big dogs," Takashi said.

"Not cooperating," J.J. replied, lowering his voice to a growl. "Competing."

"Then what the heck are we waiting around for?" Jill shouted. "Collin? Take your shot, dude."

Collin thumbed the zoom control until the face of the chain gunner filled his sights. He felt his breath catch in his throat, as though he'd just swallowed a bug. Pneumatic stabilizers kept adjusting until the deadly crosshairs were locked and floating on the target as a bright red dot, right between the girl's eyes. Collin could see the sunlight in her eyelashes, the freckles on the bridge of her nose. She was maybe sixteen.

"Collin? You good?"

He heard J.J.'s question, but he wasn't quite ready to answer. He needed a moment. Pirates were supposed to be grizzled men with missing limbs, scarred faces, and tangled beards. Not young girls with expressive eyes that stared right back into his soul.

No matter how many hundreds of exercises he'd completed against inanimate targets, no amount of training could have prepared him for the moment when he'd have to pull the trigger on a living human being. Collin wasn't a hardened soldier, after all. None of them were. They were a bunch of civilians—*nerds*, to be exact—with a government contract and a gamer's enthusiasm for engaging one another in geeky battles. However, there was nothing the least bit redeeming about shooting a young girl right in the face.

"Collin? Hello?"

"I c—" Collin said, choking on what felt like the worst word in his vocabulary. He was in way over his head, and he realized that now. The NEWT program was better off in the hands of trained soldiers than privateering civilians, just as their opposition in the SWCC had been arguing, all along.

"Alright, dolphin time's over, buddy. Move over."

Collin felt J.J.'s hands snatch hold of his headset, as Jill yanked the plug on his out-of-body experience. His arms felt too weak to resist. The strong cocktail of blood and adrenaline that once filled his head had gushed down into the pit of his stomach, and he felt like he was going to be sick. When he opened his eyes, Collin found himself surrounded by a very disappointed team.

J.J. hauled him out of the pilot's seat. He pulled the Mindbender Rift over his own head, and adjusted the visor. "Jill, patch me in."

"It's too late," Takashi said. "SEALs beat us to the punch."

Collin staggered over to the periscope, and grabbed hold of the sweaty controls. He did so more for physical support than to be of any further assistance to the mission. However, what he saw in the viewfinder snapped him back into character. Through the spraying wake off the bow of the SEAL gunboat, there was a sneering face that he knew all too well. It was none other than the spearhead of their military opposition, a warrant officer and deep-sea specialist who harbored a special kind of hatred toward the NEWTs. He'd managed to block them from training anywhere near his jurisdiction, which was here, in the heart of the Yellow Sea. A bad situation had just gotten a whole lot worse.

"Mad Hatter's on board," Collin said.

"You serious?" Takashi gaped up from his radar screen.

The foreboding presence of Miles Bent in Shanghai's field command base was akin to a rolling thunderhead through that labyrinth of corridors. While Bent disliked civilians working for the military, he particularly despised the NEWTs, because their techy approach danced smartly around those primal confrontations that epitomized his more glorified and straightforward style of combat. Over the years, the so-called "Mad Hatter" had leveraged every ounce of his clout in the SWCC in an effort to crush the NEWT program out of existence. Rumor had it he'd earned his nickname by decorating his barracks walls with the hats of vanquished enemies, and rumor further had it that he'd cleared a spot on his trophy wall once he decided to make dismantling their program his pet project.

"Topside, give me a visual," J.J. said. "Dolphin's moved out of position."

"I can't see anything," Collin replied. The Mark VII had swerved right into his line of sight. The gunboat fishtailed back and forth, as if the pilot's intention was to block his view of the situation.

"Jill, switch my feed. Rowdy's gone too deep."

"Pepper's in a good position," Takashi said.

"Switching feeds."

"Bingo. Pepper's on. Got a visual on multiple targets. We've got pirates in the water, boys and girls. Arming cannons."

"They've spotted the SEAL gunboat." Collin zoomed past the oscillating bow of the Mark VII to steal a glimpse of his teenaged girl, who was swiveling her roaring chain gun right onto the SEALs. No hesitation. Looked as though she'd been shredding people with flying lead for the better part of her young life. Collin began to feel a bit like a schmuck. It occurred to him that if any SEALs were wounded or killed in action on account of his failure to take her out, then that was going to be something rather sour to chew on for the rest of his life. The SEALs returned fire. Flames spewed from the Mark VII's deadly armaments, chopping the corridor of seawater between the vessels into foam.

"Something's wrong," J.J. shouted. "I can't see!"

Collin pulled away from the scope, and gawped at the view on the overhead monitor. Torrents of bubbles spiraled up through a swirling crimson cloud. Round and round, the camera spun. Round and round. The glowing orb of the sun waned faintly with every pass until the monitor faded into blackness.

"Switch feeds!" J.J. gripped the sides of his pilot's chair as though he'd actually felt the spray of bullets that had ripped through his dolphin's body. His stricken reaction was shared by every member of the team. This situation had somehow been overlooked in all of their training exercises. They'd failed to ask themselves what would happen to a pilot, if a dolphin was killed while the two were cerebrally synched. "Hurry! God, I'm going down!"

"You're right here, buddy. Don't believe it."

"Takashi? Which dolphins are still with us?" Jill's voice was cracking.

"I can't tell. They're all in there, but …"

"Switch my feed!"

"Switching to Moxie."

J.J. arched his back and screamed. He clawed at the visor of the Mindbender Rift headset, as though whatever sight was being streamed into his brain was actually burning his eyes. The overhead monitor was a cauldron of fire and foam. At the red heart of the inferno leered a hellish face, with lips peeled back in a joker's grin. All the dolphins were smiling, too, even as they burned. That was the irony of dolphins. Like sad clowns, they always appeared to be smiling, and they were wearing those false smiles to the grave.

"They thought those pirates in the water were us," Collin said. He felt like he was going to be sick. "They thought it was time to play."

"They're burning alive!" Jill began to cry. "Do something!"

"There's nothing we can do!" Ripping the headset away from his eyes, J.J. slammed the technology against the floor. He leapt up from the pilot's seat, palms pressed to his forehead, and stormed off in the direction of the cabin. As big and intimidating as he was, the former boxer had one of the softest hearts on the team.

Collin left the periscope. He strode up to the window, and stared in horror at the raging horizon. Swarms of drones spiraled like motes of ash over a flaming sea, where the submarine was slipping beneath the waves. Everything on the surface was left to burn. The bad guys had escaped. The dolphins were gone. The Mad Hatter had won.

"It's over. We blew it," Takashi said, shutting down his hologram displays with a single wave of his hand. "The NEWTs are finished."

"They never saw us. No one did." Jill thumbed tears from her eyes. "The world never even knew that we were here."

✳✳✳✳

With the bag of precious canisters clenched in his teeth, he seized the baboons by their scruffs. The beasts screeched with indignation as they plunged together over the bulwarks, and down into the elemental fury. They didn't linger long at the surface. He dove, dragging the hysterical apes with him, down into the deep. Bullets hacked at the water all around them, lancing past their swimming forms like pale spears. He took both of their chains in one hand, and used his free arm to thresh the water. Glancing back over his shoulder, he was amused to see how out of place baboons looked beneath the sea.

He first encountered the hideous apes on the Burmese coast, just six days ago. They were tethered to the pole of a palm wine merchant's tent, where they grubbed about in the dirt, grunting like hogs, and flashing their fangs at anyone who so much as glanced in their direction. He could hardly stop laughing at them. From the moment he'd first gazed upon those awful faces, he knew that those baboons were coming back to the submarine. They were special gifts for his employer, a man with an insatiable interest in deadly exotics, and in the terror that such monsters inspired in weaker men.

One of the baboons pulled its way up the chain, and sank its fangs into his forearm. He gave both animals a smart shaking for their trouble. They would suffer this small inconvenience before beginning their pampered lives in their new owner's compound, deep in the heart of Mongolia. Wrenching the pair of knuckleheads along by their chains, he scissor-kicked in the direction of the submarine.

A staccato of dull impacts filled his ears. Another phalanx of white spears stabbed downward from the heavens. One struck him dead in the chest. The impact slammed the breath from his lungs in an eruption of silvery blobs that wobbled toward the burning surface. A frigid jettison of water blasting wildly against throbbing chest brought him back to his senses, and he realized that a can of moon juice had saved his life. One canister had taken the brunt of the bullet, and its steel skin had been punctured. He could feel it knocking around inside the sack, spinning and tumbling, as it released its pressurized contents into the sea.

The sub looked so far away, and there was no chance for another breath of air. The surface world was a ceiling of moiling flames. When he'd first hatched the idea of raiding the patrol boat with a couple of chained monsters at his sides, it had seemed like a pretty wild gimmick. However, bringing them along had perhaps been a poor decision. They were only slowing him down. One of the baboons began to spasm in unnatural ways. Its eyes rolled skyward, and its fangs snapped at the salty torrent of fluid rushing into its lungs. A burst of bubbles escaped his nostrils. It was kind of funny to watch a baboon drown.

Then, it came to him. Like the spirit of some fallen friend, it slid out of the gloom to quell even the baboons with a portentous moment of wonderment beneath the waves. Here, met different creatures who never in the whole of their lives should've chanced to look upon the other. Its laughing eyes, its toothy smile, it appeared barely able to contain its amusement over some darkly private joke.

With his free hand, he snatched hold of the little handle on the side of the creature's vest, because at once, he'd fallen in love with it. He would have this creature as well, or he'd drown with baboons clenched in one hand, and this thing in the other. There was some remarkable intelligence behind that dark eye that peered askew into his own, almost as though this creature knew of deeper shared connections than his human mind was able to grasp. Oh, but it was true, because as though his new friend had performed the same trick a hundred times, it knew just where to take him. With a powerful thrust of its flukes, they were off, rocketing toward the submarine.

Chapter Two

The journey was long and cold. Many did not survive. Those who saw release from their frigid prison were received by the warmest of green seas, but there was no celebration. These were microscopic entities, tiny things, whose whole universe was but a droplet of water. Aware, but hardly cognizant, they went on to perform the same tricks their kind had done since time's beginning. However, something had gone wrong inside of them, or perhaps it had at last gone right, because genetic potential buried within this menagerie was unearthed in the favorable conditions of their rich, new world, and the sluggish arms race of a frozen moon was throttled up into overdrive, favoring the monstrous, and the grotesque. Strong slaked their appetites for the weak, big begat bigger, until after the first year, the enormity of the invaders was the wonder of the undersea world, and the numbers surpassed even the stars in the sky.

One sort was a lover of light. Their fondness for luminescence was a relic from the old world, where light had been a scarce resource. Trapped beneath miles of dense ice, enveloped in utter blackness, their ancestors had learned to generate lights of their own. Flamboyant rituals became their new language of love, as well as a declaration of war. Dazzling displays came to fill those frigid seas, as males strove to outshine their competition. Coupled in courtship, and in clashes, their garish spectacles didn't go unnoticed, and the flesh-eaters closed in.

***

Her eyestalks broke the surface. Dilating in the radiance, her eyes seemed to absorb the shoreline spectacle with much the same dependence as petals spread before the sun. There were lights within lights. There were streams of light that flowed. There were flickering blips, roving tracers, and complex panels of flashing nuances that continually changed pattern, hue, and intensity. Tiny lights arranged in stacked columns formed twinkling reefs of organized structures that jutted to heights that rivaled her own. Having been allured by the distant glow of this place from hundreds of miles out to sea, she remained transfixed by its ethereal beauty. She was so enraptured, in fact, that she'd failed to notice that she'd been followed.

The ocean behind her swelled. She turned, emitting a defensive rattle. A spiked carapace rose, clattering from the depths. It was a male, and a big one. Glimmering lights reflected in its expressionless eyes, eyes that possessed the same gaping awareness from the moment of its hatching until its death. The hue of bioluminescent striations that fluted his armor burned with the hellish color of a thermal vent. Hooked mandibles splayed at the light source rivalling his own display.

The female edged aside. She sensed that a fight was imminent. Her suitor reared back on his massive hindquarters, clattered his pincers at the stars, and swung his horned head from side to side. Toppling into the sea with a thunderous explosion, he charged toward the heart of the luminosity.

Every male was born with a burden of armor. The weight of weaponry hung heavily upon his head. Oppressed by the natural laws of a world poised to destroy or deny him, he'd little choice to but to embrace that decree of his being that demanded he wage a forever war against every light in his path, until every last twinkle but his own was smashed to blackness.

From the safety of the sea, she watched her mate obliterate the lights. She admired his sweeping horns that slashed through towering columns, and the rippling bulk of his sheer tonnage, as he reared and plunged into the ground. Whole sections of the colony flickered and died with every blow, as the alpha male bulldozed its core. The flowing streams of lights slowed to a stop. A massive cloud spread from the epicenter of the carnage, and spilled out over the sea. Only the spiked back of her mate's carapace remained visible above the haze. Evidently satisfied with the level of destruction he'd wrought, the alpha male's bioluminescent signature cooled to a lavender hue as he departed the smoldering ruins, and returned to the sea.

Although the destruction of lights didn't bring her the same satisfaction, she understood him, and she was aroused by his display. This one had pursued her, only her, all the way across the ocean. He'd proven himself as being focused, loyal, and very powerful. Here was a male who would defend her against the flesh-eaters of the deep, the great ones that inhabited the darkest trenches, and he'd protect their brood from the slithering hordes of scavengers. This one had passed every test. She accepted him as her mate.

****

"Order of bangers and mashed—and be careful, the plate is really hot. I'll get you a refill on that pale ale, and if you need anything else, my name's Collin."

"Is your name Collin even if I don't need anything else?"

His companions all laughed. It took Collin a few seconds to wrap his mind around the joke, and once he'd done so, he found it to be more annoying than humorous. When he was at work, he was normally running on autopilot, protecting his introverted mind from the restaurant's barrage of stimuli by steering his thoughts elsewhere, anywhere but where he actually was.

"Yeah, I guess it would be," Collin replied, forcing a terse smile. He then slipped back over to the bar to fetch what would be the comedian's sixth or seventh pale ale, as if that table needed any more alcohol. He wasn't going to waste his time fawning for a big tip from those guys. Drunks were lazy tippers, always rounding up their bill to the next ten. Kind of a shame that Collin had learned so much about waiting tables over the last two years.

It was strange. Time had passed, but Collin hadn't been able to move on. His presence of mind remained trapped inside that hovercraft, watching his future burn. He couldn't have imagined how quickly those creeping government wheels could actually turn, in the event that the military needed to save face in the public eye. The NEWT program was terminated before they ever returned to base. They arrived to find their barracks cleared, their belongings boxed and staged along the airstrip. Four drone choppers were standing by to dump them on the Australian mainland. It felt as though their failure was some infectious disease, and the Allied Navy was taking every precaution to prevent it from spreading. Their program never even existed, which reduced the two most outstanding years of their careers to a smoking hole in their work histories. Collin, being the youngest, fresh out of school when the Navy adopted their program, probably suffered the greatest impact because those missing years comprised the whole of his professional experience.

Collin returned to the table of drunks, pint in hand. The four sailors were crowded over to one side of their corner booth, where they were all squinting down at the comedian's phone. Quite frankly, Collin was relieved to find them distracted, and no longer in the mood for heckling him. Their brows were furrowed. Their jaws hung slightly ajar.

"Your refill, sir." Collin replaced the empty glass with the full one. The men didn't so much as acknowledge him. As Collin turned away from their table, he became suddenly aware of a stifling silence that had settled like a pall over the entire restaurant. Every patron in the joint was frowning down at a phone.

"Turn on the news!" one diner shouted from the bar, directing an accusatory finger at the big monitor, where the tied football game was underway with minutes to go. "Tokyo just got wiped off the map!"

Peak of the dinner rush, and the dull roar of conversation, clinking silverware against plates, and shouts from the line cooks in back had all been silenced. It felt as though a breaker on the circuit of all activity in the establishment had just been flipped. There were only whispers, and soft cries muted by hands.

"Working on it." The bartender managed to sync his phone to the monitor. The game disappeared, and was replaced by a scene that didn't at first make sense to the eyes. The headline mentioned a tsunami in Tokyo, while the news ticker scrolling at the bottom of the screen displayed an estimated death toll so large that it was beyond the scope of the imagination. Talking heads babbled in secondary windows, while the same event was replayed from every possible angle. Despite the ample coverage, not a single video drone had been able to capture it in its entirety, whatever it was behind the wave. It was just that enormous.

Collin felt his phone vibrating in his pocket, but he could not bring himself to look away from the screen. He slipped his hand in there, and retrieved it with his fingertips. A downward glance informed him that the caller was unknown.

The same event unfolded from another angle. There was the wall of water appearing out of nowhere, smashing into Tokyo with such devastating force that most of the drone feeds were terminated by the concussion. The skyline waned to gray, an instant before those structures crumbled like sculptures of ash. In an instant, millions of lives were ended with simultaneous indignity. Another drone camera fizzled out. A new feed captured the same cataclysmic blow from an even more intimate view. The drone floated between buildings, close enough that countless people behind windows could be discerned running mindlessly through their office spaces, or poised frozen in terror before the shadow of the inevitable.

Collin's phone began to vibrate again. As he glanced down at the unknown caller in his hand, he realized that he was wearing the same disbelieving frown as everyone else in the establishment. He lifted the phone to his ear, and cleared his throat. "Hello?"

As the voice on the other end identified himself as an officer with the Allied Navy, Collin struggled to divide his concentration between the caller and the video imagery that now filled the screen. The new angle was from a seaward perspective. The same mountain of water slammed into Tokyo's skyline, but from this perspective, Collin could see that his initial perception had been correct. There was something else. There was something behind that wave, pushing it right into the city. It was streaming with rows of red lights.

"This is he." Collin plugged a finger into his opposite ear. The shell-shocked restaurant recovered, all at once. The stunned ambiance became a clamor of voices. Wails keened beneath the deafening staccato of a helicopter's hacking blades. Collin could barely hear his caller. Cranking his neck around, he scowled through the windows at the patio, where a drone chopper bearing the crossed trident insignia of the Allied Navy was landing amidst the tables and chairs. Patrons fell over one another to get out of harm's way. The miniature aircraft touched down, flushing napkins from the tables like a tumult of white birds.

"I'll be right out," Collin replied, nodding his head with a sort of numbed complacency, as he loosened the strings of his apron. He hesitated, just before ending the call. "I'll need to stop by my apartment. I'm not leaving without my dog."

****

It was becoming difficult to sustain itself, out there in the open ocean. While the seas were rich and teeming with life, much of that life was too small to effectively utilize. It had grown too large, and it was starving. The algae and microorganisms that it absorbed through its permeable skin sufficed to maintain a lowly existence, but those meager nutrients were not enough to fuel its core bioreactors, and it needed to be able to defend itself. For the first time in its life, it was feeling vulnerable.

Out of water, its body was heavy and ponderous. It preferred the cover of darkness to make brief forays onto land. It could feed for hours beneath the cool light of the moon, which didn't blister its skin like the rays of that infernal sun. On account of its size, it was rarely recognized as being a great devourer of all life. It was simply so huge that the eyes of the land dwellers seemed to pass right over it in the darkness of night, as though such mountainous enormity was categorically benign in the scope of their minds.

Land was interesting. Unlike the ocean's barren floor, the world of the land dwellers was carpeted with nutritious greenery. Within the lush shags of foliage hid various creatures with new and exciting flavors. They were always fun little surprises. It rippled over rows of indigestible hives, forcing its inverted stomach through fragile portals into compartmentalized interiors, where their scuttling occupants were digested. All living matter could be devoured, from the towering canopies to the fluttering tenants of their branches, and converted into energy for its bioreactors. It tasted every petal of every bloom, every strand of hair atop a head, as the translucent mass digested all life in its path, leaving a steaming trail of refuse in its wake.

It crested a bluff, engorged with liquid energy, and scanned the horizon with a beaded whisker extended through its permeable skin. The organ oscillated back and forth, mapping the energy signature of the unexplored land ahead, and what its senses detected was perplexing. It was a pattern of energy that sprawled like a grid from one horizon to the next, racing in every direction from a nucleus of raw power so intense that it defied measurement. It appeared as a forest of energy, jutting skyward in a copse of columns emanating the collective life force of millions. It recognized their energy signatures. These were the same scuttling creatures that dwelled inside the rowed hives, and it found them to be quite delicious.

Urging its sloshing mass over the precipice, it half-slithered and half-rolled down the escarpment of rowed hives, but it didn't bother the creatures inside. It picked up speed, whipping its beaded whiskers to and fro, as it bore down on the massive colony. There was no sense in raiding dwellings that housed just two or three, not in the shadow of a place where the prey were concentrated in such vast numbers.

Things began to swarm, overhead. Its bioreactors activated. The hovering things had energy signatures, and they circled in a sentient manner, yet they were not alive. The blob didn't trust these contradictions.

It oozed between jutting columns as its defensive organs charged, forcing its inverted stomach through a thousand apertures at once. The vibrations of its terrified prey thrilled its senses, as ropes of gelatinous guts poured through hundreds of levels of compartments, liquefying everything therein. The swarm closed in. It appeared as though they were preparing for some sort of an attack.

Glowing with plundered energy, the blob discharged its bioreactors in a phantasmagorical explosion of plasma that lashed like crackling vipers at every object in the sky. The swarm plummeted, smoldering down to Earth. This place was its new feeding ground, and it had no intention of ever leaving.

****

"We cannot begin to discuss a return mission to Europa without first facing the prospect of the long and difficult journey that lies ahead. As scientifically minded people, we tend to lose ourselves in the vast minutia of details along our roads to discovery. Perhaps that's our survival technique. Perhaps, deep down, we know that if we dare to look up from the laboratory bench, if we dare to let go of that security blanket of little details, and we stare directly into the yawning abyss, we might falter. We might lose our resolve to press forward when faced with the magnitude of the mission that awaits us.

"A return trip to Europa is intimidating. It presents monumental challenges, both financial and technical. Ladies and gentlemen of the scientific community, there is perhaps no other living person more qualified to put long journeys into perspective than our guest speaker tonight. Ladies and gentlemen, I am honored to introduce a brilliant scientist, pioneer, American hero, and the sole survivor of Moonwalker Mission One, Ms. Skyler Hale."

"Break a leg," the backstage coordinator whispered, placing his hand on Skyler's shoulder. He then covered his eyes and recoiled. "Oh, my gosh. That was horrible."

"It's okay," Skyler replied, offering the mortified man a reassuring smile that she'd perfected for just this sort of an occasion. "Not a big deal."

Backstage hands swept in to open the door for her. The applause hit her like a great wave of sound. It made her heart skip a beat, and made her mouth go dry. Fortunately, she had a bottle of water. Public speaking was not exactly her forte, but she understood why she'd been selected to evoke sympathy and interest from what was quite possibly the largest crowd of scientific investors ever assembled. Before she was halfway ready, someone grabbed the handles of her wheelchair, and rolled her right out across the stage. This was happening. Skyler took a deep breath, and exhaled through her lips.

The stagehand wheeled her to a stop around three meters from the podium. As instructed, she waited patiently for the applause to subside before making her big move. The wheelchair was basically a prop. It was no longer a necessity for Skyler, after eight months of physical therapy. However, the theatrical masterminds behind tonight's New York symposium had determined that her entrance would be more dramatic, and more metaphorical to overcoming difficult journeys, if they presented her in the same crippled condition in which the world probably remembered her, following the pirate attack.

Once the audience settled, Skyler performed the trick intended to lift hearts and blow minds by rising slowly to her feet, and taking her first publicized steps. She'd been walking with the assistance of a cane for more than a year, so she felt like a bit of a phony sitting in the wheelchair, but she went ahead and played along in the big performance that someone else had envisioned.

The audience rose with her. When she took her first step, the roar of applause was so thunderous that it dizzied her. The celebrity host, a young actor from a science fiction television series that she'd heard of, but never actually watched, approached her with her trusty titanium cane that she'd stashed earlier behind the podium. She thanked him. He kissed her on the cheek, and stood escorted her to the podium.

Skyler wondered if the applause was ever going to end. The rolling sea of people showed no inclination to ever sit back down. The deafening white noise of clapping hands, piercing whistles and howls was embarrassing, to say the least, and not to mention a little bit terrifying. She'd imagined that this gig was going to be pretty scary, but if she'd just had any idea of how frightening it was actually going to be, she might never have accepted the invitation. Public speaking was rattling enough in front of a crowd of this size, but Skyler also happened to be afraid of heights.

Beyond the crowd, the glass walls of the ballroom situated on the two-hundredth floor of the Synerdyne Tower offered an electrifying view of New York City at sundown. Skyler was a Kansas girl from the American heartland, where the tallest structure in her flattened world was probably the Ferris wheel at the state fairgrounds. She maintained her professional smile, thanking the audience, but inside she was quivering like a rabbit. Over her shoulder, her own gargantuan face filled the teleprompter screen, magnifying every defect a thousand-fold. She didn't dare turn around.

Remembering the water bottle she'd hidden, she groped around inside the podium before her tongue had a chance to turn into a chunk of balsa wood, and before her lips could start sticking to her teeth, making her look like a snarling weirdo. Her knuckles bumped into something about the right size and shape, but instead of a plastic bottle of drinking water, her fingers encircled a steel canister that she recognized all too well. Its familiarity quelled her anxiety, and slowed her racing mind. At last, the crowd quieted, and audience members began to take their seats.

Skyler closed her eyes for a moment. She just clasped the canister that had traveled all the way to Jupiter and back, the only one to have survived the piratical raid, and just breathed. She recalled the roaring baboons, the slashing teeth and claws, and the sack of canisters being ripped from her hands. However, the demon didn't get them all. There was a deeper connection between Skyler and this object than she could have thought possible between a person and an inanimate object. After all of this time, it still felt like her only child.

"Ladies and gentlemen," she said, reopening her eyes and clearing her throat. The gravity of the moment suddenly crushed down upon her. "We are not alone."

The crowd resurged in a joyful cacophony.

This was one of the greatest announcements in scientific history, and it would be her voice that would carry it into the far-flung future to inspire wonder in generations to come. Tears filled her eyes, and they were strange ones, wrought of a bizarre cocktail of pride and shame. She was honored to be a part of this historic event, but she was ashamed of what she knew would be an everlasting connection between her image and this moment, when so many deserving others could not be standing up there beside her.

Thankfully, someone had anticipated her emotional reaction, and they were prepared for it. The symposium host swept in with a handkerchief. Skyler thanked him, and dabbed the corners of her eyes. Once the crowd had calmed, she continued. "Two years ago, in the heart of China's Yellow Sea, Moonwalker One recovered twelve canisters of pure water from Europa, Jupiter's frozen ocean moon, moments before we became the victims of a ruthless and senseless attack." Skyler dabbed her eyes a second time, and then placed the handkerchief inside the podium. "Although the thieves' motives remain unknown, they failed in their attempt to deprive the world of the greatest treasure of all." Skyler lifted the sample canister, and held it up for all to see. "That treasure is knowledge, ladies and gentlemen." Skyler smiled, fighting to keep her eyes from misting. "We embarked on a great quest for evidence of extraterrestrial life, and we found that evidence in abundance. Europa's oceans are teeming with life, ranging from simple unicellular forms to larger, multicellular organisms that are astonishingly compl—"

Skyler gripped the podium, as a wave of vertigo knocked her right out of the moment, and made her wonder if she would even remain standing. By the manner in which audience members were glancing all about, gripping the armrests of their chairs, it appeared as though she was not the only one to have experienced the sickening sensation of motion. She gazed past the crowd to the glass walls of the ballroom that overlooked the city in its twilit splendor, and the gentle rise and fall of the glittering horizon suggested that in fact, the building was actually swaying. This was the tallest structure she'd ever been in, and she supposed that it was probably engineered with some flexibility

"—that are astonishingly complex," she repeated, sweeping a lock of blonde hair from her eyes, "and if my friends and colleagues didn't die in vain, then Europa must become our new horizon. That ocean moon, and every wonderful mystery hidden beneath its icy crust, are our manifest dest—"

Skyler shrieked into the microphone as the building lurched back, throwing her off balance as New York's twinkling horizon disappeared beneath the windowsill, and the glass wall tilted up toward the stars. The sample canister toppled off the podium, knocking its lid loose as the empty vessel struck the floor and rolled crazily across the stage. Skyler's wheelchair took off in reverse. It bisected the stage, slammed into the backdrop, and then began racing forward toward the crowd as the building lilted back in the opposite direction. The wheelchair collided with a floor light, detonating the bulb with a pop and a flume of sparks before dumping offstage to crash into the orchestra pit. Skyler screamed again, covering her head as sharp reports like gunshots cracked the air. Fissures streaked across the walls of glass.

"Oh, my God." In her pocket, her phone began to vibrate.

The building sagged forward, scrolling downward through the stars until it offered a stomach-turning view of a glittering corridor plunging down between buildings, where something unspeakable awaited. Skyler gasped down at the rippling mass of amber, and noticed the play of lightning trapped within it. Exuding billowing clouds of steam, the mass gathered itself into a knot, and thrust forward again, oozing through the gauntlet of mirrored glass.

Dropping to her hands and knees, Skyler scrambled across across the stage as the building canted backward again. She hooked a floor light with the crook of her cane, grimacing as her legs swung pendulously over the slick surface of the stage. People in the front row toppled out of their seats like shelved dolls, tumbling toward the stage. The lights flickered, and then cut out completely. The ballroom was enveloped in blackness.

With a titanic groan, the skyscraper lurched forward again, and this time with more momentum than before. She was going to be sick. Her body swung by the end of her cane, until her heels caught the anchored podium. Bolts of agony shot up through the titanium rods in her legs. Stars raced across the heavens as the building bent at the waist to gawp down at its own footings. The snap of thick glass was as loud as a shot from a high-powered rifle. The ominous sound evoked a collective scream. The ululation of the crowd arose in one terrible wail, as the entire translucent wall of glass carved loose from its frame like jagged chunks of glacial ice. They seemed to pirouette toward the streets in slow motion, scooping great gouges of glass and steel from neighboring buildings as they knocked around, amassing a deadly avalanche of debris.

Skyler clung to her cane, staring straight down into the pits of Hell. Those seated nearest to the missing wall weren't so lucky. Sucked from their chairs by the vacuum of pressure change, they sailed stiff and strange into oblivion. The glimmering street below was a smoldering trench. Cartwheeling people vanished into the river of mist.

"Ms. Hale, I've got you." One of the backstage hands slid toward her on his belly, clinging to the leading edge of the stage. He reached for her cane, and seized its metallic crook in one hand. "Hold tight, and don't let go."

Skyler nodded. Trusting him, she released her foothold on the podium, and allowed her rescuer to drag her back, inch by inch, through the backstage door. A man wearing headphones, evidently a member of the technical crew, took notice of their situation. He crawled over to her opposite side, took hold of her arm, and together, the three rose. The building continued to sway, but it seemed to be stabilizing. Using the walls for occasional support, they stumbled through a dark maze of tilting corridors. The building moaned and popped, while the screams of the ballroom grew more distant.

"Something's happening," the stagehand said, between gasps for breath.

"What is it?"

"Nobody knows."

"Tokyo, London, and Seattle all got hit," the technician replied.

"Hit? Hit by what?"

"I don't know, but now it looks like it's our turn."

"Our turn for what?"

"There's a stairwell up ahead."

"We're on the two-hundredth floor!"

"We can't take the elevators, obviously. There's no choice but to take the stairs."

"Guys," Skyler interrupted the arguing men. "I saw something. There's something down there on the streets, between the buildings. Something strange."

"There's obviously a lot going on down there."

"No." Skyler gently pulled free of her handlers. "What I saw was something huge—something alive." She returned the men's incredulous stares. "You don't understand. We can't go down there."

"We sure as heck can't stay here," the technician replied. "I feel like this building could come down any second. Just listen." The technician hovered just outside the stairwell door. Somewhere beneath the screams and sirens, the rush of wind through missing walls, the skyscraper's entire structure emitted a basal moan, not unlike the tormented hull of a sinking ship. "It'll take us thirty minutes if we start right now. How long do you think this building will remain standing?"

"I don't want to die like this," the stagehand whispered, shaking his head slowly from side to side.

"Me neither." The technician shoved open the stairwell door. "Rather die with both my feet on the ground than be splattered all over it."

"Agreed."

Skyler's phone began to vibrate in her pocket again. The light from the screen glowed softly through the fabric. "Use your flashlights on your phones," she said, groping for hers, while the men went for their own devices.

Within seconds, beams of white light swept through the blackness of the yawning shaft. Ribbons of mist rose with a foul draft of air that billowed up from the stairwell's depths. A sharp odor burned the linings of their nostrils, and made them start to cough. The stench was sour, almost like vinegar, yet it stung the throat and lungs.

"God, what's that stink?" the stagehand asked, covering the lower half of his face.

"I have no idea."

"It smells like chemicals or something."

Skyler stepped onto the landing, where the men were peering over the rail down into the abyss, holding their noses. She moved past them, and stared down the first flight of stairs. Drawing a deep breath, she gripped the rail. One step at a time. She would just have to take it one step at a time.

"Hey, whoa," the stagehand said, as she picked her way down the first flight. "You don't have to do that on your own."

"I'm good," she replied. She supposed that the men had every reason to be confused by her capability, given the way in which she'd been presented at the symposium. Just a poor, broken cripple, fighting to live a normal life. Maybe it used to be that way, but not anymore, and she'd never for a second felt broken. The pain in her legs was manageable. She no longer suffered those excruciating bolts of agony if she moved the wrong way, as had been the case for eight months following the shooting. These days, her discomfort was more of a latent pain, an almost constant ache that throbbed deep down in the bone marrow. It bothered her most often at night, hours after she'd moved the wrong way, when she laid awake for hours wishing away the memory of the skinned face of her personal demon. Two hundred flights of stairs would ensure a week's worth of sleepless nights, but after fourteen surgeries, she'd become so familiar with nightmares and pain that it was just her way of life.

"Look at this," the technician said, casting his beam of light over a thin coating of mucus on the concrete walls. "This is where that smell is coming from."

The translucent goo appeared to be flowing. There was definitely some motion. Little particles caught in the rivulets were drifting along like debris in a stream. However, the most bizarre aspect was the flow's direction. It wasn't sliding down the stairwell walls, as one might expect from the law of gravity. Instead, the stuff was flowing up.

"What in the world is that crap?"

The ropes of slime thickened, gaining mass and viscosity as they slithered skyward like a snarl of vines. Then, after an unsettling rush of momentum, the slime paused. When the flowing motion ceased, Skyler noticed a draft of sour air rushing up from the floors below. The acidic reek intensified, until the stairwell air became ineffable. Coughing into their fists, they stood bewildered in an acrid torrent, watching the vines of mucus growing thicker. The stuff was moving again, sliding upward, reaching. It almost felt as though something down below was hauling itself up.

"We need to get out of here," Skyler said. "We can't go down there. I told you!"

The technician doubled over, retching in the fumes. He reached for the wall, as if to stabilize himself, inadvertently palming his hand in the slithering goo. His scream barely escaped his throat before a rush of slime had filled it, surging up his arm to flood his mouth and nostrils. He clawed at the invading entity, but he could not fight what he couldn't grab. The mucous tightened, slamming his body flat against the wall, where the stuff enveloped him.

"God, what the hell is going on?"

Flesh dissolved with such speed that the man's grinning skull had already deliquesced to a pale stain in the flow before his empty headset went clattering to the landing. A small collection of items tumbled down from the wall. Coins bounced down the stairs. Keys, a few credit cards, and a belt buckle were the last bits of evidence that a living human being had ever been standing beside them. In the blink of an eye, he'd contributed himself wholly to the living stream.

"We've got to get out of here," Skyler shouted, hobbling back up the staircase.

"There's nowhere to go!"

He was right. Skyler knew that he was right, but she wasn't ready to accept that the gelatinous horror that she'd seen down on the city streets was already oozing up through the core of their building with the dark designs of a serpent slithering toward a nest of helpless chicks. She wasn't ready to accept death on its own terms, so long as there remained a place to which she could flee, like the ballroom, where she could lose herself amongst the crowd. However, the dark thought that she could not escape, the one looming behind all of the others in her mind, was a sort of dread certainty that this monster was one of hers. Amidst the thousands of screaming people, Skyler alone knew exactly what was happening, and why. She'd brought the thing here. It was all her fault.

She threw open the stairwell door, where the howling of tormented souls resounded through lightless halls. It was disorienting and hellish in its dissonance. Below it all, the skyscraper released another lugubrious groan up through its stairwells and shafts. Skyler could feel it inside her chest. Her breaths quickened, and her eyes began to dart. It was happening. The monster was coming, and she wasn't getting out. No one was. The whole building was coming down.

The crowd compressed against one wall of the ballroom. They were a trapped herd of animals, paralyzed by the presence of some predator in their midst. No one dared attempt to exit the room. There were open stairwells on either side, but one glance in those directions and the reason for the crowd's reluctance became apparent. A rippling tide of amber oozed from those routes of escape, boiling up from beyond the stairwell doors to spill across the ballroom floor. The exits were choked with the same living mass that continued to haul its immense bulk ever higher into the skyscraper. These extremities were akin to its slithering tentacles. The crowd let out a scream as the building lurched toward the open wall. A few lost their balance. Stumbling, they grabbed for one another as they slid, only to raft entangled together over the precipice. The whole building was hanging by a thread.

Center stage, Skyler had become a spectator in a weird reversal that had shifted the show out into the audience. For months, she'd worried about tonight's event. All along, she kept telling herself that it was just a case of stage fright, and that everything was going to be fine. As she watched in horror as whole panels in the domed glass ceiling detonated, showering broken glass down onto the crowd, she began to wonder if her anxieties leading up to tonight hadn't in fact been a glaring premonition that she'd chosen to ignore.

Amber gel gushed from ventilation ducts in the walls. It coiled on the floor in writhing ropes. The brushed steel doors of the defunct elevators trembled and shifted in their frames. The shiny panels bulged outward, buckled, and ruptured with volcanic force. An avalanche of pressurized goo that had been building up inside the elevator shafts exploded out into the ballroom, engulfing everything in its path.

"There's no way out of here," the stagehand said, backing toward the hopeless corridors from which they'd just escaped. "We're all going to die."

Skyler didn't know what to say to him. She couldn't argue. He appeared to be right, and she wasn't in a position to offer anyone else sympathy. She just watched him go, knowing well enough, as the stage door closed behind him, that was the last time that she would ever see that man.

The phone in her pocket began to vibrate. Twice, she'd ignored the unknown caller, presuming it to be someone affiliated with tonight's event, or with the two-year research program she'd conducted for the Allied Navy. Certainly, it was bound to be someone worried about her. Even though she didn't have any close friends or family left, someone out there was watching the news, and they were concerned for her safety. It terrified her to answer that call, because if she did, she'd be forced to admit to the lone voice in the darkness just how dire her situation was, and that would be her acceptance of death. With the last spot of safe ground shrinking by the second, and the entire skyscraper threatening to crumble beneath the weight of the climbing behemoth, she was being pressed closer to the acceptance of that finality, but she wasn't quite there yet. The unknown call was filled with emotional portents, because whoever was on the line might be the last person with whom she would ever speak.

"Hello?"

"Ms. Skyler Hale?"

"Yes?"

"We've locked onto your location. Do not move. Stay exactly where you are."

The line went dead. Skyler looked from her phone to the gaping hole in the ballroom wall, where a thumping helicopter ascended from the abyss, piercing the gloom and chaos with a lance of brilliant effervescence. Groveling masses shielded their eyes like sinners before an angry god, as the chopper positioned itself over the fragmented dome. A great pop lurched the skyscraper a few more degrees, and another wail arose from the damned. A few more souls were swallowed. Arms outstretched toward the heavens, pleading. Desperate fingers raked at the shaft of blinding light.

A spot of darkness preceded unfurling cordage. A tethered harness tumbled through the open ceiling, and down onto the stage. Wails of lament escalated to primal screams. The mob turned on Skyler. With wild eyes and bared teeth, they rushed the stage. American hero no more, she'd been devalued by death's dark promise. They were going to rip her apart. The slackened line straightened, and the harness began to rise.

"Grab the rope!"

Skyler obeyed the booming command that resounded from the heavens. She seized the rope, hugging the harness to her breast, and rose as the unforgiven clambered onto the stage. Her toes left the ground as their claws raked her legs. A single shoe she gifted them. It tumbled down into their midst, as she soared like a locust from the pits of the damned, gilded in silvery brilliance.

The building emitted an agonized groan, just her body passed through the jagged portal, and the whole structure started to topple. Skyler stole a last glimpse over her shoulder, and looked upon the fate from she'd been spared. Waves of amber gel rushed in from all sides to envelope the screaming crowd, liquefying the forsaken as the gutted corpse of America's tallest skyscraper thundered upon the wasteland.

Chapter Three

The baboon licked a goober of meat off the sandstone, and sat there smacking its chops. They were such awful creatures. Each was so possessed with avarice that one could not be tethered within reach of the other during feeding time, or they would rip out each other's throats. The second creature emitted a grunt, following the scraps of thrown flesh with its eyes, with an almost childlike expression of entitlement. It should've learned by now that it wasn't getting anything to eat.

He liked to torment them. For two years, he chose to feed one over the other, until its belly was fat and round. Day after day, he would continue the treatment until the eyes of the starved began to hollow with madness. When at last the ghoulish one was unleashed upon its fattened brother, he observed the depths of a baboon's depravity. Then, their respective roles would be switched. That was his game. Week after week, he fostered a profound hatred in those animals for everything in life but an orange bowl of human flesh. It consumed them. Without windows or other stimulation, that bowl could be the only thought festering inside their rotten minds, such that his control over them was absolute. However, their master remained hidden behind a screen during those feeding sessions, such that no sense of dependence on a living person would ever corrupt the pure minds of his savage addicts to human flesh.

"Sir?"

He heard the fawning voice of his Chinese manservant, and he sucked the human blood from each of his fingertips, one by one. From beyond the black curtain, a starved ape emitted an indignant bark. No one liked to be disturbed during feeding time. That was supposed to be their time, when nothing else in the world should exist but master's floating hand, a lucky baboon, and a bowl of warmish meat.

"What do you want?"

A Bengal tiger's roar shook the corridor. The great killer smelled flesh, and a primal switch behind those burning eyes had flipped, transforming the striped cat into death incarnate. Anyone unfortunate enough to be dropped into that enclosure from one of the many trap doors throughout the palace would find themselves reduced in worth to the weight of their meat in a monster's swinging gullet. Somewhere high above, a peacock howled.

"You have a visitor."

He dipped his fingertips back into the bowl, and swirled them gently in the blood. "Who is it?"

"Mr. Krupin, sir," the manservant replied. "He insisted that you bid him to come see you immediately." He lowered his upper-half in a respectful bow. "You know that I would never disturb you down here, as you've made abundantly clear, if I didn't believe Mr. Krupin's visit to be some matter of urgency."

Volkov stopped swirling his fingers. He grabbed hold of a fatty cord of flesh. He extended his hand through the curtain, and flung the wet thing at a baboon. With a snarl and a ringing chain, it was gone. His visitor, Mr. Krupin, had in fact brought him those two baboons. He'd delivered them as gifts, two years ago. Of the hundreds, maybe thousands throughout the Red Brotherhood who received Volkov's orders, Mr. Krupin was perhaps his most inventive. Hideous to look upon, no doubt, but Krupin's fetish for facial mutilation seemed to symbolize some deeper resent for the civilized world, and perhaps a renunciation of his own humanity. It was a bold statement akin to spitting in the creator's face, and perhaps that was the proverbial point, for he that has no money needs no purse.

Volkov extended the bowl through the curtain, and inverted it. He relished the baboons' screams as their meal splattered on the floor, just out of their reach. He would let it rot there. They could stare at that denied meal until starvation had devolved them into living nightmares. That's when he'd break the Chinaman's legs with a pipe, and throw him screaming to his flesh-eating apes.

"No worries," Volkov replied, flashing his manservant a silver smile.

The man pointed a trembling finger at the floor, where a dark pool of blood crept from behind the black curtain. "Would you like me to—?"

"No." Volkov's smile fell. He dropped the temperature of his visage by fifty degrees. "Send in Mr. Krupin."

"Yes, sir. Thank you, sir." The manservant bowed his way out of the corridor, trailed by a bobbing shadow that slithered along the torch-lit wall like a dungeon ghost.

Volkov clasped his hands behind his back, and strode down his menagerie corridor. Things unloved glowered back from the shadows, their eyes glowing like twin portals into Hell. Some paced mindlessly, rubbing against the same spots on the stone walls with every turn, until their flesh was scoured down to exposed bone. Volkov paused in front of the tiger's cage. The beast thinned its gleaming eyes from the darkest corner of its cell. He and the once-magnificent cat exchanged their knowing looks of mutual hatred and respect wrought by two forever locked in a standoff. The creature blinked, turned, and resumed its pacing. Sometimes, Volkov thought about killing it, turning it into a rug. It used to be a gorgeous animal, before it defiled itself just to spite him by rubbing half its face off against the wall. The tiger turned, grinding bare skull against sandstone, and cast Volkov that baleful glare meant to haunt some unlit corner of his mind.

For years, he'd made a hobby of collecting the world's most terrible creatures, and turning them worse. The people who served him, he supposed, were no exception. Volkov strode further down the hall to an unoccupied enclosure filled with water behind a thick plate of glass. Ruddy streaks circumnavigated the walls, evidencing the slow and deliberate manner in which the creature had ground its life away. His gaze fell to the layer of accumulated waste on the tank bottom. It was all that remained of the bygone tenant.

"Thank you for coming on such short notice," Volkov said. He'd heard the sucking air being drawn through Mr. Krupin's bared teeth, but he chose not to turn around. Not yet. He never liked to look too long at that man, because to behold the self-inflicted mutilation inspired dark impulses in Volkov, and he didn't want to kill Mr. Krupin. He needed him. Mr. Krupin was family, and family had no ugly members.

The man beside him grunted. He raised a finger, and pointed toward the empty tank.

"It died," Volkov said. He unclasped his hands, and folded his tattooed arms across his broad chest. "She was like a bitter woman, and refused to find happiness here." Volkov frowned down at the layer of detritus on the tank bottom, as if reading the creature's leavings like thrown bones. "But, I suppose there is more to learn from its death than there was ever to be learned by observing it, in life." He turned toward Krupin, permitting himself a glimpse of that wired mess of a face. "I've got the dolphin's head upstairs, in my freezer."

Volkov turned away, and began to walk again. Mr. Krupin followed him, as he anticipated. "I presume you've been watching the news, yes?"

The man trailing his heels emitted a grunt.

Volkov whirled around. He seized Mr. Krupin by two fistfuls of wires, and he yanked their faces together. "I've warned you before, and I'll never warn you again. When you come to Mongolia, you will come to me as a man, or I'll show you an animal. Take this mess off your face."

Volkov hated Russians almost as deeply as he hated Chinamen, but for business reasons, his disdain was kept simmering beneath the surface—most of the time. Volkov's Red Brotherhood was as much a hybridized offshoot of the Russian mob as was he, with his broad face and Asiatic yet emerald eyes. The Mongolian blood was the only blood in his veins that he claimed, despite Volkov's known relation to a certain Russian prostitute. The last man who'd dared to call him the "Moscow Mongol" was forbidden to speak the "M" phonetic again, a penance Volkov ensured by feeding both of his lips to a monitor lizard.

Volkov shoved the ugly face with force enough to slam Mr. Krupin's bare back against the stone wall. He hung there for a moment, glowering from the shadows. His tattooed chest rose and fell. At last, he blinked. He raised a hand to dab the blood from his torn lip piercings. Unfastening the contraption buckled behind his head, the wires sprung, and Mr. Krupin's face relaxed. His slackened lips fell wimpling around his tongue.

"You know why I called you here?"

Krupin nodded. "I've seen the news." He thrust himself off the wall, slapped his hands against his pants, and rolled his painted neck. "Going to need a bigger dolphin tank."

Volkov flashed a silver grin. "Isn't it fun watching them all try to pretend they don't know where the monsters came from? It's nobody's fault. Not the Navy. Not our heroes, who brought contaminated water back from another moon."

"Europa," Krupin said, jabbing a finger skyward.

Volkov's eyes took on a shimmer. "Where the wild things are."

"Yeah. That's why I thought, like, why's he calling me, even?" Mr. Krupin said, throwing up his hands with a shrug. "'Cause I got you the moon juice already."

"That's the trouble." Volkov cleared his throat. "It's gone."

"Gone?" Mr. Krupin cocked his head. "Where'd it go?"

"Into the gullets of the European elite."

"Wait … it got drank?" Krupin frowned, narrowing his eyes. "Why'd they drink the moon juice?"

"What they drank was vodka. Very expensive vodka."

Shifting back and forth on his feet, Mr. Krupin could only frown. He looked as though he wanted to say something, but never did. No one had likely ever accused him of being the smartest man in the world.

"They sing to it, Mr. Krupin." Volkov turned to his favorite henchman, and mirrored the angle of his cocked head. "Did you know that?"

Krupin's eyes flicked over the incomprehensible map that was Volkov's face.

"The Mongolian distillers in Nantong. They sing to their water. They believe that water has moods, and so they adjust the mood before distillation begins, by exposing it to certain tones that infuse the water with the perfect energy for transformation, and before you laugh, consider that the best vodka in Russia has always been distilled by the Mongols."

Mr. Krupin stared at Volkov. He licked his lips and swallowed. "You turned the moon juice into vodka, then."

"Diluted, of course, into three hundred gallons of the most expensive vodka ever distilled."

"That's good, then. Right?" Mr. Krupin nodded, gazing at the empty dolphin tank, at Volkov, and back again. A bewildered frown remained tilled into his brow. "So ..." He licked his distorted lips. "Why did you call m—?"

"Because I had it right there in my hands!" Volkov doubled-over, fists clenched, roaring so loudly that it made the torches flicker. An unseen beast replied with a low moan. Volkov pressed the butts of his hands to his temples, his face screwed into a red knot. He rested his forehead against the cool glass of the dolphin tank. "I held the most powerful weapon in the world right in the palm of my hand, and I never even saw it for what it was."

There was no getting that water back. Not unless he could roll back time by two years, and have a second chance to make the most of that stolen cargo. Never in his life had Volkov regretted anything so deeply. He'd made an extraordinary profit on the Europa brand of vodka, enough to fund the Red Brotherhood's trafficking operations well into the next generation, but money meant nothing in the shadow of the greatest power that the world had ever beheld; power that should've been his to wield.

They were so perfect. The new creatures emerging from the sea were everything that Volkov had ever wanted from his hobby, but had never been brave enough to imagine. His attempts to create the perfect abomination, a purely destructive force that somehow remained comfortable in its own skin, had never amounted to anything more than an enjoyable diversion from his work, but his perspective changed on the day that Mr. Krupin brought in the dolphin.

The Allied Navy, as it turned out, were involved in some similar shenanigans. While tinkering with trained animals that performed terrible tricks, they'd evidently stumbled onto something huge. They'd discovered some mechanism of direct control over their test subjects, because no amount of thrown fish could ever inspire a dolphin to behave in the strange manner captured on drone footage. Something else was going on. It was something technical, and the first step was solving that mystery, if Volkov hoped to ever have anything better than a flesh-eating baboon on the end of his leash.

Volkov narrowed his eyes at Krupin. What his henchman lacked in intelligence, he made up for with pure determination. Disadvantaged in the Brotherhood by his Russian heritage, Mr. Krupin was driven to outperform the Mongols in every task. He would storm the gates of Hell and bring back the devil's pitchfork if he thought that by doing so, he'd gain some favor.

"What do you want me to do?" The corner of Mr. Krupin's mouth was quavering, his eyes brightening, like a dog anticipating a treat. This was a man who was ready for orders.

"I need you to deliver the dolphin's head to Nantong, China."

Chapter Four

Filling its storage bladders with seawater, it pumped the fluid through its gill slits, timing each surge with a whip of its flagella. In this chugging style of locomotion, the creature was able to ascend from the depths, and into the dead zone. This was a vast desert without landmarks, with no visual points of reference throughout those gulfs of midnight blue. It was an ocean layer too deep to glimpse the sun, yet it was more than a mile above the sea floor. Up might as well be down. Directions were irrelevant. Navigation was only possible if one was equipped with the ability to perceive magnetic fields, while remaining aware of subtle changes between thermocline layers. The dead zone was so devoid of life that even the scale of living things was totally subjective. A creature might wrongly appraise itself as being quite enormous, until confronted by something else drifting through the gloom. Only then could the question of one's size be put into perspective.

Chugging, whipping, it felt the pressure of the depths relaxing, but this brought no relief to the discomfort. Quite the contrary, the ocean's weight was something of a stabilizing force that helped its organ systems function properly. The nearer it drew to the surface world, the more ghostly thin it began to feel. Whole years of its life seemed to fly by as lost seconds, while some binding essence of its existence was being diluted. The great pupils of its eyes constricted to pinpoints, and then vanished. Neurological misfires rocked its body with spasms. Somehow, it intuited that the consequence of reaching the surface might be death, but if it dared to slow its pace, death was a certainty.

Leagues behind and below, the pursuer's threshing tail churned the water into foam. The massive bioelectric signature rose like a sentient thunderhead, pulsing with electrical currents that scrambled magnetic fields, and spun the internal compass of its prey like a top. This was a hunter from the extreme deep, where forever-darkened skies were searched by gaping, soulless eyes, and where the particles that settled down from above were sampled by masses of wriggling organs. It was death incarnate. Once prey had been targeted, a switch inside its mind flipped, and there was no turning its course.

The fleeing creature chugged toward the sun's brilliance, whipping its flagella with mechanical rhythm. It refused to alter its suicidal pace. It would die in motion, fighting its way upward until its heart ceased to throb in the burning sunlight. Muscle control became corrupted as the enormous predator closed in, wracking its nervous system in a field of bioelectric chaos. Stunned, its flagella could barely twitch. The chase was over. Tipping askew in the endless blue, the prey submitted itself to the inevitable.

When the moment of devouring arrived, the monster's snout instead rushed past, serrated knives gleaming in the barnacle-encrusted acreage of its jaws. For an instant, their eyes met. As one gaped into the frigid depths of the other's soul, and the other gaped back, each came to know something intimate of the other, and then it was over. The killer's vast and serpentine form undulated by for what seemed like an eternity, until the field of electric carnage dissipated with a final thresh of the great tail.

Tumbling end over end in the monster's wake, the lucky one came to the realization that the threat had passed, and that its life had not been taken. While the day had at once become something of a gift, perhaps the greater gift was that of perspective, because it understood its scale in a vaster world than it might've dared to reckon. Inflating its bladders with seawater, it dipped its head downward, and vanished back into the midnight blue.

****

The monster unhinged its massive jaws. Torrents of seawater gushed through lateral vents as its terrible mouth yawned into killing position. Bulging eyes crossed their independent fields of vision to focus on the target's underbelly. With one final lash of its tail to rocket its mass skyward, the hunter slammed into its prey, and the two breached the ocean as one. Midair, squealing steel panels shredded as the monster thrashed the inedible thing in its jaws, before crashing disappointed back into the sea.

The prey's ruin floated strangely upon the waves. The hunter circled, watching its lights flicker dimly, as a column of black smoke billowed up into the air. Its dying sounds were unlike those of any creature that the hunter had ever encountered, nor did it behave in any familiar way. The wounded thing didn't flutter upon the water, or swim dazed in mindless circles. Its cries were not one, but the collective shrieks of many. The hunter slithered around the smoldering carcass, tasting the water with its masses of barbells. The flavor was acrid and charred. While its oblong body resembled prey from down below, this thing was something else, and it was unfit for consumption. Although it was a waste of time and energy to attack what couldn't be eaten, there was still a reputation to uphold. The waters over the trench were the monster's hunting grounds, and trespassers were never tolerated.

Barrel rolling over the sea, the hunter lifted its great tail out of the water, and brought it down upon the intruder with a slap so fierce that the seas trembled. The collective squealing stopped. The flickering lights went out. At last, the invader behaved in a normal way, sinking lifelessly down into the deep.

One invader had been dealt with, but now the monster was agitated. There might be more of those things trespassing through its territory, and the monster felt compelled to show some feats of strength. It hoisted the spiny fan along its back in a crimson display, declaring dominance over its kingdom. Slashing at the water with its tail, the monster snaked over the surface, war flag billowing in the wind. It welcomed a challenge from anything that dared to cross its path.

****

The naval officer sidestepped down the row, shaking hands with a steely grip. "My name is Captain Roswell. I'll be your primary point of contact, here on the Barrier Reef. I've spent the last eighteen months overhauling your old NEWT program, and on behalf of the admiral, I'm proud to offer an opportunity for reinstatement in the Allied Navy." He pivoted at the waist to gesture toward the surreal spectacle looming in the background. "Welcome to the zoo."

It was Collin's turn to stick his hand into the flesh vise that was Captain Roswell's hand. However, he was so overwhelmed by the alien environment of the naval laboratory that he hardly even noticed the pain. Breaths billowed from their throats with every exhale, and rose into the frigid air. Ranks of glass cylinders jutted like glowing pillars from floor to ceiling on either side of the laboratory. Imprisoned inside these vessels were nameless creatures gawping back through streams of bubbles, exhibiting the benign disinterest in their surroundings that was common amongst lower forms of life. However, some appeared to be more aware of their human observers than did others. Collin awed over the whipping flagella and oscillating gills that performed single functions with clockwork regularity, while simpler specimens oozed around the walls of their cells with the dimmest deliberation.

"James Price?"

"J.J., sir."

The captain stepped back up the row of former NEWTs to stand face-to-face with their team leader. "My father was a naval pilot. He flew alongside yours in the Battle for the Bering Strait during the last months of the End War. He told me about your father. He was a true hero. It's an honor to meet you."

"Pleasure's mine," J.J. replied.

Collin's head was spinning. It was all happening so quickly. Years ago, during their first go-around with the Navy, the NEWTs had languished for months in a sort of bureaucratic limbo while the system slogged through a screening process that seemed like it would never end. Pitching their program to the Allied Navy was J.J.'s idea, wrought of some personal ambition to secure his place in a familial legacy. His one-track mind had started to become a point of contention amongst the team, particularly once it became painfully evident that their program was not being taken seriously.

From the start, they were banished to a sterile barracks where their only source of entertainment was a battered air hockey table with one short leg. Technology was forbidden. No contact with the outside world. By the time they finally set foot on the Barrier Reef, Collin felt as though he'd mentally devolved by some arbitrary differential that he feared he might never recover. This time, something was different. Red tape was being snipped. Security procedures were waived. Their admission was being expedited.

The captain lowered his chin, clasped his arms behind his back, and cleared his throat. "All of you remember that day, two years ago. You were deployed off the Chinese coast on what we all believed was going to be a routine offensive. Seemed like a perfect opportunity to introduce the world to the NEWT program, with minimal risk of collateral damage. However, as we found out, sometimes the small and manageable can evolve into something much bigger than we ever could have anticipated."

Captain Roswell turned on a heel. He strode over to a nearby laboratory bench. While his back was turned, Collin stole a glance at Jill and Takashi. It felt so bizarre to be back together after two years apart. They all looked a little different. J.J. had put on a few pounds. Takashi had shaved his head, and grown a goatee. Jill's hair was shorter. On her left hand, he noticed, when she bent to scratch Hotspot behind the ear, she wore a sparkling ring. For some reason, the sight of that ring made Collin's stomach do a flip. He wasn't sure why. It was just weird. Very weird. Just another sign of how much time had elapsed, and how vastly different their respective paths in life had evidently taken them.

J.J. had always said that there was no such thing as losing, only winning or learning, but there was nothing to learn from their program's meltdown. It was a total loss. After the big break-up, they'd all gone dark. As far as Collin knew, his former teammates had not kept in contact with one another, or at least they'd never made any attempt to contact him. Shame seemed to be the underlying reason for their reticence. However, here they were. They'd all answered the call. The band was back together, and Collin wasn't exactly looking forward to admitting that he'd done nothing with his life but wait tables, when the others had probably moved forward with their nanotech careers. While catching up was going to be a critical part of rebuilding the shattered infrastructure of their team, socializing rarely made any list of military prerogatives.

"An hour after the pirates' sub sounded, we found this floating in the Yellow Sea," Captain Roswell said, as he removed a cloth covering from a small steel canister. A round hole perforated its dented center. Looked like a bullet hole. "Found it amidst the wreckage." He picked it up, turned it over in his hand, and then brought it over to the team.

"What is it?" J.J. asked.

"That is what your team was supposed to have been protecting."

J.J. frowned down at the punctured vessel in his hand. He cast a glance at the rest of his team. "I don't get it."

"'Course you don't. You only know what you're told, on the battlefront. What you're holding is one of twelve cylinders that contained samples of pure water from Europa, Jupiter's ocean moon. By now, I'm sure you all know the same story that we fed to the press. We still don't have a clear motive for the attack, but that, right there, is what the pirates were after. That's one of two that didn't fall into their hands, and that's the one that changed our whole world, as we all once knew it."

"And this is the one that's going to make things right again."

Heads turned toward the sound of the female voice that came from the back of the laboratory. From behind the rows of instruments stepped a woman in a white lab coat. She clutched an undamaged canister to her chest. With the aid of a titanium cane, she limped through the alternating swaths of light and shadow cast by the specimen tanks. Collin's eyes widened, as she stepped from a spot of darkness into a shaft of luminescence. Her beauty was almost breathtaking. If anything, her slight physical disability made her even more alluring. Perhaps her little struggle appealed to some ancient protective instinct that he never even realized was encoded somewhere deep in his DNA. She was a fluttering bird that had fallen from the skies, and he just wanted to scoop her up.

"I would like to introduce you to Ms. Skyler Hale," Captain Roswell said. "National hero, brilliant scientist, and sole survivor of that pirate attack."

"Well," she replied, smiling, "at least one of those is true."

Collin felt his half-witted smile fall. His lips went numb, and his throbbing heart plunged into the depths of his guts. His silly fantasy had just crashed headlong into a freight train of reality. Now, he knew who she was.

"Ms. Hale defended that last sample canister with her life, and she nearly died for it. Since the day of that attack, and through her very difficult recovery, she has devoted every spare minute of her time to the analysis of the microscopic life forms that were accidentally released into our world, and now threaten its very existence. Ms. Hale had the foresight to know that if any of those life forms managed to survive in our seas, then we'd benefit by learning all that we could about them in a controlled laboratory setting. She is the world's foremost expert on the invaders. She alone knows the strengths and weaknesses of the microbes that have since evolved into giants."

"Actually, they didn't evolve," Skyler said, offering Captain Roswell a kind smile. "By definition, evolution is the gradual shift in form within a species, over many generations. 'Metamorphosis' is a more accurate term for their sudden and exponential metabolic rates, in response to our planet's level of ultraviolet radiation and higher temperature. The result is an unstable and titanic aberration." She clicked a laser pointer in the direction of the cylindrical tanks. "The Japanese are calling them, *Kaiju*."

Collin wondered if the others could hear the grinding of his emotional gears. He felt ashamed and embarrassed that he hadn't recognized her. On one hand, he was awestruck to be standing in the presence of a true hero, but on the other, the sight of Ms. Hale hitching along with a cane was no longer the least bit attractive. In fact, it was starting to make him feel a little sick to his stomach. After two years, he found himself facing the only survivor of those victims he was hired to protect, and whom he'd utterly failed.

Just like everyone else in the free world, Collin had watched the fragmented documentary of Ms. Hale's slow and painful recovery over those months of televised interviews, award ceremonies, and public appearances. However, unlike the billions of other viewers, Collin suffered a private burden of guilt every time her face appeared on the screen. Nothing could have prepared him for meeting her in person. She was smaller than he'd imagined. Seeing her struggle to walk normally evidenced every minute of pain that she'd suffered, on account of him.

"It's an honor to meet you." Jill was the first to speak. She stepped forward, and traded Skyler's offered handshake for a hug.

J.J. rocked on his heels, hands in his pockets. He was grinning like an organ grinder monkey. When Skyler offered him her hand, he nearly leapt out of his own skin to accept it, as though he hadn't been quite sure that she was going to offer him anything at all. Takashi took her hand more easily. Collin knew why he and Jill were more comfortable. As the technical wizards of behind the NEWT project, they'd done exactly what the Navy had hired them to do. If it ever came down to pointing fingers, Jill and Takashi had to know that they'd both done their jobs to perfection.

"I'm sorry," Collin whispered, when it was finally his turn. Her grip was as cold as the steel canister, yet he somehow felt her warmth. He heard his voice crack on the last syllable, and it suddenly became a fight to keep himself together. Maybe he should've gone through some therapy, and found a constructive way to dealt with the guilt, rather than hiding for two years behind an apron, just blending in, and pretending he wasn't even there. Out of everyone on the NEWT team, his failure had been the greatest. Down at his side, Hotspot emitted a thin whine.

"You must be the dolphin pilot," she said, with a twinkle in her eye.

Collin felt his ears turning red. He didn't know what to say. He supposed that she was able to guess his role in the huge disaster because he looked the most tortured by guilt, probably the most inept, and easily broken.

"They told me to not underestimate the shy guy, because you're the only one brave enough to handle the task that lies ahead."

Collin blinked. He could feel the stares of the others, as their heads all swiveled in his direction. If he'd not been embarrassed before, he certainly was now.

"It's an honor to meet you, Collin. I've watched some of the videos of your training sessions, and what you're able to do in there is nothing short of amazing. You and I will be working pretty closely in the years to come. You're going to move mountains, and I can't wait to watch you."

"Did you all hear that?" Captain Roswell returned the punctured canister to the lab bench. He set it down with a resounding clang, and turned back to the team. "She said 'years.' I presume you all have friends, families, loved ones. There can be no misconceptions about what the Allied Navy has brought you here to do, and the level of commitment that we're going to expect from anyone who accepts our offer for reinstatement."

Collin couldn't help but shoot a glance at Jill, just to check on her reaction. The others looked a bit shocked by the statement, but Jill appeared genuinely disturbed. Her parted lips and shimmering eyes kept no secrets. This looked to be bad news for her, and for whatever world she'd left behind.

"What are we here to do?" J.J. asked.

"We're rebooting your old program, but don't confuse what lies ahead with that half-baked novelty outfit that you might remember. This is the real deal. Welcome to the big leagues."

"Half-baked?" Takashi murmured.

"The NEWT program died two years ago. What's risen from the ashes is a new operation called Psyjack." Captain Roswell's steely eyes appeared to challenge dissent. "The fundamental skills and technology that you brought to the table remain in place, but the application is getting one hell of an upgrade."

"I don't get it," J.J. said.

"Shush." Jill frowned.

"Look around you. The people standing beside you will become your new family, because Psyjack has the highest level of military classification. We can't afford leaks. If the details of this program ever fell into the wrong hands, it could be repurposed into the deadliest weapon that the world has ever seen."

"Can we back up for just a second," J.J. said, tamping the air with his hands. "We're dolphin pilots. You knew that, right?"

"I'd hope so," Captain Roswell replied.

"Are you suggesting we're going to engage those things, those things the size of frigging aircraft carriers—with dolphins?"

"Not exactly," Skyler replied. Captain Roswell and Skyler exchanged glances. "Psyjack deploys monsters against monsters, and you," Skyler said, levelling her ice-blue eyes at directly Collin, "are going to pilot them."

Collin was still in elementary school the first time he read about nanobots, those microscopic robots that would make such a tremendous impact on his life. At that time, nanobot phage technology was being marketed as a sexy new tool in the field of neurology. Modelled after viruses in both form and function, the little critters were touted as the future of neurosurgery. Thousands could be injected into a patient's bloodstream. Once inside, the program took over, and they swarmed to their assigned destinations to perform specific tasks. Real-time communication between bots and surgeons, and between bots and bots, was already being slated as the next big step in their development.

The first prototypes were pretty simple. Armed with a single tool, an electrical prod, the one-trick ponies were programmed to seek out and destroy tumors that were embedded beyond the surgeon's reach. It wasn't long before the next evolutionary phase enabled them to cauterize hemorrhages, bringing new hope for patients suffering from head trauma. However, the best was yet to be discovered, and it was none other than Collin who would make that discovery.

Shortly after he enrolled at the University of Glasgow, bots were being programmed to form artificial synapse chains, bypassing damaged circuitry in degenerated brains with synthetic neurological highways. This was the last knock at the gates, before the doors to nanobot science would blow wider than ever before. All eyes in the medical world, including Collin's, were fixed in the same direction. The little robots were so much bigger than their original role, as cauterizers and cutters. Connected to one another, and connected through code to the outside world, they became microscopic miracle workers that restored cognition to those robbed of it, and redeemed souls born damned into intellectual darkness. The possibilities were endless. Nanobots marked the grand opening of the human mind.

"Hotspot," Collin whispered, clicking his tongue at the wandering animal. The dog had evidently discovered something of interest on the floor beneath a laboratory table. "Psst. Get over here."

The lab raised its head, gazing quizzically at Collin with the usual guise of feigned innocence. After a brief staring contest, Hotspot plodded back over to Collin's side. It was sometimes a difficult case to make that Hotspot was something more than an ordinary animal when the dog's snout was always snuffling around garbage cans. Some behaviors were simply more hard-wired than the circuitry in the animal's head.

While studying under the wings of J.J., Jill, and Takashi, Collin's groundbreaking discovery was made in the typical flippant manner in which the biggest turns in his road of life had always been taken. Goaded by Takashi, who was his roommate at the time, Collin self-administered an injection of customized nanobots into his own bloodstream. These particular critters were programmed to go places where no bot had ever gone before, into the prefrontal cortex of a test subject's brain. It was Collin's hypothesis that when implanted in the brain's control center for body movement and cognition, the bots could translate the electrical impulses of the subject's will into binary code. This code could then be transmitted to a synchronized nanobot colony in a second test subject, where the translated impulses of the first could be artificially replicated. In a nutshell, the will of the second test subject could be overridden by the first.

It was one of those lightbulb moments. Once in a lifetime, if he or she was lucky enough, talented enough, and positioned in just the right time and place to exploit the available resources, a person could stumble onto an idea that might leave their life and the world around them forever changed. This was one of those ideas. Collin never had any illusions about the magnitude of his brainchild, and he made Takashi his only confidant. While they worked together in secret through weeks of crunching nanobot code, they rarely ate, drank or even slept, because this was science fiction realized. This was the stuff of comic books. This was mind control, Manchurian candidates and zombies.

On the night of Halloween, freshman year, backlit by the wonderfully ironic chaos of an electrical storm, Collin found himself reclined in a chair, covered in electrodes, and strapped into a customized VR headset. The lights in the dorm room were switched off. By the glow of a laptop and Takashi's eyes, a nanobot network came online in Collin's head. With the tap of Takashi's finger against a function key, Collin found himself being dumped quite literally into the mind of an experimental test subject, located three doors down. Blissfully unaware of its significance in scientific history, the test subject's eyes flicked open, transmitting visual and auditory data back to Collin in an encoded flood of ones and zeroes. From the moment he rose shakily upon those four borrowed legs, Collin would forever have a special connection to Hotspot, the living host of his first out-of-body experience.

"Why not conventional weapons? I mean, why entertain an idea like this?" J.J. inquired.

"Conventional weapons can be effective under ideal circumstances, but we're not getting those ideal circumstances very often," Roswell replied. "We never know where or when they're going to strike, and when they do, there's no time to evacuate the local populous for a counterattack. It happens fast, and then it's all over before we have a chance to respond. While we're waiting for one of these things to show us a glimpse of its soft underbelly in some conveniently unpopulated area, the greatest cities in the world are burning. We can't afford to wait for ideal circumstances. We need to get down there, now, and bring the fight to them. We need to stop them before they ever decide to step out of the sea."

"We estimate the original population of Kaiju to be somewhere in the thousands," Skyler said. "That's the number we calculate survived the first few seconds of exposure to the new environment. In two years, we can't rule out the possibility that some of them have found each other out there, and might already have been breeding."

"There's a lovely thought," J.J. said.

"Some species don't even need a partner to reproduce. Budding, cloning … it gets a little biological in a hurry, but my point is that the original population may have doubled, or even tripled by now. The truth is that we really don't know. We're just beginning to see their first wave of emergence, as the oldest and largest of these creatures are making landfall. While the world is just starting to get an idea of what we're up against, believe me, we haven't seen anything yet. The worst species have yet to even show themselves."

"What about a test subject?" Collin asked, gesturing to the collection of living specimens in the tanks. "Are you planning on growing our hosts here in the lab, or …?"

"Yes and no," Skyler replied. "As you can see, they're relatively easy to rear in a laboratory environment for research purposes, but even under ideal conditions, a test tube titan remains two years of growth behind the original invaders. If we wait two years until we've reared one big enough to stand up to its older brothers and sisters, there's not going to be much of a world left to defend. A counterattack needs to happen now."

"So," Takashi said, clearing his throat, "are we wrangling wild ones to pilot?"

"Something like that," Captain Roswell replied.

"It's freezing in here," Jill whispered. She rubbed at the goosebumps prickling the flesh of her upper arms.

"It's below freezing, actually," Skyler replied. "The freezing point of saltwater is a few degrees lower than freshwater. Temperature and ultraviolet radiation are critical variables for encouraging or inhibiting the rate of Kaiju growth, and we want to keep the growth rates of these guys maintained, for obvious reasons."

Skyler approached one of the tanks, and she tapped on the glass with a fingernail. The spiked thing inside extended a set of eyestalks, and responded to her stimulus with a dull flicker of lavender light. "This is one of my favorites, as well as one of the species on our Naughty List. We call them longhorns. They're simple life forms, but they have a pretty complex system of communication through bioluminescence. Very pretty, when they're feeling talkative." Skyler turned from the tank, and the creature inside settled back to the bottom. "Unfortunately for us, and for them, the longhorns are highly territorial, and they tend to be aggressive toward any source of artificial light."

"That's what hit Tokyo," J.J. said.

"UV light is measured by a photoreceptor that seems to be a common feature in almost every Kaiju brain. Comparable to the pineal gland, it's the power plant of the Kaiju endocrine system.

It's the place where regulation of hormone production and release is determined, based on what the photoreceptors interpret as subtle changes in favorability in a given environment. It was obviously an unfavorable environment, back home on Europa, so their growth rates were inhibited. The UV light that penetrates the miles of ice on Europa's surface is just a fraction of a fraction of what we receive here, on Earth. To the photoreceptors in Kaiju brains, the change in environment was totally off the scale. Earthly UV and temperature sent their endocrine systems into metabolic overdrive, dumping growth hormones just as fast as they could be produced. Their alien biology demands that they take advantage of favorable growth conditions by seizing and utilizing those resources before they disappear. However, we can't explain to their photoreceptor glands that the UV light on Earth isn't ever going to disappear. So long as they're exposed to it, these creatures will never stop growing."

"What temperature range is most favorable?" Collin asked.

"All earthly temperatures are within a very favorable range for growth. Temperature regulates how efficiently their growth hormones are metabolized. Back on frozen Europa, large doses of hormones released in response to favorable conditions might've taken years to fully metabolize. Here, in temperate and tropical waters, they're absorbed in a matter of hours. Biologically speaking, it's a perfect storm."

"What do they eat?" Takashi asked.

"The longhorns? They're scavengers. Bottom feeders. Part of the cleaning crew on the ocean floor."

"I meant, like, all of the different types. Are they all bottom feeders?"

"No-no. Just as you'd find in any ecosystem, anywhere in the universe, you're going to find a diversity of predators and prey. You'll find your autotrophs, heterotrophs, and chemotrophs. Europa is no exception. So far, in the single canister that I managed to preserve, I've documented more than seventy species of Kaiju."

Collin heard his own expletive join the murmur of stunned voices. The enormous scope of the problem was just beginning to come into focus, as well as the monumental challenge of correcting it, if the problem could be corrected at all. The alien zoo in which they all stood shivering, impressive as it was to behold, was a microcosm of the situation at large. The planet itself had been transformed into a world zoo without cages, and they were being appointed as its zookeepers.

"Whoa-whoa-whoa," J.J. said, waving his hands in the air. A head taller than most men, the former boxer was always the first to step forward. With his imposing size and physique, he might've found success in any number of physical paths, including a career in the Navy. However, despite his family legacy with the armed services, it was J.J.'s pride that had always prevented him from muscling his way down what he perceived as a lazy shortcut through life. Instead, he pushed his way upstream through more cerebral challenges. "You're talking thousands of Kaiju in the seas, maybe even millions, and there are four of us standing here. One-two-three-four."

"Five," Skyler replied, raising her hand to wiggle her fingertips.

"Okay, five. If we worked night and day for the rest of our lives, we might not even begin to make a dent in this population, and like you said, they could be breeding like rabbits. What's being asked of us is …"

"Impossible?" Skyler cocked her head.

Captain Roswell cleared his throat. "Ms. Hale, if I may?"

Skyler nodded.

"Our vision for the road ahead does not account for a plan for total extermination, at least not at this juncture. Rather, we're looking for a firm policy of monster management." Captain Roswell strode up to another glass cylinder, and frowned at the rippling folds of amber gel imprisoned within. "One week ago, up in New York City, we nearly lost Ms. Hale to one of these nasty things. She was giving a talk in the Synerdyne Tower, just before it came crashing down. Thirty-thousand lives was the estimated death toll, and it took this creature less than five minutes to accomplish it." Roswell lowered his head, turned, and paced before the aquariums. "Forty-thousand in London. Sixty-thousand in Seattle." He stopped, and swiveled his head in the direction of the longhorn tank. "Almost a million, in Tokyo. Guys, this is only the beginning."

Collin's gaze traveled from one end of the unearthly menagerie to the other, studying the collection with increasing dread, and wondering if this first wave of emergence marked the beginning of the end of humankind. He placed his hand atop Hotspot's head, and scratched the dog gently behind its ear. The animal was shivering.

"Sir?" Takashi raised his hand tentatively, and then brought it back down when Captain Roswell's eyes rolled in his direction. "How exactly do you go about injecting nanobots into a fully-grown and wild test subject?"

"I don't. But you do. That's why you're here."

Takashi furrowed his brow at the captain, and blinked.

"Harpoon syringes were an obvious starting point." Roswell sighed, and smeared his hands across his face. "We tried for the better part of a year to dart one of those things from high-speed watercraft, aircraft, even submarine deployment. No success. These things are fast, elusive, and fiercely territorial. You can't get anything larger than a gunboat anywhere near them without provoking an attack, and trust me, you don't even want to know how many lives we've already lost, trying."

"Maybe go with a smaller, stealthier watercraft," Collin said, "like a one-man submersible."

"Not fast enough. That's the catch twenty-two. These things are out in open water, way out of range of smaller watercraft. Once you've pinpointed their location, you've got minutes to get the jump on them. Basically, our failures have taught is that you've got to be there to begin with, before one ever appears."

"Drone submersibles then, cooperating with drone choppers."

"Negative. Even slower. They're not designed for pursuit."

"So, out of everything you've tried, what's been the most effective?" J.J. asked.

"We're currently monitoring the coastlines with military drones equipped with sonar, and armed with depth charges. You could call it a safety net. When one of those things gets too close to making landfall, we do our best to turn it back out to sea. We've had some success with that method, but it's not enough. When we encounter more persistent individuals that decide to breach our net, it never seems to happen in a location where a weapon of mass destruction is a practical backup. We need something smarter than a big boom. We need you." Captain Roswell's dark gaze tracked across each of their faces.

"You inquired about a test subject," Skyler said, "and how we might successfully engage one in the wild for a nanobot injection." She strode over to one of the tanks, where a frilled serpentine creature resembling a Chinese dragon writhed against the glass walls of its enclosure. When Skyler placed her palm against the tank, the little monster hoisted a crimson fin along its spine, and flared its jaws. "The region of the Yellow Sea where the pirate attack took place still harbors the highest Kaiju density. These particular creatures, the bloodfins, are so territorial that they've all but shut down the world's busiest trade route, off the coast of Shanghai. Out of all the Kaiju, the bloodfins in this region are perhaps the most predictable, in the sense that they will attack any ship that passes through their hunting grounds. It's not much, but a predictable behavior pattern is something to exploit. In my estimation, it's the best place to start. China's Yellow Sea will be ground zero in our war against the titans."

J.J. pinched at his nose, chuckled, and shot a sardonic glance at his team.

"Is something funny?" Skyler asked.

"No," J.J. replied. "I'm just hearing a lot of dramatic monologue, but I haven't heard a single straight answer to any question we've asked." J.J. threw up his hands. "You said you've already tried everything, and nothing works. How do you expect us to do any better than the Allied Navy?"

Skyler cocked her head and smiled. "You're dolphin pilots, right? How about we deploy some dolphins?"

Chapter Five

Mr. Krupin leapt from the mail drone, and sailed into the stormy skies over Jiangsu. He spread his arms and legs, drawing the flaps of his black wingsuit taut against his limbs, and he harnessed the battering winds. The sensation of electricity fishing through his flesh and bones made his skin prickle. Fairy lights flitted along the wire manifold that peeled back his pierced lips, and flitted from his teeth as sparks of light. Wind filled his cheeks to resonate with a mournful howl. With each flash of lightning, he could see the other members of Team Beta. Red Brothers tumbled from mail containers clamped beneath the drones to spread their wings and soar through the Plum Rains. Cloaked by a tempest so violent that even the Chinese airlines were grounded, it was unlikely that they would be detected. The timing was perfect, and the storm felt amazing.

Mr. Krupin hefted his right arm to bank sharply around a jag of lightning that lanced through the clouds to send an unluckier Red Brother plummeting in flames like a hawk-struck pigeon. The wing suits were highly flammable. They were designed as such, for the purpose of being disposable upon landing with the aid of a small incendiary device, but that feature of their commando gear had one obvious drawback.

Gaping his wired mouth, Krupin bellowed into the maelstrom. He felt so grateful, so filled with joy that it overflowed as tears of ecstasy that melded at once into the rain. It was one of those poignant moments that sometimes caught Mr. Krupin by surprise, when he was reminded of how blessed he was to have been born at exactly the right time and place to find himself in the servitude of a man like Maxim Volkov. Tonight, he would make his employer proud.

Below, at the heart of the Jiangsu province, the sprawling port of Nantong bejeweled the banks of the Yangtze, a river so black that it swallowed all light cast upon it, denying even the electric bolts that arched over its impenetrable darkness. The contrast was stark between the vast and glittering brilliance of a civilization that raced from the river's banks to sparkling horizons as far as the eye could see.

Nantong was the last Mongol foothold in the Chinese mainland, and it was slipping, month by month, and year by year. Hidden amongst those twenty million Chinese lives down there in that field of gems was another insidious presence. It was one that ran deeper and darker than even the river that flowed through it. Relics of the End War who refused to give up the fight, the Chinese insurgents had been slaughtering foreigners in the Yangtze Delta for the last twenty years in bloody protest against their conqueror's military presence in Shanghai. It was an underground militia of deranged patriots who called themselves the *Jaw-long*. They were down there. They were everywhere, and they were always waiting.

Battered by some new elemental layer, he fought against bullying torrents intent on blasting him back up into the sky. Krupin growled at the resistance, struggling to keep the great bulge on his stomach from shifting, and throwing him into deadly imbalance. The cumbersome piece of cargo was the only aspect of this operation that Mr. Krupin found detestable. Although it was key to their mission, the thing was bulky, and cold as the grave against his guts. He was proud to have been selected to bear the burden, and to lead the Beta Team, but there was a part of Mr. Krupin that wished another Red Brother had been strapped to the severed dolphin's head.

A web of electric brilliance flashed below him like a lethal net. Streamlining himself by clasping his legs, and slapping his arms to his sides, he transformed himself into a living dart that whizzed unscathed through the gauntlet. He shielded his face as he rocketed through a cloud of burning debris where a less fortunate comrade had just been incinerated. Once past the warring elements, the city of Nantong erupted into stunning detail.

The rectangular shape of an ancient moat formed by the Haohe River was the landmark he'd planned to use to train his descent in the direction of a darkened stadium situated at the heart of Nantong Medical University. Krupin flapped his arms and barked. The Red Brothers obeyed, converging into a tighter formation. They were coming in fast. Details flowered into view as they plummeted toward campus. Between semesters, the university was dark and lifeless. Only a few cars were scattered throughout the empty parking lots beyond the ranks of college halls that rose lightless and abandoned.

The Brothers were looking to him for leadership, awaiting his signal. Through the corners of his eyes, he could see their heads flicking in his direction, eager hands ready to snatch for the ripcords of their parachutes. Not yet. He'd make them wait until the last possible second, because those moments when an underling's loyalty could be tested came few and far between, and he intended to make good use of this opportunity.

With a great flap of expanding fabric, one Brother was jerked skyward from the squadron by the cords of a prematurely released parachute. Mr. Krupin flinched as the coward's boots swung past his face. He looked to the other Brothers, the loyal ones who'd earned his favor, and he clenched both fists in a gesture that permitted deployment. Billowing flumes of black fabric and straightening cordage yanked them all back from their deadly trajectory.

Together, they floated down to the stadium turf. Mr. Krupin glanced over his shoulder, taking a moment to identify the man who'd released his chute early. It was Baichu, the slab-faced troll from Ulan Bator who'd made a business of selling turns with his sister, in exchange for chocolate.

"Don't touch him."

Krupin turned toward the veiled threat to find Jochi glowering down at him, hands balled into fists. Tall for a Mongolian, and proportionately broad across the shoulders, Jochi was built to be intimidating. No other calling would've suited the ham-fisted brute quite as well as pummeling other men into a bloody pulp.

Grinning up at the big ape, Krupin unfastened the clips on his harness, sloughed his parachute and cordage, and then unzipped his wingsuit. The stench from within was more than a little bit distracting. The reeking bundle strapped to his belly had begun to thaw. No sense starting a fight with Jochi too quickly, he guessed, not when Baichu should first be deprived of some dignity. Krupin loosened the straps of the bag that contained the dolphin's head, and with much indignation, he slung the sodden stinking burden at Baichu. It bounced and tumbled end over end until it came to rest at Baichu's feet. The boy seemed to understand. He clasped his hands and bowed, before snatching up the satchel with evident relief, and throwing the straps over his shoulders. He smiled at Mr. Krupin, nodded, and bowed again. Appeased, the giant Jochi turned and lumbered away.

The men of Team Beta emerged from their wingsuits already dressed in the counterfeit uniforms of Chinese soldiers. Each unpinned a dress cap from his waist, and situated it atop his head. Rifles were assembled from discorporate parts. Wing suits and parachutes were gathered for into a pile for incineration.

While they worked, lightning shattered the skies. Thunder trundled over Nantong with mighty resonance. The Plum Rains were a seasonal phenomenon, owed to a persistent stationary front that drenched China for the first two months of every summer. However, another more ancient explanation accredited the annual monsoons to the water dragon, Yinglong. Legend had it that Yinglong had created the channel of the Yangtze River with a good thrashing from his serpentine tail.

Mr. Krupin snapped the incendiary vials hewn into the collars of a few wing suits, and stepped back as chemical reactions spat and sizzled in the rain. In an instant, despite Yinglong's torrential downpour, the heap of chutes and clothing combusted in a ball of greenish flame. In a matter of seconds, all that remained of their infiltration gear was a black scar on the turf, and a few dozen plastic clips and buckles that would probably puzzle some superintendent for the rest of his life.

Krupin shouldered his rifle. He barked at his men through the wire mask. With a sweeping gesture of his arm, he began marching toward the stadium gates. There was no time to lose. Team Beta had exactly one hour to secure the College of Neurological Sciences building before a midnight rendezvous with Team Alpha, rumored to be under the command of Maxim Volkov, himself.

Mr. Krupin was forged of stronger stuff than the men around him, for having carried the burden of his Russian heritage for nine years in a gang predominantly and proudly Mongolian. He needed to be crazier, tougher, and more vicious than any Mongol in the Brotherhood, as Volkov cut another tie to the Russian Mob with every white corpse he sank to the bottom of Lake Khovsgol. While their nomadic faction seized control of the opium trade to the West, and the trafficking of distilled spirits into the Middle East, Mr. Krupin strove to remain close to his half-breed benefactor, knowing he'd have to elevate himself above the Russian heritage that Volkov obviously resented, if he hoped to survive. Volkov's mother was a weak and corrupted example of a Russian, whose addictions allowed her to be used like a toilet while her half-breed son was raised as a mobster by her Mongol pimp. She was the fountainhead of Volkov's hatred for Russians, and while Mr. Krupin understood, he was still driven to prove to Volkov that there was no reason to be ashamed of the Russian blood in his veins.

Hitting the stadium gates running, Krupin ensured he was first amongst his team to seize the rail, and launch himself over to the opposite side. It was a small victory, but in fact his champion status amongst the Brotherhood was determined by collective little wins, where he proved in small ways, minute by minute, that he was just a little bit faster, meaner, and more driven than any Mongol in the ranks. In a contest of physical strength, he might be outdone by a beast like Jochi, and that's why it was critical to keep stronger men like him off-balance through regular intimidation. He'd altered his face with the wires and piercings to ensure he'd stand apart from the Mongols in a way that wasn't a deadly liability. They couldn't be allowed to see him as being a white Russian in their midst, or the dogs of war might decide to turn on him. No, they had to regard him as a monster, a savage, who was imbued with a disposition that was even more frightening than his face.

As they charged across the darkened campus through flapping sheets of rain, the little confrontation with Jochi began to niggle in his mind. The brute had challenged him, called him out in front of the others, and their brief engagement had ended without a violent repercussion. He'd let Jochi get away with overstepping his bounds, and amongst a gang of cutthroats, that failure to react was an unforgivable moment of weakness. Already, his underlings were probably recalculating their appraisal of him, and feeling their own urges to test the stretch of their own leashes against the power of his grip.

Mr. Krupin dropped to all fours, and he ran like an animal. Just a little treat for anyone who happened to be watching. Just a little reminder of what exactly he was, or was not. Every flash of lightning revealed Krupin at the head of the pack, a galloping creature of the night, the alpha male who alone knew where they were going. After studying the map, he'd lied to his men by telling them that Volkov's explicit orders were to ask no questions about the mission, and to blindly follow his lead, because perception was everything.

The Hall of Neurological Sciences loomed over dark gardens, backlit by the elemental spectacle in the sky. Strange things happened here, Mr. Krupin suspected. Beyond that screen of plum trees, those walls and tinted windows, all manner of perversions were being exacted on squealing test subjects with logged assurance of repeatability, all in the name of science. His pupils constricted in a flash of lightning that was followed by a thunderclap that he felt against the walls of his chest. Yes, this was the womb where a thousand nightmares had been conceived, and where a new child of the Brotherhood would soon be born.

In the plum grove, Mr. Krupin attacked. Confused in a snarl of dripping branches, the killing went unseen. Only the smallest sound escaped Baichu's throat before Krupin's bared teeth had ripped it from beneath his chin. A blood fountain flowered pink in the plum rain. Krupin's hand followed the eager blade beneath the ribs to stir things slowly, almost sensually, inside the cavern of Baichu's chest. It was a rather intimate killing.

The other men stood stricken beneath the boughs when Krupin pulled out of the quivering boy, dripping, and smeared the warmth from his forearm across Baichu's hollowed chest. Pinching the plastic clips on Baichu's shoulders, he rose with the dolphin head dangling from one arm, licking salty remnants from his teeth, and he pointed the tip of his dagger first at Baichu, and then toward an open storm drain.

Jochi's sledgehammer fists relaxed. Having found the ends of their leashes, his dogs obeyed. No need for words, after that sort of action. The Mongols fell upon their slain Brother. Rising together, they lifted Baichu from the mulch, and carried his corpse to the gaping hole.

Mr. Krupin was aware that Jochi could beat him to death with his bare hands, but he never would. Not after this. It was all about perception, about flipping his racial distinction into an asset, rather than a liability, and manifesting their perception of the white monster into a stark reality. His life depended on their conveying a regular message to Volkov of their subservience to the white monster, be it through body language and sly nuances of the eyes, that he was in some way their superior.

Baichu's boots followed him waggling down into the bowels of China's underworld. With any luck, he'd be halfway to Shanghai by sunrise. Krupin doubted whether the discovery of a uniformed body in the Yangtze would even raise an eyebrow. Just another casualty in the war on smugglers. Just another gruesome message to the Chinese central government to withdraw their military from the Jaw-long's domain.

Krupin barked, and the Red Brothers followed. Around the backside of the building, they ascended a steel staircase to a landing adjacent the loading dock. There were almost certainly cameras watching. Krupin withdrew a cordless multi-tool from a belt holster, snapped out the serrated blade of the reciprocating saw with the flip of a thumb switch, and slid the blade over the deadbolt. The saw was noisy, but their detection hardly mattered at this point. Team Beta's part in tonight's performance was nearly complete. Their job was simply to deliver the severed dolphin head to laboratory 110, and Team Alpha would take it from there. Sparks jettisoned from the saw's vibrating teeth, until the bolt transected with a loud pop. Krupin grabbed the handle, and opened the door.

Dim beams projecting from their phones were the only lights they were authorized to utilize. The Brothers trained their lights on the backside of the broken door, while Krupin switched the multi-tool's function to cordless drill, by swapping the serrated blade for a screwdriver bit. He removed a set of steel brackets from his pocket, and picked at the black electrical tape that bound the steel-tapping screws to their backs. He wasn't sure how Team Alpha was supposed to get into the building once he screwed the brackets to the steel doorframe. This was the only aspect of their mission that he'd found to be confusing, but he knew better than to question Volkov's orders. His employer always knew what he was doing. Perhaps Volkov and his team were already here, waiting for them in the laboratory. By the wavering spotlights of a half-dozen beams, Krupin tapped screws through steel, and sealed the door behind them. No one else was coming in.

Grunting at his men, he strode across the loading bay. They followed him through a swinging set of double-doors, past a warehouse reception office, and out into the main hall of the first floor. There were no wet footprints on the tile, no evidence that anyone from Team Alpha had arrived ahead of them. Anxiety whistled up through Krupin's core. Something seemed off. He began to worry that perhaps he was in the wrong building, or if he'd misunderstood some critical aspect of the mission. He was sure that he hadn't. He'd always prided himself on his keen attention to detail, loyalty, and unstoppable momentum, but when he stepped into the appointed place of rendezvous and found it empty, Mr. Krupin quavered with an uncertainty that he'd never experienced before. Rows of strange and incomprehensible instruments were revealed in a flash of lightning, but there was no one waiting in the laboratory to greet them. The place was deserted.

Krupin's tongue quested anxiously over his teeth. The next and final step in the instructions were to seal the laboratory door closed behind them with a second set of brackets and hardware, just as they'd sealed the loading dock door. His Red Brothers were watching him, quietly awaiting the next phase of a plan he'd deprived them. Slotted Mongol eyes borrowed wildness from the lightning, but their stoic faces were devoid of effect. Perhaps a bit soured by his rough treatment of Baichu, but he supposed that in time, they'd get over it.

Krupin heard a shrill shriek reverberate through the laboratory. When the Brothers dragged him to the floor by his mask of wires, and pinned his arms behind his back, he realized that the scream was his own. The laboratory door slammed shut. They were enveloped in utter blackness. Boots smashed his teeth. Fists pummeled his head. When Volkov found out about this treachery, he'd have them all gutted, and toss their innards to the baboons. Krupin tried to warn them, but in the flurry of blows, the only sound his pinioned lips could produce was a phlegm-bubbling wail.

When the beating ended, Krupin had no fight left in him. He felt plastic ties being zipped around his wrists and ankles. He heard the whine of a cordless drill securing brackets to the back of the laboratory door. The amiable chatter of his backstabbing brethren was the most terrible sound of all, as they chortled amongst themselves over the success of what appeared to have been a setup, all along. The lights flickered on. Through the rivulets of blood that stung his eyes, Krupin found himself staring up into the gloating faces of his Red Brothers.

"Surprise, Mr. Krupin." Jochi bent down, and spat right in his face.

Arching his neck, he opened his throat to emit a roar that he hoped they would hear all the way in Shanghai. He didn't care who heard him. The mission had been compromised. The Brothers had betrayed him. They probably intended to slice his throat, to send him downriver after Baichu, long before Team Alpha ever arrived, and agree on some fictitious tale of his demise. If these traitors thought they were going to kill him without a fight, they were sorely mistaken. Inching his way back into a corner, Krupin struggled into an upright position. Chest heaving, ropes of blood swung from his chin. The Brothers found his fortitude amusing, but he didn't care. He drew his knees up to his chest, and glowered back at them. The first traitor to approach him was going to join him for a ride down into the storm drain.

Jochi lifted a remote from the laboratory bench, and aimed it at a large video monitor mounted high on the wall. The screen blazed to life. Krupin winced in the pale brilliance, as the face of Volkov appeared. Krupin could discern by the crimson lights in the background that their employer was transmitting his live video broadcast from the submarine. His green eyes fell onto Krupin, as did the smile from his face. "Congratulations, Mr. Krupin," he said. "Welcome to Nantong."

Krupin blinked his eyes. They felt hot, and on the verge of overflowing. He glanced from one Brother's grinning face to the next, and he realized that he was alone in his astonishment. Volkov was in on it, whatever it was, and Krupin's years of experience assured him that when someone found themselves singled out by the Red Brotherhood, death was never far behind. A strangled hoot escaped his throat, and the tears began to flow. He didn't deserve to die like this. He'd done nothing wrong.

"Don't feel betrayed, Mr. Krupin," Volkov said. "I simply couldn't afford your refusal to participate in the next phase of this mission, because you're the perfect man to fill the role." Volkov offered him a smile. "I see you've brought the dolphin's head."

Krupin glanced down at the oddly shaped satchel on the floor. Pinkish water pooled around the sacking. Swallowing a mouthful of blood, he nodded, after some hesitation. There was an almost fatherly benevolence in Volkov's eyes, as though his mistreatment had in some way hurt Volkov even more than it had hurt him.

"You're the only man I could entrust with the task of getting it here, to this laboratory, in the heart of the most dangerous province of China." Volkov leaned inward, leveling his gaze with a sort of sternness that conveyed respect. "You're the most fearsome bastard I've ever known, Krupin, and best of all, you're loyal. If every one of the Brothers possessed your mind, there's no doubt that I'd be the most powerful man on earth. However, there is only one Mr. Krupin, isn't there, and I'm afraid that there will never be another." Volkov placed his intertwined fingertips to his lips. "Pity, that such a wonderfully dangerous mind as yours should be trapped inside the body of a Russian. That's your only flaw, if I had to name one, but it's not your fault. It's just the way that God made you."

Krupin cocked his head, frowning at the screen. He had no idea where he stood anymore. Was this to be his end, or some new beginning? He glanced down at the dolphin sack, and then back up at Volkov. His employer's smile appeared genuine, but that did little to change the fact that he remained handcuffed and beaten, bleeding all over the floor of a Chinese laboratory.

"Dr. Wu? I think that you can come out, now," Volkov said, his roving gaze searching the lab. "Come out, come out, wherever you are."

A restroom door at the back of the laboratory creaked open. In an instant, every Red Brother's rifle was shouldered, cocked, and trained in the direction of the individual who'd been in hiding. By the shocked expressions of the Brothers, Krupin reckoned that they'd not expected this twist in their plan, and he found their confusion to be somewhat satisfying.

"It's alright, Dr. Wu. Don't be afraid. They won't harm you. Brothers, lower your weapons. Show Mr. Wu a little bit of comradery. He is your Team Alpha."

Krupin rolled his head against the wall, and observed a timid man in a laboratory coat step slowly through the aperture, hands quivering in the air. Jochi lowered his rifle, and shot a glare at the overhead screen. Krupin snorted. This was getting more interesting by the minute.

"Mr. Wu, say hello to your lovely wife." Volkov reached to one side, and yanked a tearful, shuddering woman into view. He forced her in front of the camera, gripping her by her upper arm. "She decided to accompany me on a romantic cruise at the bottom of the Yangtze River. If you're not expedient and cooperative, then this is where I'll dump her body, right after you get to watch her die."

The scientist crumpled at the sight of his wife. He folded his hands, fell to his knees, and began to plead. The Red Brothers stood baffled and speechless, glancing at one another, and down at Mr. Krupin. Blood bubbled through his teeth when a chuff of unexpected laughter escaped his throat. He had no more idea about what was happening than did they, but he was pleased to help himself to a share in their intimidation.

"Tonight, Mr. Krupin, you're the star of the show. The procedure you'll undergo may be painful, and it is not without risks, but in the end, I believe that any suffering you endure will be worthwhile to our cause." Volkov nodded at the Red Brothers. "Pick him up. Put him over there on the laboratory bench."

They lifted him from behind, by his shackled arms and legs, and they conveyed him through the laboratory to the central table. Crimson slobber whipped from Krupin's chin. They laid his battered body facedown atop the table. Krupin rested his bruised and throbbing cheek against the cold slab of stainless steel. It felt good. No matter what happened from this point forward, it felt good.

Chapter Six

The Devil Ray detached from the C-550's underbelly. Snatched by the howling winds, it spiraled toward the Yellow Sea. It was a stomach-churning freefall that stiffened Collin against the backrest of his seat, crushing his lungs against the walls of his chest. If these descents had always felt so sickening, so far out of his own control, he couldn't recall, but he remembered J.J. doing a better job at the helm than the SWCC pilot that had been assigned to them for their first mission. Lightning slashed at the spinning windows. Hailstones clattered against steel. The voice of the storm was a titanic groan that swallowed the aircraft in a furious vortex. Collin squeezed his eyes shut, spinning and spinning. Every panel of the supersonic hovercraft chattered against its rivets. It felt as though the Devil Ray would be ripped to pieces at any instant, and it was too easy to imagine the sound of rending steel that would precede their bodies being flung out into the Chinese skies.

From what Collin thought he'd understood, the Plum Rains were mild seasonal storms that gave the region an annual soaking. A little turbulence was to be expected. However, the magnitude of the tempest outside didn't even begin to be described by the Navy's forecast, which fell short enough to inspire distrust. When Collin heard a shriek as the aircraft was slammed in the gut by a rising thermal, he hardly recognized the voice as being his own. It took a few seconds to collect his senses. Interior lights flickered. The smell of burning plastic hung in the air. Collin blinked, and glanced back over his shoulder to check on his team members. J.J. was doubled over his armrest, getting sick in the center aisle. Jill and Takashi, looking more than a little shell-shocked, groped for technology that was dangling by cords, and lay scattered all over the floor. Christ, even if they managed to survive the landing, it was going to be a miracle if their equipment functioned at all. Sometimes, it seemed as though the Navy was always behind it all, just setting them up for certain failure as part of an ongoing practical joke.

A mechanical thump underfoot indicated that the electromagnetic turbines were finally being engaged. Interior lights blazed brightly, as all six engines came to life with a powerful whine. The craft immediately stabilized itself amidst the elemental chaos, and at last the team breathed a collective sigh of relief. Hotspot rose from his bed at the back of the hovercraft, ears pricked, and emitted a long and baleful groan.

"What was that all about?" J.J. shouted from the back of the aircraft. "Why'd we wait so long to engage the turbines? Was he trying to kill us?"

Obviously, there was some anger in the emotional cocktail, and for good reason. Piloting the Devil Ray was supposed to be J.J.'s job, and this time, there was a stranger in their midst. They'd barely had time to glimpse their nameless chauffeur, let alone establish some basic level of trust. It seemed so typical of the Navy to put their lives in the hands of an inexperienced pilot, and just shove them out the door before anyone had a chance to realize the danger. Takashi's hands were trembling, as he did his best to remain calm while reassembling the tangled mess that had been made of his equipment. Jill was sending a text message on her phone. Her face was crumpled. She wiped tears from the corners of her eyes. Collin turned back around in his seat, and took a deep breath. This had all happened so quickly that they'd not been afforded the luxury of time to really think about what they were getting themselves into, and perhaps that was all part of the plan.

"Sorry about that." The pilot's voice through the overhead speakers was punctuated with an electrical pop.

"You should be!" J.J. wiped the back of his arm across his mouth, and then hauled himself up off the armrest.

Collin glanced back at Jill again. She had the phone to her ear, still tearful, whispering to her caller and nodding her head. It appeared as though she was assuring someone that she was alright.

When she swept a lock of hair behind her ear, that sparkling ring on her finger never seemed more portentous. The person sitting there in Jill's usual seat looked a lot like Jill, but it wasn't her. It was someone else, someone new, whose best interests were invested elsewhere. Their reunited team, if there was even a team at all, was hanging by the thinnest thread. Nothing was set in stone. No contracts had been signed. No terms had been discussed. "Psyjack" was nothing more than a cool brand name slapped upon the sort of rushed and disorganized mess where human lives were likely to be lost.

"Is everyone alright?"

Collin turned back to the front of the aircraft, where Ms. Skyler Hale had emerged from the cockpit. There was something about her presence that induced an immediate calming effect. Whether it was because she inspired confidence as a celebrity hero, or simply because she was a vision of beauty in an ugly place, Collin couldn't be certain, but he liked looking at her.

"What's up with that pilot?" J.J. asked. "Did he just earn his wings this morning, or what?"

"No. We took a direct hit to the main electromagnetic drive from a bolt of lightning. He had to manually reboot the system from a portable drive that we're all very lucky he'd brought along. He's good. Captain Roswell assured me that he's the very best."

Skyler edged her way toward the team, gripping an overhead handrail for support. Although it was strange to see someone in civilian clothing aboard their Devil Ray, or anyone else in addition to the usual foursome, for that matter, Skyler didn't throw the dynamic off balance, because her presence was critical. She seemed to be the missing link between their fledgling program and the military brass, as well as a voice of reason.

"What's the matter, hon?" she asked, as she approached Jill.

Jill shook her head, wiped away another tear, and lowered her phone to her lap. "I just don't know if I can do this. I mean, I really shouldn't even be here." As Skyler took a seat in an empty chair next to her, Jill drew a deep breath, exhaled, and cast an imploring glance to the ceiling.

"You want to talk about it?" Skyler asked.

"This is all just—crazy." Jill threw up her hands. "I mean, what is this? What's even happening here?"

Skyler frowned, shook her head, and placed her hand atop Jill's. "I guess I don't understand what's bothering you right now."

"What's bothering me? Well, one minute we were all just living our normal lives, and now, here we are, flying right into what's probably the most dangerous place in the entire world. Nobody saw this coming. Nobody warned us. We haven't had time to talk to our families about what's going on, or when we'll be coming home."

"There is no time," Skyler replied, as gently as possible, "and those normal lives you mentioned? They're over now, and I mean for everybody. Here, at least you have an opportunity to make a real difference."

"You know. I get that, and I appreciate the opportunity, but some of us have other responsibilities and higher priorities."

"What priority could be higher than this one? We're talking about the fate of the entire world, and you're—"

"My entire world is my daughter."

Collin felt his stomach drop like a sack of pudding. He knew it. Some part of him knew it the very instant that he saw that ring. They weren't what they used to be. They weren't anything at all. They were like the cast in a really bad joke, where a waiter, a housewife, an ex-boxer, an engineer and a crippled scientist were all aboard a plane in a storm …

"We've got a problem," Takashi said, as he cross-checked one of his laptop screens with the one in front of Jill. "You're not coming up in my feed."

"What does that mean?" Skyler asked.

"I'm not exactly sure. Something may have been damaged when everything fell. I'm just not getting Jill." Takashi pulled up his hologram instrument panel, and gestured toward a dark area in the main stream between the dolphin pilot and the available hosts, where Jill's familiar icon was missing.

"Double-check your connections," J.J. said.

"I did. I've double-checked them all a dozen times."

"She's showing up online on her end."

"That's what's confusing me. If it's not the connections …"

As the eyes of all his teammates flicked in his direction, Collin swiveled toward the empty mounting bracket where his Mindbender Rift headset should've been secured. It wasn't there. Panic seized hold of an indefinite part of him, at his core. He located the missing headset quickly. It was down on the floor, near his feet. It must have been jarred loose along with everything else when they were hit by that thermal. Collin retrieved it, and flipped it over in his lap to examine the wireless receiver. A blackened halo burnt onto the side of the helmet explained the odor of burning plastic he'd smelled.

"Oh, boy." Collin turned back to the team, holding the helmet up to display the damage. The most critical component was smashed. The collective feeling of doom was the same stricken mask worn on each of their faces. Without a functional receiver, there would be no communication with Jill, and without Jill, there would be no piloting of dolphins. He could of course borrow a headset from one of his teammates, but that meant reintegrating new hardware into Jill's system. Some of those headsets had never even been used in the field. Years of updates had been missed. No telling what operating systems they were running.

"See? This is the whole problem," J.J. said. "I'm actually glad that this happened. There's never been any sort of built-in redundancy with this program. No protocol for this kind of a situation. I've been telling them this for years, and nobody ever listens. Maybe they'll start listening now."

"You guys don't need me," Jill said.

All eyes fell on her. Jill's face relaxed, as if the admission brought her some sense of relief. She wiped away the last of her tears, and reached for a duffle bag that she'd brought along with her. She pursed her lips and nodded, as she unzipped the bag and began removing items. "I'm glad that it happened, too." She placed a component that Collin didn't recognize on the desktop in front of her. "See, I realized that I was expendable in the first few months of the program, back when we were all stuck in those stupid barracks with nothing to do but think." She sniffed, and cleared her throat. "That's when I came up with the design for this."

"What is it?" Takashi asked, examining the technological trinket through his glowing eyes. "A new type of receiver?"

"I call it a 'mouse piece,' because it fits inside the pilot's mouth, like a mouthpiece, but it functions like a touchpad mouse. One cable jacks straight into the receiver port on the Mindbender Rift, and these plug into the audio and video feeds. All the options are now available to the pilot rather than here, in front of me. Collin will use the tip of his tongue to toggle between hosts, and he can drop himself into a host wherever and whenever he chooses. I built four of them. One for each of your headsets." Jill passed them out to each of the stunned team members.

Collin stared down at the ingenious component in the palm of his hand. "Are you telling us that you've had these things—the entire time?"

Jill nodded. "I'm sorry."

"Why did you sit on them for so long?"

"Why do you think? I'd just made myself irrelevant. Basically, I invented my own replacement. Too smart for my own good. Isn't that what you always used to say to me, back in college?" She smiled at J.J., and shrugged. "Obviously, I wasn't going to advertise what I'd discovered, but I knew that one day the need was probably going to arise, and today just happened to be that day."

"Jill, we do still need you," Takashi said.

"No. I promise you. You really and truly don't, but thanks." Jill folded her hands atop the duffle bag, and sighed. "The only person in this world who really needs me is my daughter. I'm a mommy, y'all, and I need to get back home to my baby girl."

"What's her name?" Skyler asked, after a long moment of silence.

"Luna."

Collin fumbled the headset in his lap. His hands were quivering, and he wasn't sure why. He disconnected the wiring from the fried receiver, and snapped the dead component off the side of the helmet. If Jill's new tech worked—and there was no doubt in his mind that it would, because Jill was nothing short of brilliant—then it was going to be a huge leap forward for the program. That should've made him happy, but it didn't. In fact, it was making him feel a little sick to his stomach, almost as though he'd just witnessed Jill sacrificing her own life for her friends. He didn't want the new tech. An infantile part of him kind of wanted to smash it to pieces, and to pretend he'd never seen such a thing, but that wouldn't change the fact that Jill was leaving their team behind. Collin plugged the red cable into the receiver port, and connected the auxiliaries to the audio and video feeds. Of course, everything fit perfectly.

"Go ahead. Try it on," Jill said, beaming, her eyes twinkling with excitement. "I'm as excited as anyone to see if it actually works."

Already, her state of mind seemed to be improving by leaps and bounds, while Collin was feeling sicker. It was as though he'd just been dumped, and now that the hard part was over, she was happily assuring him that they would still remain friends. It was unfair to judge her. Collin knew that. He couldn't possibly relate to her parental obligations from his own limited life experience as a dog owner, but he couldn't help it. This all felt so messed-up and wrong. He lifted the newfangled helmet over his head, dropped the visor, and then hesitated before inserting the device into his mouth.

"Yep. Just pop it in there, and switch it on."

"Takashi, we got any dolphins out there?" Collin asked.

"Oh, right." Jill chuckled. "I guess I was putting the cart before the horse."

"Umm—yes. Wow. We've got several, and I'm not familiar with any of them."

"How is that possible?" J.J. asked.

"Surprise. We've been preparing for you guys for a long time," Skyler replied. "We've got a fleet of close to fifty dolphins now, with a dozen stationed right here in the Yellow Sea. All subjects have been trained to respond to coordinates, and they're all already armed with nanobot harpoons."

"I'm getting eight swimmers, right now."

"Guys, I realize that from your perspective, it might've seemed like the Psyjack program was thrown together in haste," Skyler said, "but, in fact, we've been busy laying the groundwork for you guys for eighteen months, and I've been here for every step of the way. This is a program that I'm very proud of, and I truly believe that it's the best and only way forward."

Collin switched on the Mindbender Rift. When the visual display leapt up on the backside of the visor, an unexpected matrix of independent feeds nearly made his eyes cross. He was seeing everything that had once appeared on Jill's screen. Sweeping the tip of his tongue across the touchpad of the so-called mouse piece slid the highlighter cursor from one available dolphin to the next.

"When you're ready to select a feed and stream, just double-click."

The name and vitals of every dolphin appeared in the upper corner of their windows, as did their location on a separate radar screen that seemed to be streaming from Takashi's station. It struck Collin that Jill's brilliance had not only marginalized her own role in the team, but J.J.'s and Takashi's as well. The pilot no longer needed a support system. It was as though a leash around Collin's neck had just been unfastened. For the first time, he realized, he was free. All of the tools now belonged exclusively to the pilot, who was in complete control. Collin grabbed for the headset, and pulled it off, wide-eyed and out of breath.

"What's the problem?" Takashi asked.

Collin leveled his gaze at his old roommate, but he didn't know what to say. He could only stare back into those soulfully robotic eyes, and feel pity for him. Due to his physical handicap, Takashi was unable to receive the replicated stream of visual data from the nanobots associated with the optic nerves. While J.J. would still be able to serve Psyjack as a secondary dolphin pilot, Takashi didn't exactly have that option. As Collin stared at him, he wondered how you were supposed to tell your best friend that he'd just been made irrelevant, and while you're about to move up in the world, he'd be moving down.

"Well, what's the word? Does it work?" Jill asked.

Relieved for the opportunity to look away from Takashi, Collin nodded softly at Jill. "It works," he replied. "What you've done here is amazing."

Collin knew that he'd have to warn J.J. before he ever strapped on a headset. Together, they'd swear to never breathe a word about their newfound independence from their technological handler. The Navy was bound to figure it out eventually, but that didn't need to happen right away. By the time that bit of redundancy in the program was discovered, they'd hopefully have developed a new and important role for their friend.

"We're reaching position off the coast of Shanghai," the pilot said, his voice crackling over the speaker. "I'll maintain an elevation of five hundred feet throughout the operation. Just off the port side, the decoy is being launched from the harbor. Be advised, things are bound to happen fast."

All heads swiveled toward the windows on the hovercraft's port side, where the Pearl of the Orient's garish skyline rose bejeweled in neon trimming. Hot lancets of lightning jagged down through swarming drones to bridge the angry skies with architectural marvels that appeared to defy the laws of physics. Shanghai's harbors, once congested superhighways of commerce connecting every corner of the earth now stood at a standstill, choked with the thousands of landed ships that idled at their moorings.

"There it is," J.J. said, pressing up to a window. "There's our decoy."

Dripping with strings of glittering lights, a single ship plied the waters of Shanghai's harbor, headed out toward open sea. It was still recognizable as a battered Chinese hulk beneath all of that sparkling décor. Its hull was blackened by fire. It listed on its keel from the tons of seawater in its bilge. Looked like a casualty from the End War, and it probably was. Enmeshed in flickering lights meant to invite a Kaiju attack, the old warrior chugged toward its fateful rendezvous with an almost admirable deliberation.

"Alright," Collin said, sliding the Mindbender Rift back over his head. "Let's get this show on the road."

Except now, there was only Collin. He could hear Takashi's fingertips rattling away on a keyboard, pausing now and again to swipe through his floating layers of hologram windows. It pained him to know that whatever the wizard was doing back there was no longer necessary. Collin popped the dangling hardware into his mouth, scrolled through the dolphin feeds until the one nearest the ship became highlighted in red, and he tapped the mouse piece with the tip of his tongue. Collin heard himself suck a sharp breath through his teeth, and just like that, he was freefalling into his host.

A culture of nanobots being activated inside your brain was a sensation that was more than a little strange. Their electrical feedback alone felt like streams of tiny bubbles inside your head, or crawling bugs. It took some getting used to, but the incoming flood of visual and auditory data took your mind off of those nanobots in a hurry. Without the headset, streaming would be neurological chaos, mixing the pilot's sensory experience with everything streaming in from the host. The Mindbender Rift was both a filter and a stabilizer that softened the experience of the stream. Technically, it wasn't necessary, but Collin couldn't imagine the psychological torment of existing in two bodies at once.

"I've got three dolphins within range of the decoy," Takashi said.

Collin knew that. He'd discerned which of the three available hosts would be utilized and started streaming in a fraction of the time that it normally took the combined efforts of Takashi and Jill to patch him in. The new tech was unbelievable. Collin was soaring beneath the waves inside the head of a dolphin named Daisy, and he had the decoy ship in his sights.

"Wait, are you already in?" Takashi asked.

Collin hesitated before answering. It looked like his buddy's irrelevance was probably going to be discovered sooner than later. "Yeah. I'm streaming Daisy right now."

"Oh."

Takashi's voice sounded a little strange. Collin was glad that he was wearing the headset, because he didn't really want to see Takashi's expression fall, as the slow realization set in. This situation was not unlike watching some wounded thing dragging its carcass around the floor, unable to put it out of its misery.

"Well, I guess if you've got radar and streaming covered with the new tech," Takashi said, "then I'll just shift my primary focus over to sonar and thermal imagery. Come on, kids. Let's go on a monster hunt."

Collin laughed. Clearly, he should've given Takashi a little more credit. His value to the team would never depreciate, no matter what the changing circumstances.

"How is it down there?" J.J. asked.

Collin smiled. "If I told you, you wouldn't believe it. I'm afraid that you're just going to have to experience this for yourself."

Collin tipped his dolphin snout and plunged into the polluted depths of the Yellow Sea. The water was so turbid that it possessed an almost fuzzy quality due to the massive amount of suspended solids rushing past the screen. Light scarcely penetrated fifteen meters, and thirty meters was absolute blackness. It had been a long while since he'd used the functions of the handgrip, but Collin's thumb found its way toward the switch that activated the dolphin vest's submersible lights. The screen leapt into sickening brilliance, providing every detail of the stew through which he traveled.

"I'm picking up massive structures on the sea floor," Takashi said.

"Kaiju?"

"I don't think so. I'm not getting any heat signatures. What I'm seeing are formations. Almost looks like a lost city down there."

"Shipwrecks," J.J. replied. "Probably the Chinese fleet lost in the Battle of Yangtze. Turning point in the End War. We're over a graveyard."

Collin slowed his pace to avoid impaling his dolphin host on a piece of debris. He could see forms thrusting up from the sea floor, but it was difficult to make out much of anything in the murk. Clearly, Takashi had a better view of this crucible of bygone things deliquescing back into primordial sludge. It crossed Collin's mind to inquire if Jill could add sonar and heat signature options to the new tech, but he decided that bumping Takashi out of his second job in five minutes was probably not the best idea.

"Some of those wrecks may be more recent than the End War," Skyler replied. "In the last year, hundreds of ships have been lost in this region."

"What do we need to know about these things we're dealing with?" J.J. asked.

"Of all the organisms brought back from Europa, bloodfins are the most predictable," Skyler replied. "They're the bullies of our interactive tanks, where we introduce different species in a controlled environment to observe their strengths and weaknesses. Bloodfins are fiercely territorial. You can count on them to defend what tends to be a rather entitled amount of personal space. Anything that strays too near what they perceive to be their hunting grounds will immediately be regarded as one of two things: a rival challenger, or foo—"

"Wait a minute," Takashi said. "We've got something."

"What is it?" J.J. asked.

"Hard to tell, but it's big. It's showing up on several drone sonar feeds."

J.J. rushed for the gunner's station, where he alone had clearance to the Devil Ray's deadly arsenal of cannons, as well as views from multiple external cameras. Buckles clicked across his chest. Pneumatic valves hissed as he lowered the periscopic viewfinder from its storage position on the ceiling. Those familiar sounds of rehearsed actions performed countless times by the well-oiled machine that their team used to be was like comfort food to the ears.

"Can you guide me in, Takashi?" Collin asked. "I'm kind of flying blind over here."

Visual streaming was worthless in such a dense and lightless miasma. If not for the depth readings derived from the water pressure on the dolphin's vest, it would've been impossible even to discern which way was up. Daisy's oxygen levels had dropped from the green to the yellow zone. She'd need to surface soon.

"Forty-five degrees to the east. Approaching the decoy head-on, at a speed of about forty knots."

"That doesn't do me any good down here."

"Start veering starboard. I'll let you know when you've got the right trajectory."

"What do I do once I'm on this thing? Skyler?"

"Go for the gill slits," Skyler replied. "Bloodfins have huge masses of capillaries just behind the gill plates, on either side of their jaws. That's where you'll want to aim your harpoon. A dolphin ought to be small enough that you won't be perceived as either a threat or a food source, but maintain a safe distance and be careful, all the same."

"Sounds easy." Collin wasn't sure if they'd detected his sarcasm. Beneath the headset, a pilot was robbed of the luxuries of eye contact and facial expression when trying to make a point, and that imposed some limitations on conversational nuances. The truth was that he wasn't even sure if he was being sarcastic or not. To his teammates, Collin did make dolphin piloting look easy, because for him, it was. Collin had no difficulty speaking casually to those seated around him while streaming dolphin data. J.J. was more clunky and wooden in the dolphin suit, and Jill was even worse. They twitched and contorted their human bodies in a grotesque rendition of their host's vicarious movements, as if the whole experience was just as uncomfortable and disorienting to them, as it was liberating to Collin.

It sounded like this operation was going to be pretty similar to the old torpedo training exercises in many respects. The only significant difference was that his target wasn't likely going to be moving in a nice linear pattern like that of a ship or a submarine. From what he'd observed in the naval laboratory, the bloodfins swam like conger eels, writhing and undulating their serpentine bodies through the water. Lining up a direct shot on a small area of a moving target like that was going be difficult. It would be tough even in crystalline waters, and this sea was like a bowl of dirt soup.

"Alright, stop turning. Straighten out. There you go. You're on it. You got this, man."

Takashi's reassuring words did little to extinguish the rising trepidation that ignited Collin's nerve endings afire from the first instant they'd boarded the Devil Ray. He couldn't easily forget how things had ended the last time he'd buckled into a pilot's chair. They'd taken an awful beating. It required something of an athlete's psychology to rise above that last defeat, and to march back out onto the playing field. However, Collin wasn't much an athlete, aside from those hours he'd logged on an off-kilter air hockey table.

"How close am I?" Collin asked.

"Closing … I'd expect a rendezvous in less than thirty seconds. Better head for the surface."

"Headed that way. My girl needs a breath."

"Got a visual!" J.J. said. "It's headed right for the decoy, and—oh, man. This thing is a monster!"

Collin could actually hear the smile on J.J.'s face. He was getting anxious for a glimpse of anything besides polluted water. His visual was a torrent of what looked like coffee grounds and chewing tobacco. Depth readings indicated that Daisy the dolphin was going to breach the surface in a matter of seconds.

"Good God almighty." Collin heard his own muffled exclamation resonating apart from his host's rubbery squeals and clicks, as Daisy's head burst from the waves. Collin felt quite suddenly like the smallest minnow in the world, swimming alone in the Kraken's shadow.

The bloodfin slashed its upraised head from side to side, displacing mountains of seawater with every sweep. Eyes like portals to some alien world took turns offering glimpses into that frigid oblivion, while fathoms of its endless body unreeled forever behind. At every turn of that battle-scarred chin, the great jaws gaped, revealing a forest of translucent teeth. Higher still, and billowing with great folds of vermillion, a hoisted dorsal sail seemed to send a declaration of war that was just as clear to the inhabitants of this world as it would've been in any other. The foreboding banner flapped against the dark and brooding skies.

"Look at the size of those gill plates," Collin said, gaping up at a mountainside fissure, splitting and resealing with clocklike regularity. Each parting of that wall of flesh flashed a glimpse of the target. It was almost as though the monster was aware of its weak spot, and made access to that slot of crimson viscera into a deadly game of perfect timing. "What's the range on my weapon? I don't want to get cut in half."

"The harpoons are effective out to fifty meters," Skyler replied.

"We've got some kind of a strange issue, here," J.J. said.

"What is it?"

"I don't know. I've never seen this warning come up before. Some sort of a contingency on your weapons protocol."

"My weapons protocol?"

"Yeah. Somebody toss me my radio, would you?"

"I don't know how long I can keep up with this thing." Collin swung Daisy's head in the direction of the bloodfin, and with a hard thrust of her flukes, swept alongside the oscillating cliff that was the monster's head. He could hear J.J. shouting into his radio, presumably at Captain Roswell, but it was difficult to remain in touch with the world inside the Devil Ray when the Yellow Sea was roaring in Daisy's ears. He watched the vacillating gill slit, mesmerized and repulsed by the red tonnage of exposed veins. The shot would have to be perfect.

"Tactical field commander's approval?" J.J. yelled. "What field commander? I'm the only commander in this field!"

"J-man, what's the story on that contingency?"

The dolphin's stress levels were edging up into the yellow zone. Not difficult to imagine why. Daisy probably wouldn't be able to maintain her breakneck pace alongside the slithering wall of death for much longer. Dolphins exhibited incredible endurance under normal circumstances, but this situation was anything but normal. The animal was terrified. It was wanting to tap out, and go somewhere else.

"Got a bogie coming in fast at four-o'clock," Takashi said.

"Are you serious?" Jill replied. "Who'd be crazy enough to come out here right now?"

Through borrowed eyes, Collin watched a dark mass of angled steel descend from the swirling clouds. Like the Devil Ray, the flying weapon was designed to thwart radar detection. An array of rockets bristled from the undersides of downturned wings. Only one thought burned in his mind. "Is it pirates?"

"No," J.J. replied. "It's the SEALs."

"Stand by to be boarded." The terse voice of the Devil Ray's assigned pilot emanated through the speaker system. "Tactical field command has arrived."

The gunship lowered through skeins of mist until it hung nose to nose with the Devil Ray, mere centimeters between their cockpits. The intimidation did not appear to be accidental. With the pugnacious aircraft's wicked arsenal aimed right in their faces, it was made plain to see that they were outgunned and outmatched.

"What the heck is going on?" Takashi asked.

"I'm going to lose him!" Collin gritted his teeth, pushing the stressed dolphin to her physical limits in order to remain within range of that champing gill slit, but the bloodfin was beginning to pull into the lead. Daisy's stress levels were entering the red.

"It's over," J.J. said.

"What? What are you talking about? Like heck it's over!" Takashi shouted.

"This ain't our show anymore, bud, and I'm not sure it ever was."

Collin eased back on the control, engaged the vest's pneumatic stabilizers, and floated the spent dolphin atop the waves. Daisy's stress meter continued to flash in warning at the top-right corner of the screen, while the undulating sea dragon bore down on the decoy amidst swarms of video drones. Collin couldn't bring himself to watch. He closed his eyes just as the bloodfin's sabered maw gaped wide, and listened to the sound of rending steel and explosions as its jaws slammed shut around the ship. Massive coils churned the seawater into foam, as the monster took the vessel for a death roll.

The cockpit of the SEAL gunship yawned open with a gaseous hiss. Backlit by the electrical storm, a dark figure arose from the aircraft's throat. Collin blinked in the flash of distant explosions, the flickering strings of decoy lights, as armed flanks of Navy SEALs marched across a boarding plank.

Collin switched off the Mindbender Rift headset. Although he welcomed the enveloping blackness, he found no real sanctuary within it. Invaders stormed through the cockpit. Their trundling military boots reverberated through the fuselage, accompanied by a reeking cloud of sweat, brine, and gunpowder. Hotspot laid down his ears, and emitted a low growl.

"Easy, boy."

There was no mistaking the foreboding presence aboard their ship. Here they were, once again, being punished for trespassing in the Yellow Sea. The warrant officer in charge of this boarding could be none other than Miles Bent, the Mad Hatter of Shanghai.

Chapter Seven

The severed dolphin head tumbled from its sacking onto the laboratory bench in a slurry of pinkish ice. Rivulets of stained water spilled from the counter's edge to pool on the tile floor. The Red Brotherhood loitered in the wings, as Dr. Wu approached the remnants of the defunct sea creature, and placed his hand with a paternal tenderness upon its sunken cheek. The room's silence was broken only by the spatter of water droplets, and by the constant hum of the incandescent lights. The dolphin's bleary eye stared up into the appraising face of the Chinese scientist with the dullest regard. The doctor's hand slid over the mottled flesh until it came to rest upon the animal's bulbous forehead. The hint of a smile curled the corner of his mouth, as he patted the dolphin's crown. He glanced up to the overhead monitor, where Volkov's image lingered. "I think I know this one. I will have to digest," Dr. Wu said.

Volkov frowned.

"Digest head—in acid." The doctor was struggling just a little with the Tong-Tai dialect of the lower Yangtze, a tongue more closely related to its Mongolian linguistic roots than to any brand of Mandarin, evidencing a foreign presence that had endured for centuries in Nantong. Rumor held that the foothold was originally established by a colony of Mongolian criminals whose descendants were never extirpated.

The doctor nodded and smiled. "This one mine."

"I don't understand," Volkov replied. "What are you talking about?"

The doctor patted the dolphin's head. "Nanobots in here. Very tiny. I get them out."

"Don't damage anything. Understand? No damage."

"No, no damage." The doctor shook his head. Scurrying over to the large steel cabinet covered with corrosive placards, he swung open the double-doors with a terrible squeal of rusted hinges. Inside were rows and rows of glass jugs, amber and clear. As if in afterthought, the doctor darted off to a cluttered corner, seized a plastic tote and overturned it where he stood. Nameless contents rained to the floor with a terrible clatter. Once emptied, he returned to the acid cabinet, and dropped the empty tub on the floor. "Put head in here."

Still shackled upon the central examination table, Mr. Krupin watched as the Mongol giant called Jochi obeyed Dr. Wu's command. He seized the dolphin by its serrated snout, and raised it to give it a sniff. Jochi wrinkled his nose. He then swaggered in the direction of the plastic tote. Dr. Wu was already cracking the seals on glass jugs, and pouring their steaming contents into the tub. Jochi ambled right into the rising cloud. He reared back coughing, drawing his forearm across his nose and mouth, and shot an incredulous glare at Dr. Wu. The doctor noticed his reaction, and as though he'd just been reminded of some critical step he'd forgotten, he flipped a nearby switch into an upward position. An overhead fume hood came to life with a hollow whine. Currents of air began to slither through the laboratory, drawn up into the vortex created by the spinning fan. The doctor resumed his work, emptying jug after jug of acid into the vessel until he'd procured a volume that he deemed satisfactory. "You put head in now," he said to Jochi, pointing at the steaming container. "Very gentle."

Jochi glanced uncertainly at the doctor, as though he'd never done anything gently in his life. Goaded by the doctor's expressionless stare, Jochi leaned lowered the severed head into the fumes. Received by furious fluids, the smiling face of the dolphin disappeared into the boiling cauldron. Jochi was quick to step back a few paces, as some violent reaction was triggered by the strange ingredient he'd just added to the witch's brew. Unaffected by the sights and smells before him, as though he'd experienced the same situation a thousand times, Dr. Wu stared straight down into his angry concoction, hands folded behind his back, while the lenses of his glasses steamed over.

Krupin's eyes crept around the room, studying each of the Mongols. Two still held their weapons. The others had shouldered their rifles, and holstered their pistols. They leaned against walls and counters, transfixed by the gruesome science.

A dance of death was composed with inside Krupin's mind. A lifetime of fighting and killing had transformed his brain into a computer of violent choreography, where every strike, every contortion of his flying form accounted for all possible reactions and counterattacks with automatic precision, until each enemy was neatly dispatched—all but one, anyhow. Krupin's eyes came to rest on the broad back of Jochi, lingering at the front of the room like a spellbound ape. His thick knuckles were still ruddy with blood, stained from the beating he'd inflicted. Jochi would die last of all, and he would die in some spectacular fashion. Krupin smiled, as dark artwork splashed against the walls of his mind.

Dr. Wu probed his stew with a measuring stick, frowning down into a reaction that had stilled to a simmer. As though he'd already arrived at some conclusion, he relocated to a table dedicated to a large manifold of glass filters and funnels. He fussed with the complex system, opening and closing valves, switching on little vacuum pumps, and releasing flows of distilled water through coiled tubing.

"Okay," he said, placing his thin hands on his hips, and scrutinizing over his contraption. When no one moved, Dr. Wu spun around and glared at Jochi. He threw up his hands. "What you wait for? Bring me it."

"Oh," Jochi replied, lurching into motion. He retrieved the steaming tub from the floor. Grimacing, he turned his nose, and transported the awkward sloshing container over to the filtration station, where the doctor instructed him which vessel was going to receive the dolphin slurry.

Pinkish froth slopped against the glass as the level rose. Fragments of bone clinked musically against the bottom. Dr. Wu used a water wand to rinse the vessel walls, as a vacuum pump pulled the thick amalgam through coiled tubing into a magnetic separation chamber. He flipped a switch, and a centrifuge began to spin, pulling all of the solids down into the vessel's concave paunch. After solids and liquids had been separated, the dregs dissolved, separated, and filtered through several stages, the end result that was captured in an ordinary test tube appeared to be nothing more than a shot of clear water. Dr. Wu inserted a hypodermic needle into the final test tube, and drew back on the plunger. Once the syringe was filled, he held the gleaming needle aloft before Volkov's digital image.

"What am I looking at?"

"Nanobots." Dr. Wu smiled up at the screen.

"Looks like nothing to me. How can you tell?"

"Because I talk to them." The doctor tapped his temple with his index finger. "Mine talk to them."

"You're communicating with them? Right now?"

"Of course." Dr. Wu nodded. "I the master. These slave."

Volkov's jade eyes widened. His image moved a little closer to the screen. He tapped his chest with two fingers. "I want to be a master."

Dr. Wu's smile fell. His gaze hardened on Volkov, as though some silent judgement was being passed. After a moment, he turned away from the monitor, and he strode over to a refrigerator located at the back of the laboratory. Disappearing inside the open door for a moment, the doctor reappeared with a second hypodermic syringe. He held it up to the monitor. "This one make you master." Lowering the new needle, he held aloft the first one. "This make you slave."

"Can I enslave something other than a dolphin?"

The doctor scowled. "You don't like dolphin?"

Volkov cleared his throat, and pressed his fingertips together. "Dr. Wu, you were the best and the brightest in this field of study. For over a decade, you were head of the College of Neurology at the University of Glasgow, where all of the major breakthroughs were being made. You were standing at the top, on the cutting edge of nanobot technology, and then, something happened."

"What happen?"

"You tell me." Volkov leveled his eyes at the doctor. "You left Glasgow and returned to China, leaving behind a good life and an outstanding reputation. After you left, Glasgow's nanobot program fell into ruin. Why?"

Dr. Wu shook his head, clinging to his two syringes. "I don't know."

"The Allied Navy shut you down. Once they'd stolen your technology, your ideas, they made sure that no one else would ever get their hands on it. They took your work, your inventions, and even your best and brightest students, and they poured all of those stolen things into the heads of dolphins." Volkov narrowed his eyes. "That's why I don't like dolphins, and neither do you. We need something superior to the Navy's swimming clowns. Something bigger."

"Kaiju," the doctor whispered. His eyes returned to the quivering hypodermics in his hands. Their needlepoints were reflected on the lenses of his glasses. "You want Kaiju."

Twisting, twisting, Krupin rotated his wrists against their bindings, working the plastic straps down against bone. This was a silent performance. His expression never changed, even as meat peeled away, and blood flowed from his wrists and ankles. He felt warm droplets falling from his fingertips, but bone wouldn't give. Bone was something that he could pull against with all of his might. Twisting, twisting, he replayed the steps to that deadly dance inside his mind, visualizing every violent change of partners.

"I want to see your technology work," Volkov said. "I want to see it work here, now, before we ever take it out into the field." Squinting one eye, Volkov pointed a finger at Mr. Krupin. "Test it out on the Russian. I want to see you enslave his mind."

Dr. Wu glanced back at Krupin, and then implored the looming face on the screen. "Helmet," he said, gesturing to the sides of his own head. "Must have helmet. Too much data for human mind."

"What sort of helmet are you talking about?"

"Receiver. Data filter." The doctor frowned, shaking his head, still frustrated by the limitations of the linguistic barrier. "Protect mind's eye. Too much data. Must protect mind's eye with helmet. Too much data cook brain."

"You can build me one."

"I don't—" Dr. Wu stammered, backing a step away from the monitor. "Don't know make helmet." The needles trembled in his hands. He backed into the central island where Mr. Krupin was still and prone.

"You can get me a helmet, then. Steal one. I don't care. You can get me whatever I need." Volkov turned his head to one side. A hitch of his chin prompted the agonized wails of a woman who was evidently staged somewhere just off-screen. Dr. Wu folded his needled hands, begging, pleading, but the Moscow Mongol appeared distracted. Volkov's smug expression had just plunged like a hanged man through a gallows. Volkov leaned forward until his face filled the monitor. His bulging eyes searched the laboratory, as though he'd just lost track of something of real importance. "Mr. Krupin?"

Blood and snapped plastic ties were all that remained of the subject on the examination table. The room shook with rhythmic concussions before a flashing muzzle. A rifle bolt snapped back. A stolen pistol joined its former owner on the floor. A second barrage commenced before the Red Brothers' collective minds could even grasp what had just transpired. Groveling bodies fountained blood from red cavities. One dragged loops of glistening entrails away from the source of the destruction. Not a single scream was emitted, as bullets shredded lower cabinets to tear hot tunnels through cowardly flesh. Gore painted the walls like a gallery of abstract artwork. One hung quivering in the filtration apparatus, missing the better part of his head. The crawling were stilled, the vocal silenced, as Mr. Krupin paid brief visits from a rifle's length to each Red Brother, until the fat head of Jochi at last filled his sights.

"Please," the giant said, hiding behind those softball mitts for hands.

"Mr. Krupin," Volkov said, in a voice broken with uncharacteristic cracks, "I brought you here to be a part of this. This is something much bigger than you or I. This was all for you, Krupin. I did all of this for you."

Mr. Krupin whipped his wired head in the direction of the monitor, laughed, and licked the blood from his bared teeth. This was just the sort of situation where his mechanical mask provided him with a peculiar advantage, because he could not speak, and therefore, was rendered unable to negotiate. He was a beast, a force of nature that could only run its course. Blood streamed from his lacerated wrists and ankles, spattering the floor at his feet as though he walked through a shower of rose petals.

"You were the only one I could trust to deliver the dolphin here. You're my best, my very best, and I need you now more than ever."

Krupin glanced down at the shuddering form of Dr. Wu. Still hunkered at the base of the examination table, the scientist clenched his pair of quivering needles as though they were the antidote to death itself. However, all Krupin had to do was to start swiveling the barrel in Wu's direction, and the needles were extended as a peace offering.

"Mr. Krupin?" Volkov said, his voice rising in timbre by at least two octaves. "Would you like to be the master?"

Licking his teeth, he flicked his gaze back up to the looming face of his employer. There was the man for whom he'd risked his life on so many occasions, the one to whom he'd delivered so many gifts, for whom he'd suffered so much to please. In the end, no matter how hard he'd fought, no matter what lengths he'd traveled to earn that bastard's respect, Krupin would never be anything more than a Russian, like Volkov's mother.

"You can be the master. You deserve that honor, for all your years of service to the Brotherhood. I want to prove my sincerity," Volkov said, displaying more emotion than Krupin had ever suspected the man had in him. "What better way could I prove my trust in you, and my respect, than by placing the most powerful weapon in all the world right into your hands? It's yours. I mean it. Take it."

Keeping the rifle trained on Jochi, Krupin outstretched his hand. Red droplets quavered and fell from his fingertips, as they encircled the thin hypodermic that was still cold from refrigerated storage. Strange, that something so immensely powerful could hide itself in a shot of what looked like pure water. Krupin held the syringe to the incandescent lights for a moment to admire the invisible monster within. Satisfied, he rotated the instrument in his fingertips until the needle was inverted, and then he slammed the steel point into his rump and depressed the plunger.

"Now, I can get you safely out of Nantong." Volkov's voice had lowered to a steadier pitch, as though he was feeling assured of some incremental return of control over the situation. "If you'll take Dr. Wu out back to the loading docks, I'll send over a drone." Volkov cleared his throat. "Just hop aboard the drone, and come back to me. Things will be different between us from here on out. That's a promise. You have my word."

The face of Volkov disappeared. The monitor faded into blackness. The only sounds in the laboratory were the buzzing of overhead lights, and the rattling breaths of a dying man. A queer sort of intimacy had fallen over the laboratory where Krupin now reigned king, and after so much drama, the new quietude amongst corpses struck him as being kind of funny. A naughty child who'd just committed some terrible mischief might've experienced a similar giddiness, having realized that there weren't going to be any repercussions, whatsoever. Emitting a chuff of laughter, Krupin tossed the spent syringe over his shoulder. Things had worked out rather well.

Dr. Wu rose to his feet, and relinquished the second syringe. Holding it up to the light, just as he'd done with the first, Krupin squinted into the living emptiness of the slave serum. Although teeming with wonderful things, once again, there was nothing to see. Slightly pink with dolphin essence, this one felt warmer to the touch. It also felt somehow corrupted. Krupin's gaze slid down the point of the needle, and at its end, he found the cowering mass of Jochi.

***

"What are you doing boarding our ship?"

J.J. slammed the periscopic viewfinder against the ceiling. He rose from his battle station to meet the Mad Hatter in the center aisle. From this stark perspective, and for the first time, it was possible to compare the men in size. Collin was surprised to see that J.J. was in fact much larger than their rival, whose indomitable persona and violent reputation had always made him seem much bigger than he actually stood, lean, wiry and unwavering.

"This hovercraft is the property of the SWCC," Bent replied, with a voice coarsened by boat exhaust. "You're civilian support, subordinate to field command, and I'm the tactical field commander in these waters. I own you." He strode right past J.J., deeper into the Devil Ray, as though any threat that J.J. might've thought he'd presented was dismissed.

The dog began to bark, flashing its teeth at the invader with every snap of its jaws. Collin collared Hotspot, and pulled the animal close. His eyes fell to Bent's uniform, where the blue bars of a chief warrant officer had been replaced by the silver leaf of a field commander. He wasn't bluffing. During their two-year hiatus, the Mad Hatter had evidently earned quite a promotion. Although Captain Roswell still outranked him, by entering the Yellow Sea, they'd left the underside of Roswell's protective wing. Here, Bent could and probably would stymie their fledgling program into irrelevance. However, unbeknownst to Bent, Collin had just flipped his power toggle, and was back in the game.

While J.J. and the Mad Hatter roared in each other's faces, Collin spurred his dolphin in the direction of the bloodfin, circling its vanquished prey. Daisy's oxygen readings were normal, and her stress levels were back in the green. Cresting over waves, and plunging through the valleys between, Collin angled his animal for a perpendicular attack on the target's vacillating gill. A flick of his thumb unlocked the weapon guard. He armed the nanobot harpoon. The weapon snapped into forward position. The familiar sight of those digital crosshairs nucleated his private screen, as he entered shooter mode.

"Who's doing that?" Bent's voice was a sawblade through rusty metal. "Who's doing that, up there on that screen?"

Collin had forgotten about the overhead monitor, where his dolphin's perspective was being broadcasted for viewing by the rest of the crew. He could only imagine what Bent must've been thinking, as he veered in alongside the writhing wall of flesh, but it wasn't going to take the Mad Hatter long to determine who was in control. Leaping through the monster's wake, he closed the distance between Daisy and her intermittently exposed target.

"Well, I guess if you sit down, we could try to explain all of our technology to you," J.J. replied, with a condescending inflection, "but I'm afraid it might take all afternoon. Kind of complicated."

"Is that a drone? I told you to shut it down!"

"It's not technically a drone. I don't know how you'd classify it. What would you call it, Takashi?"

"It's way cooler than a drone."

"Shut it down! Ground it, whatever it is!"

"I can't."

"What do you mean, you can't?"

J.J. had run out of ways to stall him. The mission was coming down to a matter of seconds, and Collin knew it. If he didn't squeeze off the shot, then a decoy had just been scuttled for nothing, and another a golden opportunity to prove themselves would be squandered. He gritted his teeth and bore down, driving Daisy just as hard as her body could take it, until the monster's yawning gill slit was within range.

The gill slammed shut, extruding gouts of seawater like a clam. Then, it relaxed, and began to reopen. Collin locked the crosshairs onto the slot of crimson innards, and squeezed the trigger on his handset. The weapon's discharge blew the dolphin askew, filling the viewfinder with a kaleidoscopic whirlpool of darkness and light. Collin lost all orientation, and didn't know whether to bring her up, or take her down. The animal's stress levels had pegged the vitals meter, sending Daisy's biomonitoring system into a cheeping chaos of alarms, until the whole screen crashed to black.

"What happened?" Jill asked. "Are you still with her?"

Collin gasped for breath, feeling as though he'd suffered some vicarious blow in the dolphin's stead. This was a hard point of separation, ripping loose from the psyche of another being after you'd just become one. It left you feeling disoriented, drained, and disconnected from the rest of the living world.

"You!"

Collin felt the Mad Hatter seize two fistfuls of his shirt, before being hauled straight up from his pilot's chair. Hotspot lunged. Clamping his teeth on the cuff of Collin's flight jacket, the animal began tugging with all its might. Collin dropped the wireless handset to the floor with a clatter, and spat the mouse-piece from his lips. The headset swiveled around sideways, until he was staring into an earhole, wondering what on earth he was looking at.

"Let go of him now, or I'll knock you out," J.J. said. His voice was close enough that it made Collin's stomach do a flip. It felt like he was caught in the middle of a bare-knuckle brawl between two heavyweight contenders.

"What did you say to me, pogue?"

"Let him go, now."

Collin was released the same instant that arms began to grapple. Boots squeaked against rubber flooring, and huge bodies crashed into seats. He struggled to straighten his stupid headset and crawl out of harm's way, when he noticed that a new window option had appeared in the tiled selection of available hosts. A new host had just come online.

"Stop it!" Jill shouted.

This view stream was different from a dolphin's. Instead of the usual submarine view of an oceanic world, this feed was a bird's eye view of the situation. Collin was a floating eye looking down at the Devil Ray and the SEAL gunship, sistered by boarding planks and ratlines, five-hundred feet above the sea. Far below, he noticed the transected pieces of a mutilated bloodfin thrashing mindlessly in a spreading stain of monster blood. It didn't make sense.

Collin popped the mouse-piece back between his teeth. He crawled between a couple of seats where he wouldn't be crushed by the brawlers. Toggling past the new aerial perspective, he re-selected the stream of Daisy, who was still swimming near the surface. He double-clicked to drop back into her stream of consciousness, and the sight towering before his borrowed eyes stole his breath away.

"Look out the window! Look out the freaking window!" Takashi screamed.

It was as though one of Shanghai's architectural wonders had come suddenly to life, tore loose of its footings in the city skyline, and just waded out into the sea. The teetering thing balanced atop those columned tentacles for legs was something incomprehensible to an earthling mind. Blood, black as squid ink, streamed down the upturned bowl of a shell from a harpoon wound just beneath its cyclopean eye. Evidently, the monster had surfaced right between the dolphin and the bloodfin, just as Collin squeezed the trigger. Horned mantis pincers folded prettily before its breastplate clung to a wriggling segment of the bloodfin that had been snipped all to pieces. The creature conveyed the chunk of meat into a grinder of busy mouthparts. It appeared as though the Chinese dragons of the Yellow Sea were nothing but a snack for this gargantuan monster that didn't seem much bothered by the harpoon near its eye.

"Charybdis," Skyler said, almost laughing in disbelief. "It's a Charybdis."

"Kah-what?"

"This is one of the ones … so perfect … regenerates limbs, and—"

"Good God almighty," Commander Bent said, blurting his exclamation as he staggered a couple of steps away from the window.

Collin toggled down the row of available dolphin streams, until the cursor came to rest upon the looming eye in the sky. He had him. He really had that monster as one of his streaming options. This odds of such a fortune resulting from collateral damage was staggering, but Collin felt as though he'd just unlocked the big boss character in the greatest fighting game ever created. He double-clicked with his tongue, and went tumbling back into the destroyer's immense head.

"Oh my God, it's getting closer." Jill turned to shout down the corridor at their pilot, who seemed to be sitting awestruck in the Kaiju's shadow. "What are you doing up there? Get the ship out of the way!"

"We can't move," he replied. "We're tethered to the SEAL aircraft."

"Get the hell out of here," J.J. shouted in Bent's face. "You're going to get us all killed!"

The host's body was so alien, in every sense. How to maneuver such a top-heavy and lilting creature upon a clutch of tentacles was not a task that Collin was able to wrap his mind around. It wasn't anything like piloting a dolphin, given the whole mess of awkward appendages. The pincers were easy enough to see through his mind's eye, but the legs were another story.

"It's going to fall!" Takashi said.

"Get back to the ship. That thing's injured. We can take it down." Commander Bent's voice prompted a thunder of boots toward the cockpit. "You people." He pointed at J.J., narrowed his eyes, and then swung his finger around at the others. "You land this aircraft at Shanghai field command. Now!"

"Wait," Skyler shouted after the departing SEALs. "It's on our side!"

"Ohhh, cheese and crackers ..." Collin's whole world teetered like an inverted pendulum. The incoming data stream suggested that its tentacles were entangled in some sort of debris on the sea floor. Probably all of that wreckage. It made the challenge of learning to walk on numerous legs a nearly impossible feat. Bloodfins writhed through his undercarriage like a bed of eels, but due to the position of his single eye, surmounted directly atop the great mushroom cap of a shell, he couldn't see them. It blocked the view of anything beneath the rim of its carapace. The creature seemed to be designed as a bottom dweller, an armored tank with a watchful topside eye for a turret, scanning the skies above for any sign of danger. Those tentacle legs would've been more effective in the weightless conditions of the deep, where the monster could leap tiptoed through lightless abysms, poised to snap its claws at anything that might fit inside of its mouth. Encumbered by the gravitational pull of the surface world, it was decidedly more unsteady.

"Wait a minute. Is that you?" J.J. smacked Collin in the shoulder.

"What are you doing? Collin, look out! You're going to crash right into us." Jill grabbed hold of his upper arm.

"Guys, quit touching me." Collin yanked his arm away, and rose from the floorboards between seats to his feet. They were bumping him out of the verisimilitude of the stream. He rose from between the seats. "I think I need to stand to be able to do this."

The world from his Kaiju perspective steadied, as he divided the multitude of legs to better portray his familiar bipedal posture, thereby convincing his mind's eye to grasp control over the halved appendages. Moving several with each step, he edged his way out of the entanglement of sunken ships, and away from the danger zone around the Devil Ray. "I can do this," he said, in a whisper.

"Lean back a little," J.J. said. "You're pitched too far forward. That's what's making you off-balance. Just lean back."

"Shut up," Jill said, in a hiss.

Although he couldn't see his own feet, the tentacles were highly sensitive. Once he was able to recognize the sensory feedback from his appendages, his muddled orientation in the alien body began to clarify. J.J. was actually right. Leaning back, and tipping his shell forward not only felt more comfortable, more balanced, but also afforded him the protection of walking behind a massive shield. Collin raised his arms, and unhinged his enormous pincers. Snapping them shut produced a thunderclap that evoked a few cries of alarm.

"Collin," Takashi said, "you are one bad mamma jamma."

"The Charybdis is one of the toughest fighters in the interaction tanks," Skyler said. "Those pincers possess incredible crushing force. They sliced right any species we ever pitted Carl against."

"Wait, what?" Takashi replied. "Did you just say, 'Carl?'"

"Yeah. Carl the Charybdis." Skyler shrugged. "I told you, I had my favorites."

Takashi reached out to knuckle-bump Jill. "That's awesome."

"Look out, buddy," J.J. said. "SEALs are tacking around behind you."

"Call them off, then. Don't let them mess this up!"

J.J. dragged the periscopic viewfinder back down from the ceiling, and patched over to the military radio band. "Psyjack to Commander Bent. That's a friendly target. I repeat. That Kaiju is a friendly target. Hold your fire."

"He's not going to listen," Jill said. "Get Captain Roswell on the line."

"SWCC Devil Ray to Barrier One. Psyjack to Barrier One."

"There's no time. They're swinging around into firing position," Skyler said. "Collin, you need to get out of there!"

"How?" he shouted.

Plodding forward without stumbling was becoming a familiar articulation, but rotating his top-heavy bulk upon that precarious and teetering scaffold was quite another story. Collin could see the engaging gunship. When he leveled his carapace, his turret eye afforded him a commanding field of vision that was every bit of three-hundred-sixty degrees. By tipping his domed shell at the waist, he could angle the natural shield to provide his underside protection from an attack in any direction. That was helpful. However, rotating the whole show dipped his balance off-kilter.

"Here they come."

A white flash from the gunship preceded two spiraling projectiles that burned intertwining trails of cordite through the air. It looked like it was going to be a direct hit. Collin angled his armored carapace in the direction of the incoming missiles, and braced himself for the blow. At the last second, he discovered that he was able to withdraw his cyclopean eye beneath a protective hatch. Two concussions rocked through his cavernous enormity. Their shockwaves shivered down his weird appendages to the tips of his tentacle feet.

"You're going to fall."

Collin reopened his armored eyelid in time to see shelves of storm clouds racing past, from one horizon of his vastness to the next. The effect of the explosions hadn't exactly hurt, but they'd certainly left him feeling dazed, and his ungainly new form had been knocked into a state of imbalance that could not be corrected. The ocean received his toppling enormity with a thunderous embrace.

Chapter Eight

"Stay down, dude," Takashi said. "Let those tools think they nailed you."

Blinking his single eye in the new environment, Collin was amazed by how well this strange creature was able to see through the polluted murk of the Yellow Sea. Evidently well adapted to life in the darkest of conditions, its vision seemed to be bolstered with filters and light-gathering photoreceptors that enabled clear vision, even through the worst turbidity. As his stolen body sank deeper into the shipping channel, his vision became no more obscured than if he'd been immersed in tap water. That wonderful eye kept making adjustments for the dimming conditions, harvesting ample light from a barren field of vision.

"What's your depth?" Takashi asked. Clearly, the others were also baffled by what they were seeing on the overhead monitor.

"Eighty meters. The sea's pretty shallow here. I need to get out into deeper water, and fast."

"No-no-no. Don't you even move," J.J. said. "That gunship's circling right over you. They may be packing depth charges."

"Sounds like a good reason to move, if you ask me."

"That's why I didn't ask you. Play dead."

Collin descended to the bottom of the channel, where he settled heavily into lost centuries of nautical detritus. A voluminous curtain of silt unfurled from beneath the periphery of his bulk, and rippled out over the wasteland like fallout from a meteor impact. Disturbed for the first time in perhaps forever, carcasses of wayward ships groaned and crumbled before the pressure wave. Even the visual filters of the Charybdis' amazing eye were overcome in the swelling cloud of debris.

"I really don't like it down here," Collin said. "I can't see."

"You don't have to like it. Just be still, and hate it all you want."

"I can feel things moving around underneath me."

"It's just those old shipwrecks settling. Hulls collapsing. Trapped pockets of air escaping. Hang tight, buddy."

"No. No, I don't think that's what I'm feeling at all." The fog began to dissipate, revealing a twisted jungle of forms fallen from the surface world. Grim testimony to the ocean's timeless might, the world's oldest shipping channel was an eerie crucible of tangled remnants from every age. Ancient Chinese junks hung preserved and encrusted with sea life. Wooden masts lanced through folds of steel skin. Slain warships rusted enmeshed in the old ribs of merchantmen, battle wounds grotesque and gaping.

"Just be cool."

"I can feel them," Collin said, panting for breath. "They're all around me."

"That's not you down there, buddy. Remember that. You're right here with us, inside the Devil Ray."

Collin fixated his borrowed eye on the ruin of a cruise ship. Brightly painted, it stood out against the funereal backdrop as a relative newcomer to this lost world of the dead. He was not alone down here. He could see them. Ghostly faces pressed against portals, leering through tenantless sockets. It looked as though they too were spellbound by the masses of slithering forms that were now closing in.

"They're all over me!"

"There's nothing down there but some old wrecks, hon," Jill replied.

"For crying out loud. I don't know why we're even pretending that we can't just stand up right now and swat that stupid gunboat right out of the sky."

"Takashi!" Jill replied. "Are you kidding me right now?"

"I'm not even kidding, Jill. We are literally moments away from becoming a worldwide phenomenon—that is, *if* we take charge—and quit hiding on the sea floor like a fat punk. We're standing at the biggest crossroads of our lives. Right here. Right now. You guys seriously want to turn in our keys? That's what'll happen. We land in Shanghai, we're through."

"That's some really dangerous talk, dude," Jill replied.

"Dangerous? Who exactly are you afraid of? We're the dangerous ones. Wake up and see this moment for what it really is. We're either on the brink of international stardom, or fifteen minutes from being grounded again."

"Who's up for six-months of air hockey?" J.J. said.

"Exactly. Screw that. This game has just changed, boys and girls. We've got the big gun. We don't need the Navy. We don't need this hovercraft. We can operate right out of a hotel room in Shanghai. Who's with me?"

"You need to be careful," Skyler said, shooting Takashi a glare. "Jill is right to be concerned with where you're going with all of this."

"Well-well-well," Takashi said, returning Skyler's glare with a more unsettling one. "I guess we all see whose side you're really on."

"I'm on Psyjack's side, always and forever. It's as much my program as yours."

"Sure you're on Psyjack's side, regardless of the roster. I don't guess it matters to you whether we're sitting in these seats tomorrow morning, or four SEALs."

"Stop assuming the worst." Skyler jabbed a finger at Takashi's chest. "Bent is the best fighter in the open ocean. Right now, he's just got a wounded ego needing stroked."

"Well, then I nominate you, as the stroker of Bent's— whatever."

"Oh, my God." Jill slumped back into her seat, closed her eyes, and slapped her hands over her face.

"We don't need them, you guys. The gate is wide open. Just run through it!" Takashi glanced around the aircraft. "We're not a bunch of college kids anymore, begging for a stupid contract. We've been there, done that. Our future holds bigger things than depending on a government paycheck. I'm talking about us standing up in defense of our world, with our technology, and without any military assistance. First thing we need to do is show those SEALs who is running the show, and there's only one language they'll understand."

"That's enough." Skyler lowered her voice to a near whisper. "I know about you, Takashi. I've read your file, and I knew what we were getting into by bringing you along."

"Ouch, sister."

"Look, what I meant was I know what you've been through, and I know you've got every reason to resent the system."

"You don't know what I've been through." Takashi's eyes burned like a pair of embers in his skull.

"I didn't mean to downplay anything."

Takashi grinned. "Psyjack is streaming live now, baby. Our puppet strings? They just got snipped." Takashi spread his arms wide, and rotated on his heels to deliver a zealous leer at everyone. As he did so, the Devil Ray lilted gently toward Shanghai's garish skyline. "This is our moment. Right here. Right now."

"I think that we all just need some time to discuss this," Jill said, "and to decide what all of this means."

"There's no time for discussions," Takashi replied. "The last time those SEALs tried to manhandle our program, we all lost our jobs, she lost her legs, and we all watched our dolphins burn."

"He's right," J.J. said.

"I don't know much more of this I can take!" Collin shouted.

Serpentine bodies oozed through every hole in the ruins. They spilled through the guts of rotting vessels, exploring Collin's prone form with the worst sort of curiosity. He could feel the graveyard worms writhing up through his tentacles, probing his underside for soft spots. Collin ducked his turreted eye back beneath its protective hatch as one of the braver beasts wriggled over the top of his shell.

"He's not delusional," J.J. said. "There's something else down there."

"What are those things?" Jill asked.

"Bloodfin larva," Skyler replied.

"What are they doing?"

She hesitated, before avoiding Jill's question. "This is the evidence I hoped I'd never live to see, but it's true. The Kaiju are breeding."

Collin let out a shriek. It didn't really hurt, but the sensation of a chunk of meat being twisted loose from one of his tentacles was not exactly a pleasant one. He could feel dozens of them clamping their serrated jaws and spinning, spinning, tearing loose ragged mouthfuls of his flesh. "They're eating me!"

"Don't freak out," Takashi replied. "You're ginormous, remember? Unstoppable. You're Godzilla. Those little maggots can't possibly hurt you."

"They *are* hurting me!"

"Switch him off," J.J. said. "Pull the plug. Whatever you've got to do."

"Are you crazy?" Takashi said. "We can't turn the big gun loose. The SEALs are right there. They'll light him up!"

"Collin's in too deep. You need to back off, man. Back out of that thing's head, or I'm serious, I'll yank the plug."

There was no backing out. Not now. Collin was the Charybdis, at one with a body that was under attack. Gathering his lower extremities beneath his domed carapace, he spread his gill slits and filled his internal bladders with seawater.

"What's he doing? What are you doing?"

"I've seen this before," Skyler replied, eyes brightening, "in the interaction tanks."

"He's swelling up like a balloon."

"Yes," Skyler whispered, a smile curling the corner of her lips.

Collin expanded his inner chambers until every hollow was filled, every diaphragm stretched taut as a drum. His mantis blades clattered fair warning, but the pain refused to cease. Tormented, enraged, he swiveled his great shield of a head until his proboscis mouth was aimed like a great cannon at the swarms around his feet.

"What are you doing, bro?"

At once, he discharged every bladder through whorled channels in his shell. A massive system of internal hydraulics compressed the fluid against a vocal bellows, converting the forced seawater into a titanic blast of sound. As though an atomic bomb had just been detonated, an expanding shockwave across the sea floor erased the nautical graveyard in a dilating ring of destruction that spirited shipwrecks into silt. The ocean's surface dropped to expose the glistening carapace of the monster, if only for a second, before the sea backfilled the void with a slap and a foaming geyser that swallowed the hovering SEAL gunship. When the pillar of water collapsed, the Mad Hatter's aircraft was gone.

***

Something was wrong. Volkov outsmarted him, tricked him into injecting some sort of a poison into his body. The magic juice hadn't enhanced him in any noticeable way. Rather, it seemed to have crippled him. There were all kinds of voices and noise inside his head, and muddled visual effects that threatened to melt his brain into gray porridge, and bring him howling to his knees.

Mr. Krupin gaped at his own hand through the falling Plum Rains. He was seeing double, but it was far worse than just a duplicate image. Somehow, he was seeing his hand from two entirely different perspectives. The first was his own perspective, but superimposed over his normal view was the alien perspective of someone else, someone distant, who was hitchhiking along in Mr. Krupin's brain, observing everything through a second set of disembodied eyes. Through this perspective, Krupin saw himself staring at his own hand. When he spun his head in the direction that he half-expected to see a phantom copy of himself hovering, what he saw instead was Jochi, staring back at him, and laughing.

Mr. Krupin collapsed to the deck of Volkov's submarine. He rolled onto his back Spattering rain bullied his face, and confused his ears. That was the other problem. He was also hearing double. As the drone chopper lifted off into the stormy sky, leaving the three survivors of the Nantong operation afloat on the Yangtze River, Krupin heard two overlapping staccatos of rotor blades pouring into his head from different directions, but there was only one chopper in the sky. It was enough to make a man lose his mind.

The sound of dueling laughter brought him back around. One source of the sound was appropriately distant, emanating from Jochi, while a second source seemed to erupt right out of the middle of his own face. It was a terrible sensation. He wanted more than anything to kill Jochi, if only to end this bad experience, but he was too disoriented to stand, much less to pick a fight with the giant.

Krupin moaned, wincing at the sound of his disembodied and doubled voice. He pushed himself up from the cold steel, and swiveled his mixed-up head away from Jochi's smirking face. He was going to puke. The only conclusion that he could come to was that he and Jochi had somehow been cerebrally fused by those injections of magic juice, but for whatever reason, Jochi didn't seem to be suffering any ill effects from the needle that Krupin had stabbed into his neck. In fact, Jochi seemed fine. Krupin cursed himself for failing to kill that man when he'd had the opportunity. Now, that opportunity might never present itself again. He was worthless in this new condition, and for the first time since he was a child, he presented no danger to anyone.

A pressurized valve on a topside portal emitted a gaseous hiss. After a moment, the manway cover lurched upward with the sound of broken suction, and swung ajar. Krupin lolled his head in the direction of the portal. There, poking up through the portal like a tattooed gopher with silver teeth, peered Volkov. Krupin smiled. A snort of laughter got the better of him. It was a queer situation, after all.

"What's the matter with him?" Volkov asked. "He doesn't look right."

"I told you. Too much data," Dr. Wu replied, thrusting his thin arm under Krupin's back. He attempted to lift the limp body from the deck, but he did not possess the strength. "Too much for one human mind."

"Jochi, bring him in here," Volkov said.

Jochi lumbered over. He bumped Dr. Wu aside, rolled Krupin facedown, and picked him off the deck by the backside of his belt like a sack of wet barley. Krupin dangled cursing from the giant's grip, even as Jochi lowered his drooling carcass down into the submarine. Below, a team of Red Brothers outstretched their arms to receive him.

"It didn't work," Jochi said, almost smugly, once all three were below deck, and the manway was closed. He pointed a thick finger at Krupin. "He tried to make me his slave." Jochi smiled. "I ain't no slave."

As Volkov stared up at Jochi, the corner of his mouth gave a quiver. Krupin noticed that slight movement, and he knew what it meant, even if Jochi was too stupid to realize that he was tromping over some very thin ice. He'd seen Volkov make that face a dozen times, minutes before someone was being fed in chunks to some snarling animal.

The Red Brothers lifted Krupin by his arms. He wagged his head and emitted a grunt of laughter. He couldn't help it. This ridiculous mess struck him as being kind of funny. Volkov had failed his own secret mission. He'd underestimated the fight in his best henchman, and as a result, he now stood sulking in his submarine. Whatever it was that he'd been so desperately seeking in Nantong was now something lost inside of his and Jochi's bodies, and powerful as he was, Volkov couldn't do a damned thing to get it back.

"Do you feel anything?" Volkov asked, staring into Krupin's eyes with a pained expression. "Do you feel anything different at all?"

Krupin couldn't hold back the swollen river of laughter. The levee broke, and it surged up his throat in great bubbling waves. The Red Brothers who handled him wore terrified expressions as Volkov jammed both of his thumbs into Krupin's windpipe.

"Think this is funny, do you? Yeah? You won't be laughing when that ugly head of yours is dissolving in a bucket of acid," Volkov said, cursing in Krupin's face until it was flecked with spittle, "What's the matter? Didn't think about that? No, if you can't control what you stole from me, then you're useless to me. Someone give me a blade." Volkov maintained his burning eye contact with Krupin, while his right hand shot to one side, and sprung open to receive the thing that he'd requested.

Krupin saw his murderer from two perspectives. Volkov's hateful face filled the first perspective like an enraged demon, but from an alternate angle, he found himself staring down at the back of Volkov's head, looming over his employer like a juggernaut. Of the two, this was the more preferable option. Krupin focused. He closed his eyes, and abandoned himself wholly to embrace the alien angle, because he had little use for the body of a strangled vegetable when there was a much more powerful body standing by. Krupin's soul rushed into the giant, and seized hold of the controls.

"What do you have to say for yourself, hmm?" Volkov raised the borrowed blade, and he pressed its gleaming edge into the flesh of his victim's throat. "What, have you gone to sleep? Decided to take a little nap? Well, I know how to wake you up." Volkov lowered the point of his dagger to the unconscious Krupin's crotch.

Lurching forward on new and massive legs, solid as the trunks of twin oaks, Krupin slammed his vises for hands around Volkov's tattooed neck, and lifted the mobster's boots straight off the ground. The experience was amazing, and intensely arousing. He wanted to do savage things, bestial things that lurked in the most primal recesses of the mind.

"Who do you think you're threatening?" he said, in a voice he didn't even recognize as his own. It was deep and powerful, born on the winds of a massive chest that could've exerted enough force to snap Volkov's neck like a pretzel stick. "I'm here, and I'm there. I'm right in front of you, and I'm behind. I am everywhere." His laughter was that of a demon.

The Red Brotherhood stood paralyzed in the cloud of black magic that had seemingly settled upon their ship. The hatred between Krupin and Jochi had always been obvious, mutual, a permanent underlayment of the Red Brotherhood's culture. To see Jochi rush to Krupin's defense and threaten their leader's life must've looked pretty peculiar to them.

Krupin emitted a great baritone laugh, because it looked so funny to see Volkov hanging helplessly in the air. Strange glottal pops escaped Volkov's throat. His boots knocked together, as his dancing legs performed a jig of death. The knife fell from his hand, and clattered to the floor of the submarine.

"This is what you always wanted, remember?" Krupin whispered through Jochi's lips, right into Volkov's ear. "My only flaw was my Russian heritage, wasn't it? That was always such a big problem for you. Not anymore. Now, at last, I'm a purebred Mongol—unlike you, you green-eyed son of a Moscow whore."

"This impossible," Dr. Wu said, stammering. "You do this … with no helmet."

One Brother found the strength to break the bonds of the spell, and the first pistol was drawn from its holster. It was followed by others. Hammers were thumbed back into firing position. Rifle bolts snapped back into their action, as their employer gasped for air, eyes bulging like a snared rabbit. Something trickled warmly from his pant-leg. It spattered and pooled beneath him on the submarine floor.

"Is this the best idea you could all come up with?" Krupin said, through his new puppet's mouth. "Shooting a bunch of holes in the walls of our submarine?" Their mortified expressions struck him as being a little bit funny. Great hacks of demonic laughter erupted from his throat, as he felt Volkov's windpipe collapsing beneath his fingers. It felt so good, so exhilarating to squeeze the life from the bully's body. Despite the years of abuse he'd suffered at the hands of this man, he'd always managed to respect Maxim Volkov, all the while overlooking just how badly he really just wanted to strangle him to death. Now that understood himself better, there was no turning back. The sensation of Volkov's life oozing through his fingers was too arousing to quit. He wondered, at that moment, if he was strong enough to squeeze Volkov's head completely off? With a fit of cachinnating laughter, he bared his teeth, and crushed down with all his might.

All bodies upheaved, limbs flailing midair, before crashing back down to the floor. The submarine reeled from a tremendous impact. Crimson lights interior lights flickered, died for an instant, and then blazed back to life. Strewn like a roomful of children's toys, the Brotherhood collected their weapons, rose uncertainly to their feet, and peered around at the walls and ceiling of their vessel, looking, but mostly listening to the rush of spraying water.

"Where my wife?"

Krupin turned toward the sounds of Dr. Wu's mewling. The scientist was kneeling beside Volkov's fallen form, shaking the motionless man by a shoulder. If Volkov was dead, it was interesting how he still remained embedded in the center of others' pain and misery.

"Please. Where my wife?"

One Brother corrected him with a rifle butt to his temple. Dr. Wu rolled to the floor, and balled into a fetal position. His glasses went spinning across the floor.

Like ten-thousand raking nails on a chalkboard, something outside the submarine in the Yangtze River rasped against the steel hull with a long and sickening caress. The unbelievable length of the passage was as indicative of the size of the unknown object, as the potential danger that it presented them. No one dared voice the common fear, but surely they were all filled with the same dread. They were under attack by one of those things.

Volkov's body jerked with a spasm. His arms unfolded until he was spread-eagled on the floor, arched and convulsing. The eggplant color of his face was less disturbing than the bloodstained aspect of his eyes. Foam bubbled between his lips, as an awful rattling sound emanated from his crushed throat. No one but Dr. Wu seemed much interested in him, or his deplorable condition. Their collective attention remained focused on whatever river monster was romancing their vessel.

Dr. Wu gazed imploringly at Volkov's distracted henchmen, but they paid him no mind. "He can't breathe. Throat ... is damage." He jabbed his fingertips at his own throat in an ambiguous gesture. When no one batted an eye, Dr. Wu removed a pen from his shirt pocket. He popped the endcap loose with his teeth, and withdrew the tube of ink and the little spring. Positioning the tapered end of the sharp plastic tube at the base of Volkov's windpipe, Dr. Wu humped over the homemade tracheal device, and pressed down with all of his weight. Volkov's throat tented inward, and the tissue gave with a hollow pop. The whistle of inflowing air through the tube accompanied the rising of Volkov's chest. The purple color of his face began to wane.

"He breathe." Dr. Wu smiled, but he knew better than to look to the Brotherhood for any sign of affirmation. He stroked Volkov's forehead, and patted his tattooed shoulder with an almost paternal tenderness. "You be alright, now. You give me my wife."

Darkness enveloped the submarine interior, as an incredible blow struck the underside of the bow like an uppercut to the chin. Flying bodies smashed into a far wall astern. The room strobed to the deafening reports of an automatic rifle. Still engulfed in utter blackness, men's screams joined the squeal of rending metal, spraying water, with an awful dissonance. A new lake of cold water boiled up from a sudden spring. It crept across the floor, sluicing through their tangled forms.

Krupin crawled through the darkness, groping bodies with his huge borrowed hands, until his thick fingers settled upon a familiar face behind a mask of taut wires. He hesitated, with his new hand resting upon his old cheek. It was strange to hear your own voice emanating from somewhere afar, and to see yourself through another set of eyes was frightfully surreal, but the most mind-bending sensation of all was to touch yourself, while being touched by your other self.

"Please! Where my wife?"

Gathering the limp body into his immense arms, he clutched the precious bundle protectively against his broad chest. It was a poignant experience that overwhelmed him with a rather peculiar emotion that he'd never experienced before. It was a tormented and vulnerable feeling that demanded closeness of some kind, but he didn't know how to process the compulsion to hold and rock himself. His addled mind boiled into red fury, demanding blood, and then, it simmered back down again.

He'd made an art of hating himself, and he put that hatred on display. He glorified the results of all the abuse he'd suffered, ever since he was old enough to start blocking it out. Now, it all came pouring through his mind in a horrific montage, every minute of it. He clung to the body that had endured it all, rocking himself gently as the water rose. Not one of those memories ever included a guardian angel, or a moment of divine intervention. Not a single tender interlude with a loving parent, or a hug from a sibling, or a pat on the shoulder from an understanding friend. Never. Not even once. No one had ever shielded him from the torment he'd learned to channel into violence, forging the sweet child he'd once been into a weapon of blackened metal. Had the world had treated him fairly, he might've developed into a decent human being. His life had once held as much promise as that of any other child, but that promise was something broken in a lifelong struggle against indignity and pain.

Krupin rested his cheek upon that wired brow, as terrified shrieks reverberated through the shifting blackness. The water level climbed, yet he'd never felt safer. At last, the motherless child could rest for the first time ever in a loving embrace, and that embrace could've only come from himself. Krupin felt his borrowed eyes misting over. Warm tears spilled down the cheeks of both faces. Together, they felt the same cathartic release of so much poison, so much hatred for the living world, and together they cried in the darkness. No harm would come to them, not ever again. This motherless child's guardian angel had finally arrived, and he'd crush the skulls of anyone who dared raise a finger against him.

The submarine canted, sloshing a wave of floodwater against the leeward wall. Sparks spewed and flitted from a new fissure. Steel collapsed with an awful groan, popping rivets like corn against the walls. Screams arose to whatever gods might hear them, as a new cascade came blasting in with all the force of an opened fire hydrant. It was time to go.

Krupin heaved his former self over one broad shoulder, and plodded up out of the deepening water. He hoped that there might be a larger pocket of air trapped somewhere in the upper chambers of the submarine, a little sanctuary built just big enough for two. The lightless conditions actually helped, by eliminating one of the doubled assaults on his senses. The darkness enabled him to focus on just one of his twin perspectives. It was getting easier. He was learning to exist in two places at once.

Flailing hands clawed at him in the darkness. Shrieks of terror filled both sets of his ears. These doomed and terrified souls, he shoved right out of his way. He'd never suffered much from the effects of fear or panic, like other men. Hurt, he understood, but not fear. Whatever creature he'd devolved into, after so much suffering, was something mercifully beyond that whole experience.

His free hand met with the steel rungs of a ladder. This was what he'd been searching for. It led up into the officers' quarters. As he took the first step, he felt a man pushing past him, trying to cut ahead in line. Krupin snatched a fistful of the guy's topknot, and yanked him back with such force that the man's scalp ripped loose from his skull. His screeching body toppled back into the drowning pool with a splash.

As Krupin climbed, the submarine crumpled, collapsing inward, as though monstrous coils wrapped around the vessel were constricting. Electricity flashed underwater beneath him. Droves of the damned attempted to follow him skyward. Howling from the pits, they groped at his legs. He felt the desperate masses of reaching arms, and he thrust his boot heels back into their screaming faces. No. This sanctuary was not for them. With the broken body of the motherless child against the breast of his guardian angel, they ascended together, as one, by occasional strobes of light.

Chapter Nine

Luna was a clever little monkey. Yes, she was. Climbing was her new and favorite thing. Scaling the laundry hamper in Nana's bathroom was her specialty. This advanced skill empowered her with access to almost every nook and cranny throughout her Nana's apartment. Kitchen cabinets were a wonderland of forbidden treats. Every drawer was a treasure chest waiting to be opened. You never knew what fascinating items might be amongst the jumble of things inside a good drawer, but there was always something of interest. Upon discovery, a new treasure was immediately subjected to taste testing.

Nana called her a "little stinker," sometimes a "holy terror," whatever that meant, but Luna's mischievous smile reflected in Nana's twinkling eyes every time she was snatched from atop the laundry hamper, and whooshed right up into the air with Nana's gasp of exaggerated surprise. It was all part of their little game. Nana's job was to chase, and to restore order to chaos, while Luna's job was to stay a step ahead of her, disrupting all organization, and squealing with delight whenever she was captured. The adorable contest of larval skills versus wizened intuition began the moment Luna's feet hit the floor, every morning at around five a.m., and it never ceased until the evening birds began to twitter.

Luna planted her chubby palms atop the laundry hamper. She reached as far across the lid as she could stretch, and struggled to pull herself up atop the thing. This was the hard part. It was tall, and it presented quite a challenging maneuver. Her diapers crinkled as she grunted and pumped her legs, wriggling on her belly like a slug. Almost there. She reached out again, further this time, and succeeded in grabbing hold of the far edge. With a firm handhold, it was easy to haul her torso across the cushioned lid, to swing her lower-half up beside her, and soon enough, to have those sturdy little legs beneath her, once more. Standing atop the laundry hamper, she felt like the biggest giant in the world.

Luna could hear her Nana in the kitchen, calling her name. Nana did that so often that it was almost background noise. Luna gripped the wooden windowsill, and she pressed her lips and tongue to the cold, smooth glass. Sometimes, on the inside of the bathroom window, there was the thinnest layer of crusty ice that could be licked or even scraped off in cold filings with one's bottom teeth, but no window ice was available today. Outside, cars crawled along the road. Their tires slung ropes of tea-colored slush. She licked at the window and watched the cars go by until their repetitive motion lulled her into a trance.

"Luna?"

Her eyes brightened. She popped loose of the window, and turned in the direction of the voice. Her Nana was standing there in the bathroom doorway, arms folded across her chest. She was trying her best to look cross, but Luna knew better than to fall for that act. Nana never got cross with her. Not really.

"Cars!" Luna said, pointing to the window. Seemed like a pretty brilliant distraction from her naughty behavior.

Her Nana smiled. "You see some cars out there? Are they driving? Vroom-vroom?"

"Out there."

"Yeah, out there." Nana entered the bathroom, and sat down on the clothes hamper. She snuggled in beside Luna at the windowsill, and removed her phone from her hip pocket. Nana took a moment to watch the cars, too, but she didn't appear to find the sight of moving cars quite so exciting. In fact, she seemed a little distant. Adults could be funny that way.

"This." Luna pressed her finger to the window. She wanted her nana to have a taste of it, and feel how cold and smooth it was against her tongue.

"That's glass."

"Gas."

"Gl-ass."

Sometimes Nana didn't understand things quite so well. She was a sweet enough woman, but there was something of a language barrier between the two of them that Luna never had to overcome with her mama, or her daddy. Luna frowned at the cars. She hadn't seen her daddy in quite a long time. Just the thought of him and his inexplicable absence tended to make her irritable. She placed both palms against the window, and managed to smack them against the glass several times before Nana caught her by the wrists.

"No-no." Nana shook her head.

"No-no."

"We don't hit glass. Glass will break. Cut Luna's fingers. Ow!"

Luna rubbed her fingers together, appraising the unapparent dangers of the window with an expression of contrived concern tilled into her brow. "Gas bake."

"Yeah. Glass break."

Since her mama had dropped her off with Nana, she'd asked many times about her mama's whereabouts. Nana had never given her a straightforward answer, but then, Luna wouldn't have known what answer would've been satisfactory when something that should always be there simply was not. However, Nana didn't seem to be alarmed, and each time she reassured her that her mama went "bye-bye," and would be back soon. Those prompt and cheerful responses certainly didn't give off anything resembling the funky signals that Luna had come to expect whenever she asked about the whereabouts of her daddy. Questions regarding him produced such uncomfortable reactions in adults that after a month or so, Luna just stopped asking about him. Some things were better left alone, she'd begun to learn. However, even though she didn't ask about him, her daddy was often on her mind. There were times when her mama just wasn't enough, when she wasn't the person for whom Luna yearned, and her frustration over a missing daddy could culminate in an emotional meltdown over something so taboo that she couldn't even talk about it. No one seemed to be able to understand her. She was complicated.

Luna sighed. "Mama bye-bye."

"Yep. She'll be home soon."

Always, that same reply. She might've expected that it was coming. Luna didn't know why she even bothered to bring up the subject anymore. In its own way, the more recent problem of mama's absence was just as impossible as that of a missing daddy.

Luna chewed on the windowsill, a thread of drool swinging from her chin. Cooing a little tune for the day that she'd just composed, she stared out past the cars, and over the row of beige houses lining the opposite side of the street. Beyond those seaside villas of Turnagain Arm, a forest of masts in the harbor lilted and straightened like trees in the wind. Luna's chin stopped grinding. She blinked, straightened up, and pawed at some grit stuck to her lower lip.

"That," she said, pressing the pad of her index finger against the window. She turned toward her Nana, but Nana was busy, staring down at her phone. Luna poked at the windowpane, but she did so gently. She didn't want to break it. "That, Nana. That."

Nana glanced up momentarily. Her gaze tracked down Luna's extended arm to the tip of her finger. "That's glass, remember?" She looked back down at her phone again. "Nana already told you about that."

Luna frowned. Finger still pressed to the cold surface of the window, she looked back out over the snowy roofs of the villa into the forest of swaying masts. Nana could be frustrating, sometimes. She wasn't inquiring about the glass again, obviously. Her curiosity, with respect to glass, had been satisfied. This question was in regard to the glistening monster that had just risen up from the sea to a height that eclipsed the sun. It was just knocking around out there through the fleet of moored ships, sifting through vessels in a haphazard manner that was not unlike Luna's method of exploring a new drawer.

"That," she whispered.

***

Skyler slipped in opposite Jill to assist Collin down the Devil Ray's ramp. Given her unstable legs, the ramp itself was a little intimidating, but Collin had earned her best effort. Still woozy and disoriented from streaming, his legs weren't quite beneath him.

Skyler noticed a rivulet of blood trickling from beneath his headset, in the vicinity of his left ear. Her eyes widened at the sight of the crimson trail winding down his jaw, but she thought it wise to refrain from mentioning it until they had him seated.

Takashi and J.J. marched out in the middle of Shanghai's SWCC field command hangar, where Commander Bent met them like a fighter emerging from the corner of his hometown ring. The roar of their voices filled the enclosed space, as accusations and threats began to fly. Nose to nose with the Mad Hatter, J.J. held a clenched fist ready in the chamber, while Bent's stiffened arms were locked straight at his sides. Water pooled on the hangar floor beneath Bent, who'd just been hauled out of the sea by a drone chopper. The SEAL's gunship was never recovered, along with a few members of Bent's crew.

"You will stand down in my hangar, pogue, or you'll never see the light of day! You disobeyed a direct order from the SWCC to shut your program down!"

"We were operating under a higher authority than you," J.J. said, shouting back.

Bent stabbed a thumb against his chest. "I am the only authority in the Yellow Sea!"

"We'll see what the Barrier Reef thinks about that, and your attempt to compromise a mission of the highest priority with friendly fire. We've got a guy who can barely walk over here!"

"I've got a missing gunship, and three SEALs!"

"That's all on you. You put those men in harm's way."

Skyler tried to remain in lockstep with Jill, but old wounds were throbbing up in her legs. It was difficult to keep up, but she managed to do so. Together, they ushered him over to a bench outside the locker rooms, and eased him down onto the seat. Still strapped into his headset, Collin slumped over at the waist. Hotspot trotted over, and licked at his master's chin. It appeared as though the loyal dog sensed that something wasn't quite right.

"Is this normal?" Skyler whispered.

"Disconnecting from an active streaming session is never easy. Especially for him. He dives in more deeply than the rest of us. I really don't see how it can be good for the human mind, but the science is already a decade ahead of the health studies," she said, emitting a sigh.

"I saw some blood." Skyler tapped at her own left ear.

"Blood?"

Skyler nodded. "Coming from beneath his helmet. I think it's coming from his ear."

Jill knelt before her fallen teammate, and unfastened the snaps beneath his chin. Popping the mouse-piece from his lips, she lifted the Mindbender Rift from his head. "Jesus," she whispered.

The left side of Collin's head was badly bruised, as though he'd sustained a powerful blow. However, the pattern beneath the skin was curiously geometric, rather than the amorphous and blotchy appearance typical of a bruise. It almost looked as though a pattern had been printed on the backside of his skin. Skyler watched Jill use the cuff of her flight jacket to wipe the blood from Collin's cheek and ear. "Have you ever seen anything like this before?" Skyler asked.

Jill shook her head.

"How do you think it happened? It didn't happen in the Devil Ray, did it?"

"I don't know. He did get in the middle of that fight between those two," Jill replied, gesturing to the ongoing shouting match between J.J. and Commander Bent, "but I didn't see him take a hit, did you?"

"Not really." Skyler touched his temple, tracing the queer rays of bruising across his cheekbone. The coloring almost looked pixelated, like a dot matrix. "Look at this. It almost looks computer generated. Right?" Skyler glanced at Jill, whose lack of response to the obvious seemed to be an unspoken confirmation. "Do you think he brought this back from the other side—like, from something that happened during his cerebral experience?"

"The headset is designed to protect against certain types of collateral damage," Jill replied. "Every neural signal in the host's brain is being translated from electricity into binary code. That's a massive stream of information, and most of it is useless to the pilot." Jill patted the crown of Collin's helmet. "The headset works something like a filter for all that noise, but we've learned through trial and error that some of the extraneous sensory data should be allowed to come through, for the most realistic shared experience."

There was something strange about Jill's response. It almost sounded rehearsed, like a statement memorized by some product representative, stashed away in a mental file to be retrieved if something ever went terribly wrong with the product. In case of emergency, break glass. "Pain," Skyler said, hardening her eyes. "You're talking about pain."

"Psychosomatic pleasure and pain reception," Jill replied, brushing her hair behind her ear. "Does it exist? Yes and no. We've discussed our experiences after training sessions, and we've seen some evidence for it, yes. Personally, I've felt it." Jill nodded, eyes widening. "This is why I'm not the best pilot. I feel too much, if that makes sense, or maybe I just don't handle what I'm feeling as well as he does. The whole experience is totally overwhelming to me, and not in a good way. I get nausea, migraines, and vertigo that last for days … and I mean, this is exactly what I'm talking about. The studies haven't even begun on how this new science will affect pilots twenty years from now, when we're all developing brain tumors from this crap." She closed her eyes, and shook her head. "This is why I just can't." Her bottom lip began to tremble. "I can't do this anymore." Jill rose, hands pressed to her forehead, and disappeared into the women's locker room.

"You detonated a weapon of mass destruction in the middle of my jurisdiction!"

"Where's your proof? Huh?"

"The SWCC controls every engagement in the Yellow Sea!"

"I can't wait to watch you try and explain that to Captain Roswell."

"Ms. Hale," Takashi shouted from the sidelines of the fight. "Can you get the Captain on the line? Like, immediately?"

Skyler nodded, and rose to her feet.

"Who detonated the bomb that took down my gunship?" Bent shouted. He stabbed a finger at Collin. "Was it him?"

"It was me," J.J. replied, taking his Mindbender Rift from beneath his arm, and pulling the headset over his head. He planted his hands smartly on his hips.

"No, it was me," Takashi said, donning his own.

"I see. Fun and games. You all want to go down together for this? Fine. That's exactly the lack of accountability that I'd expect from a civilian program." Bent aimed his finger at everyone in the hangar. "None of you are setting foot off this base until further notice. You're grounded!"

"Yeah, we kind of saw that coming," J.J. replied. "You don't happen to have an air hockey table around here, do you?"

Skyler peered down at Collin, trying not to question everything that she was doing. She removed her phone from her hip pocket. Roswell hadn't been answering any of her calls or messages. Skyler went a different route, by accessing the iFly app. A list of available military drones popped up on her screen. When drones weren't working on the Barrier Reef, they were accessible to military personnel as couriers, messengers, and, of course, for fooling around. She scrolled down until she located one loitering in Captain Roswell's office wing. Skyler selected the drone, and entered her security password. With a fluting riff, the drone's POV filled her screen. The "voice command" icon was flashing in the top-right corner.

"Find: Captain Raymond Roswell," Skyler said, speaking slowly and clearly into her phone.

"Finding Captain Raymond Roswell," the drone replied, in a soft-spoken female voice, complete with an Australian accent.

Just like that, the drone named RACHEL-1023 was off, winding through the labyrinth of corridors, scanning every face that it encountered. Drone messaging was wildly popular, back when Skyler was a kid, but just as the fad caught the eyes of advertising executives, it began to lose its initial appeal. People simply became annoyed with haranguing robots that carried inane messages, insults, and personalized advertisements tailored to a consumer's purchase history. A backlash of drone bashing was the end result. Ad campaigns tanked. Drones backed-off to a respectful distance. Life went on. However, sending a messenger drone was still a viable option when someone wasn't answering their phone.

Skyler looked away from the dizzying drone feed on her screen. No need to watch the search. The drone would alert her, if and when it found Captain Roswell. Watching a drone feed for only just a few seconds made her sympathize with the sensory onslaught that dolphin pilots endured. She slid the phone back into her hip pocket, and watched Commander Bent storm out of the hangar. Once he was gone, she rose, and followed Jill into the locker room.

"Hey."

Jill was standing at the sink, blotting her eyes with a paper towel. Her sharp and deliberate movements, the flatness of her visage, every aspect of Jill's behavior swore an oath of resignation. She sniffed, pulled her hair back into a bun, and secured it behind her head with a few bobbies.

"Want to talk?"

Jill's head gave an involuntary twitch, and her eyelids fluttered. She cleared her throat, sighed, and planted her knuckles upon the counter. She stared into the leveled eyes of her own reflection in the mirror, and then shifted her gaze onto Skyler. "Do you have kids?"

"No."

Jill shook her head, as though affirming what she'd already suspected. She looked down into the sink, balling the wet paper towel inside her clenched hand. "Those other guys out there," she said, gesturing toward the door with a tilt of her head, "they wouldn't understand. This is their whole life. When I saw them for the first time in two years, it was like nothing whatsoever had changed. They were all ready to jump right back into the program like we were all just coming back from lunch break." Jill wadded the paper towel, and slung it into the wastebasket. "Not me. I'm not even the same person anymore."

"Parenthood changes your whole life. I totally get that."

"No," Jill replied, shaking her head. "I'm sorry, but you really don't. None of you do." She folded her arms, and leaned back against the counter. "When you reach the last trimester of pregnancy, and the big day is looming, that's when all the other mommies really start chattering, preparing you for what's coming. Up until that point, it's all about names, colors, furniture for the baby room, but the conversations don't start getting real until those last three months. That's when you begin to learn what you're really in for."

Skyler stepped further into the locker room. She slipped her hands into her pockets, turned on a heel, and leaned against a row of gray lockers. Jill wasn't giving her much of an entry point into the conversation, and that was probably intentional, to illustrate her point of feeling alienated.

"They all say that motherhood is going to change you, and that you won't even resemble the person you used to be after the first six months. They say you'll look at photos of yourself before your child was born, and you won't even be able to empathize with that person from your past anymore. You hear those kinds of things all the time, and yeah, you nod your head and smile, but you're not even capable of understanding what they mean until that baby is born. That's when everything they've been warning you about really clicks."

"How old is she?" Skyler asked, attempting a smile.

"Luna will be fifteen months, next Tuesday." Jill looked down at the floor. She toyed with the ring on her left hand, and then glanced back up with a raised eyebrow. "Yeah. Go ahead and do the math."

"Wasn't planned?"

"Are they ever, anymore?" Jill dropped her chin. "Her father and I have been trying to make it work. We got married when we found out. Maybe not the best idea, but it seemed like the right thing to do at the time—for her. I felt like it was our parental duty to at least make an effort to hold it all together, but yeah-no. We've been living apart for the last six months. Luna and I moved back up to Anchorage, to be closer to my mom. Just took a job at a fish canning factory." Jill wrinkled her nose, and nodded her head. "So, that's the glamorous life I've been living ever since the band broke up."

Skyler left the lockers, and eased closer to Jill. She took a seat on the counter beside her. "You've just been doing what you needed to do. Accidents happen." Just as soon as that word left her mouth, Skyler regretted it.

Jill's head snapped up. "I really don't like to use the word 'accident.'"

"I'm sorry, I …"

"Luna wasn't planned, no, but she's a wonderful oops. She's my very best thing. Seriously, she's the best thing I've ever done."

"That was a stupid choice of words. I'm sorry."

"Luna is my everything. I guess that's why I don't feel at all ashamed of my situation, even though some part of me knows that I probably should be."

"No, don't even say that."

"It's okay. Seriously. I get it, but it is what it is. I mean, I imagine that the guys probably all went on to do awesome things after the break-up, advancing science, making tons of money, whatever, and I'm happy for them. Genuinely happy. I hope they each found whatever redemption they needed to help them get past that huge failure, because we all needed something to move on. Luna was that, for me. When I saw her for the first time, all was forgiven. The mistakes of the past were erased, because the person I used to be—was gone."

"Honey, I don't think that the guys fared half as well as you might imagine they did," Skyler said. "In fact, I think they were all really struggling to pick up the pieces. Out of all of you guys, I think you're the only one who was spared the whole identity crises, and you've got Luna to thank for that."

Slapping footsteps approached the women's locker room door. They were punctuated by an insistent knocking against the metal frame. "Jill? Ms. Hale?" Takashi's voice.

The girls looked at each other. "We're in here," Skyler replied.

"Two things. Thing one: we're all grounded until Captain Roswell straightens this out. Thing two … can I come in?"

"Yeah," the girls replied simultaneously.

Takashi staggered into the room. He took a second to steal a glance at his new surroundings, and then he raised his hands in a tamping gesture. "Thing two: we've got a Kaiju attack happening right now, just a couple of clicks up the Yangtze River." Takashi grinned. "We've decided we're going to do something about it, before the SEALs have a chance to respond with conventional weapons. We're streaming Carl right now, right out there in the hangar."

"Are you freaking kidding me?" Jill replied.

"Not one bit." Takashi snapped his fingers. "J-man's got this one."

"I'm going to see Commander Bent," Jill said, marching past Takashi toward the locker room door.

"Wait. Whoa-whoa-whoa. Why?" Takashi spun, and grabbed her by the forearm. "What are you doing?"

"I'm leaving. That's what I'm doing." She twisted loose of his grip. "I'm going home to Anchorage to be with my child, and obviously, I need to put in for my resignation now, before you guys get me into even more trouble. Seriously."

"Wait," Takashi said, grabbing hold of her arm again. He flinched when she turned, as though he expected her to punch him. When she didn't, he lowered his defenses. "Don't say anything about what we're doing."

"Of course I wouldn't." Jill curled her lip, and scowled.

"Here's the best part," Takashi said, releasing Jill's arm. If his artificial eyes could've glowed any brighter, they might've set his eyebrows on fire. "Get this. The Kaiju attack is involving a double-hulled Russian submarine from the millennial-era, and the serial number is an exact match for the same one that slipped through our fingers two years ago, just a few miles offshore."

"You're joking," Skyler whispered, eyes widening. Her heart was hammering against the backside of her chest like some desperate stranger wanting in. She covered her gaping mouth.

Takashi nodded. "It's our pirates. We've got them."

Chapter Ten

"How're we even going to see what's happening? We don't have a monitor," Collin said, dabbing at his temple with a wet cloth that Skyler had procured for him.

Skyler's thoughts were still with Jill. She wished only the best for her. She understood why Jill had left, embarking down a path that she felt she'd no other choice but to take. Hopefully, Bent would arrange for her release. However, as she sat in the circle of Psyjackers, on the floor of the women's locker room, Skyler couldn't help but feel as though a new spot had just opened up on their four-person team. Ever since their arrival on the Barrier Reef, she'd felt as though they didn't trust her, as though they regarded her as belonging to some separate division of their program that would never enable her to sit at the cool kids' table. Obviously, as the inventors and charter members, they were entitled to a clique, but Skyler hoped to prove to them that her involvement would mark the next step in Psyjack's evolution. "We can watch through our phones," Skyler replied.

"Bingo," Takashi said. "I'm seeing a private drone, MINGYU-0613. Looks like she's right-smack on the scene. Awesome coverage. Bit of a diva, though. Looks like you'll have to 'Like' her before she'll let you on board."

Skyler sidelined the window streaming her Barrier Reef drone that was still searching the Barrier Reef for Captain Roswell, and she opened a new window through her maps app. She zoomed in on the Yangtze River, and pulled up a list of available drones. MINGYU-0613 received a tap from her thumb. A cute, animated character with an oversized head of flouncing pigtails hopped up and down in the middle of her screen. Her flashing "Like" tab had already been translated to Skyler's preference for the English language.

"Yes-yes, I like you," Skyler said, tapping the tab. The animated girl emitted a squeal of delight, clapped her hands, and blew Skyler a kiss that was accompanied by a spray of fluttering hearts. The character spun like a dervish, and disappeared in a puff of glitter. MINGYU's feed sprung open, and Skyler couldn't believe what she was seeing on her screen.

"What the heck is that thing?" Collin asked, gawping down at his phone. "Have you ever seen one like this before, Sky?"

The black cylinder barely recognizable as a submarine was being crushed in a many-legged bear hug. Four sets of blunt and wrinkled appendages, the color of boiled crayfish, terminated in owlish claws that raked furrows through the vessel's steel walls. Not unlike an enormous caterpillar clinging to a floating twig, the inverted monster's body rippled sluggishly while rows of feet adjusted their grip. Although the creature's head could not be seen beneath the river, a curious snout broke the surface to probe around on the submarine's bow.

"That thing is repulsive," Takashi said.

"It's a tardigrade," Skyler replied, sounding a little breathless. It was impossible for her to hide her fascination with the *Kaiju* creatures. She could watch them for hours on end in the laboratory, and she'd come to love each and every one of them, in a purely scientific way.

"A what?"

"I named them after a similar species of microorganism native to earth. Some call them tardigrades. Others call them water bears. The similarities between the earthly version and the Europa strain are so stunning that I'm almost inclined to believe that—"

"Nerd alert. How the heck are we going to pry the sub loose from that nasty bugger?" Takashi asked. "J-man, what's your twenty?"

"Mouth of the Yangtze. How the hell did you manage to walk on these tentacles, Collin? It's like herding cats down there."

"Don't lead so much with your head. You're top-heavy. Keep your feet out in front of you where you can see them. Pivot at the waist. Use your pincers for balance."

"Like you're dancing the calypso," Takashi said.

"That's not helpful," J.J. replied.

"Earthly tardigrades are fantastic organisms, found everywhere from boiling vents in ocean trenches to the heart of the Antarctic. Freeze them, boil them, expose them to massive doses of radiation, even blast them into the vacuum of space, and they do just fine. They're basically indestructible."

"Also not helpful," J.J. replied. "Takashi, can you get a bead on the target for me."

"Aye-aye."

It was obviously going to take some finesse to edge her way into the group, and to find her place amongst the team. Not only was she a biologist working amongst technical engineers, but they functioned like a well-oiled machine, while she was just a loose bolt bouncing around in the machine's cogs. Psyjack was commissioned to seek and destroy monsters. She understood that. Her role in the project as the *Kaiju* biologist was key, but that didn't make her feel any better about butchering them. The truth was that most of these creatures were harmless, even beneficial, when inhabiting their proper ecological niche. It wasn't their fault that they'd been displaced, and had become a nuisance. That was her fault.

"Sky. Weaknesses. Do they have any?"

"Um—they're not armored, so there's that, but I don't think you're going to want to try and pry anything loose from its grip, because that's probably not happening. You're better off coming around from behind. Central nervous system on these guys is like a braided rope of nerve endings running from the back of its head to its rump."

"A spinal cord."

"Sort of. Except that it doesn't have a spine."

"How does something that huge support itself without bone structure?" Collin asked.

"Awesome question," Skyler replied. "None of the Kaiju have a skeletal structure, yet their musculature is built to withstand that enormous weight. It's almost like they were designed to reach this potential, if the right set of circumstances ever presented itself."

"But, why would those circumstances ever present themselves on a frozen moon?"

"Exactly," Skyler said. "They wouldn't. Not in a trillion years."

"Then why is the growth potential even there?"

"You're getting closer and closer to what I call, 'the curtain.'"

"The curtain?"

"Push far enough in a single scientific direction, odds are you're going to come to the curtain. If you ever reach that curtain, do you dare throw it back? That question itself is perhaps more important than whatever answer might be waiting on the other side."

"J-man, you're moving in on the target," Takashi said. "One kilometer and closing."

"I can see it!"

"Already?"

"Damned straight, I can. This thing's eyesight underwater is incredible."

"Nothing like it in all the world," Collin said.

As the deadly Charybdis bore down on its unsuspecting prey, Skyler felt a twinge of desperation grip down on some vital part of her. This marvelous durable survivor from a faraway world was just trying to understand the environment in which it had been so rudely transplanted, and now, because of Skyler, it was probably going to die a violent death.

"You might not actually need to kill it," Skyler heard herself blurt.

"What?" J.J. replied.

"I'm just saying, the most important thing is capturing that sub. Just give it a good pinch, and it will probably let go."

"Oh, I'm going to give it a lot more than just a pinch," J.J. said. A grin spread beneath his visor. "That tub of lard doesn't even see this coming."

"Woohoo!"

Takashi's whoop reverberated throughout the hangar, as the armored slab of *Kaiju* might slammed broadside into the soft flesh of the water bear. Its stumpy legs sprung wide in shock, releasing the hostage sub without a fuss. Paddling its appendages in an effort to right itself, the injured animal churned the river into foam.

"Didn't see that one coming, did you, fatso?" J.J. said, as he extended his left pincer like a boxer setting up his opponent for a right hook.

"Guys ..."

When the opening presented itself, the spiked forceps slashed out to connect with the water bear's gummy face with a slap so thunderous that the distant shockwave was felt through the hangar floor. J.J. clamped his left pincer around the dazed creature's throat, and proceeded to pound on its head. Indigo blood flew from its whipping snout.

"You're letting the sub get away!" Skyler shouted. "What are you doing?"

"Just having a little fun," J.J. replied.

"Our heads are already on the chopping block. You can't afford to be screwing around. Let those pirates get away again, and we're all headed straight for the brig."

"Alright. Settle down."

She seriously wanted to punch him. What these geeky cowboys couldn't possibly understand, and what Skyler had refrained from telling Jill, was that parenthood wasn't the only life-changing experience that had the power to render a person unable to relate to whomever they might've been beforehand. The Europa mission had lifted Skyler to the highest point of her life, and the pirate attack had slammed to down to her lowest. By the time she'd found the strength to rise up from that experience, and hitch painfully forward into new realms of understanding of the alien menagerie inadvertently unleashed into the seas, she could no longer relate to the woman she'd been before the accident than Jill was able to appreciate her pre-parenthood self. The creatures, while dangerous, and threatening the entire civilized world, felt somehow connected to her, even if that connection was steeped in projected guilt.

"Got the sub," J.J. said. He clamped his massive blades around the battered ship's waist, and lifted it from the roaring river. Tons of brownish water cascaded from its ruptured hull. In the hand of Carl the mighty Charybdis, the nuclear submarine looked no bigger than a cigar.

"Just set it over there on the bank for now," Takashi said.

"Don't just set it on the bank for now. Are you kidding?" Skyler screwed up her face at Takashi. "Get that thing back to base right now so they can start searching it."

"Always pandering to the Navy," Takashi said, in a low mutter.

"I'm not pandering to anyone. I'm making perfect sense. What more important things do you have to do?"

"Kicking ass. Taking names. You know, our job."

"No, she's right," J.J. said, rotating his bizarre immensity downriver, and taking his first cautious steps. "If anyone's still alive in there, they've got some explaining to do."

Skyler watched the pinkish form of the water bear depart the scene of its merciless beating. It tumbled stiff-legged downriver. Rolling, spinning, it disappeared beneath the current in a cloud of indigo blood.

In the lab, water bears were the clowns of the interaction tanks. You couldn't help but smile at that frenzy of paddling legs, that restless snout that explored every crevice for a bite to eat, because they were always hungry. Social creatures, they glommed together, intertwining their trunks and trundling legs. They seemed to actually enjoy meeting the other species, and interacting with their human observers. Water bears were nice.

"Heads-up, big guy," Takashi said. "We've got a squadron of Navy gunships coming in fast, at three o'clock."

"Don't fight them," Skyler said. "Those conventional weapons can't hurt you."

"I don't know about that," Collin replied, still daubing his temple with the wet towel.

"Is that how you got that bruise?" Takashi asked.

"Had to be."

"We've never seen psychosomatic trauma like that before."

"No one ever took a hit like that before."

"Sure you didn't just bump your head against something in the Devil Ray?"

"No." Skyler put her hand on Collin's wrist, and lowered the towel. "Take a closer look at his injury."

Takashi leaned in. Collin's face was set aglow by those unnatural eyes. For the first time in forever, Takashi appeared to be at a loss for words. He seemed reluctant to believe that their technology presented a possibility for danger to the pilot. Maybe too reluctant, even defensive. "J.J. was piloting a dolphin that got killed two years ago, and nothing whatsoever happened to him. How do you explain that?"

"I don't need to explain anything, Takashi. I'm presenting evidence with pretty obvious interpretation. There's a very real risk associated with wearing this helmet."

"They're circling around," Collin said.

"I see them. I see them."

"They're banking in attack formation."

"I can't exactly hide, and I've got a pretty long walk ahead of me."

"Hold up the submarine. Surrender. Raise your pincers. Do something!"

The Charybdis teetered as J.J. lifted its massive claws into the sky. Torrents of water rushed through the underling scaffold of tentacles. Although the creature appeared capable of walking on land, it was a better designed for vaulting in great leaps over the bottom of the sea. Balance was not one of its better attributes.

"Keep your legs out in front of you. Your head and arms are too far forward."

The squadron swung low, and unleashed a volley of flaming spears. Lancet shafts of smoke and burning cordite screamed through the silver haze of falling rain. This time, they weren't aiming for the creature's impenetrable shield of a head. Rockets skirted beneath the armored carapace, and detonated in succession against its vulnerable undercarriage. The Allied Navy was learning.

"Damn it!"

"You're going down."

"Don't you dare drop that sub!"

Smoke billowing from beneath the edges of its shell, the titan reeled on its ragged mess of legs. Tentacles hung shredded and writhing, spurting ropes of indigo blood, while only fleshy stumps remained of appendages that were missing altogether. A great shadow passed over the seaport of Nantong as the behemoth reeled, toppled, and met with the Yangtze in an atomic belly flop. An entire section of the river left the channel as cataclysmic waves that arched high over the harbors, before smashing down upon them. Blocks of structures were flattened by the shockwave. Buildings crumbled as though they'd been sculpted from sand. The Charybdis wriggled in the mud, while incoming water slowly refilled the chasm.

The Psyjack team cowered, as the resonance of the shockwave trembled through the metal panels of the Shanghai hangar. Uproarious cheers and howls were soon to follow, emanating from elsewhere on base. J.J. emitted a moan. He was sprawled on his side.

"Talk to me, buddy. You alright?" Collin crawled across the floor, and slapped gently at the side of J.J.'s helmet.

"He's unconscious," Skyler said. "Don't even say I didn't warn you."

"Carl got knocked out cold," Takashi said. "Dropping all the breakers on cerebral activity during a streaming session is just a little disorienting. That's all. Wake up, buddy."

"He's got to get up," Skyler said. "The gunships are circling back around. God, they're going to kill him!"

"J.J.?" Collin shook him by the shoulders, but the team leader only emitted a groan. "It's no use. He's out." Collin popped the mouse-piece out of J.J.'s lips, and flipped the toggle on the side of his helmet to force a manual crash on his nanobot colony. "I'm going in."

"Don't go too deep, man," Takashi said. "That thing is badly injured. You're going to feel every bit of the burn."

"Here they come!"

Collin mouthed the controls. He slapped the toggle on his receiver. His spine jolted straight, and his eyes rolled back, as he plunged back into the monster's head.

Having never piloted another living creature, Skyler could only imagine the freefall, as they referred to that harrowing drop into the mind of the host, when streams of sensory data came pouring in through the mind's eye, and the pilot's body image began to blur. Described in their technical bulletins as an expansion of awareness, an outward rush of the pilot's innermost being, Skyler imagined stardust blasting outward from a supernova's core. Unlike J.J., who piloted just as casually as if he were test-driving a new car, Collin's freefall was decidedly harder to watch. He twitched and shivered, grimacing as though in pain. This was what they meant by deep diving. Neurons fired, synapses bridged, and a monster's cerebral network came online inside his head. When his eyes reopened behind the visor, Collin *was* the Charybdis.

"Defend yourself! Get up!"

Skyler watched the drama unfold on her phone. The sunken monster beneath the swollen river emerged. Tons of polluted water poured from its vast periphery, as the discus head rose atop that skirt of mangled legs. Mantis claws drawn beneath its hood, it clenched the submarine protectively against its chest. Collin swiveled the great shield in the direction of his attackers, just in time to deflect the deadly barrage meant to put him down. Missiles thumped against the armor plate. The smoldering carapace swung skyward, exposing that vulnerable underside just long enough to purge the stored water in the bladders for a blast of weaponized sound. Skyler covered her mouth, as the squadron of Navy gunships went spiraling out of the sky to become great balls of fire in the streets of Shanghai.

"Oh my God," Skyler whispered. "We are in so much trouble."

"They didn't give us any choice," Takashi said. "They were going to kill him."

"Just bring the sub in. Bring it in."

J.J. moaned, and reached for the sides of his helmet. He was starting to come around. "What happened?" he asked. "Did we win?"

"Yeah," Takashi replied. "We won, alright, and you can consider this to be our last gesture of good will toward the Allied Navy. It's time to cut our ties."

"I can see the base," Collin said. "I'm coming in."

"They've scrambled fighters."

"Blast them," Takashi replied.

"Don't blast anything! God, would you stop saying crazy stuff like that for just five minutes?" Skyler glared at Takashi. It was difficult enough to discern emotion in his expressions, due to his ocular prosthesis, but deciding whether or not his statements were intended to be taken in a straightforward manner was even more challenging. It didn't help that he always seemed to be trying to uphold his reputation as being some sort of a wild card in the team. Skyler wondered how often Takashi received bewildered stares after speaking, and what might be the psychological effects of living in that world he'd created, one populated by uncomfortable people. Takashi's ego seemed to indicate that keeping people off-balance only fueled his delusions of grandeur. She was beginning to dislike him.

"I'm not blasting anyone unless they fire on me first," Collin said.

"Thank you," Skyler replied.

According to the personnel files, Takashi's family were victims of China's chemical warfare attack on Japan. He was orphaned, and as a result, he'd spent a significant portion of his childhood bouncing around in the system while battling cancer. Skyler supposed he'd suffered far greater anfractuosities than most other kids could even imagine. On top of that, he might've struggled to fit in, due to his ocular prosthesis. Skyler recognized all of this, and she tried to cut him slack for his outbursts, but it sure wasn't easy. Collin, if anyone, seemed to have the best handle on Takashi, as well as the highest tolerance for his penchant for pushing boundaries.

"We need to give them every opportunity to be the better ally, buddy," Collin said. "Hopefully, they'll come to see that we're all on the same side."

Still trailing wisps of smoke, the pendulous monster lumbered down the Yangtze River amidst a stain of dark blood. Fighters screamed around the behemoth at a safe distance, circling high and wide, as if inviting a test on the range of its sonic weapon. Their white contrails striped the skies over Shanghai.

"They can't touch you," Takashi said. "You're too far into the city. If they drop you now, they're looking at billions in damage, and probably another insurgency."

He was almost certainly right. China had remained politically precarious since the last days of the End War, when the combined air strikes of eight countries finally took the fight out of the rogue regime, almost twenty years ago. Any tip to the constant state of imbalance was employed as leverage by the restless cells of underground Jaw-long freedom fighters who seized opportunities to incite another backlash against the occupying forces, and to push the beleaguered country ever closer to the brink of civil war. China was a book of matches floating on a lake of gasoline.

"I don't think I'm the one they're after," Collin replied. "Look downriver. You seeing what I'm seeing?"

Just off the harbor of SWCC field command, in the mouth of the Yangtze River, a strange assembly of monsters was forming in the brackish water. There, a brooding herd gathered around their fallen calf, encircling the little one in a protective wall of wrinkled, pebbly hide. Breakers crashed against their flanks. Fighters rumbled through the skies overhead. Indifferent to the changing mood of the world around them, they caressed the body of their lost one with gentle, prehensile snouts, dabbing at the wounds, as if trying to stop the streams of indigo blood.

"It's that water bear I fought, right there in the middle," J.J. said.

"Look at the size of those other ones," Takashi replied. "They're frigging huge!"

"I didn't know it was just a baby."

The creature that suffered the beating had been close in size to the Charybdis. Comparatively, the adult attendants that dwarfed the dead cub might as well have been of a different species. Great humps domed their backs. The herd of water bears loomed over the sea like a rugged mountain range, swinging their great heads from side to side.

"What the heck are they all doing out there?" Takashi asked.

"Grieving," Skyler replied.

"The hell they are. Those are oversized bugs," J.J. said. "They don't have the capacity to feel loss."

"I'm not so sure about that. Of all the species I've studied, the water bears are the most deeply devoted," Skyler said. "They remain paired to the very end, even in a laboratory environment, and they're very protective of their own."

"They don't sound so bad, when you put it that way," Collin said.

"That's because they're not bad," Skyler replied. "In a perfect world, water bears are pretty wonderful creatures. None of this was their fault. They just happened to be in the wrong place, at the wrong time."

"Well, looks like they're in the wrong place at the wrong time yet again," J.J. said. "Those Navy fighters are about to crash their little funeral."

"That's an extraordinarily bad idea," Skyler replied.

"Don't worry about them, bro," Takashi said. "You ain't got a dog in that fight."

"Agreed." Collin lifted the captured submarine over the rim of his shell, so he could admire his little prize through his cyclopean eye. "What do you say we crack into this tin can, and see if we can shake out a few pirates?"

Skyler had been trying her best to hold back her excitement over the submarine's capture, but this moment was huge for her. It was more than just a victory for the team. This was her overdue vindication, and the redemption for which she'd awaited. Her wildest expectations for this team's assemblage would never had accounted for the possibility of capturing the same bunch of bad guys who'd destroyed all of their lives. This was redemption for all of them. She noticed a smile spreading across Collin's face, and she wondered if the Charybdis was smiling too.

Chapter Eleven

"Luna, come with Nana," Diane said, trying her best to maintain some composure. She snatched her granddaughter off of the laundry hamper, and rushed out of the bathroom. "We've got to go bye-bye, right now."

"Dat, Nana?" Luna pointed over Diane's shoulder. Her sapphire eyes remained riveted to the spectacle beyond the bathroom window. "Dat?"

"I don't know, sweetie. We have to go."

Diane grabbed her purse off the back of a dining room chair, her keys from the blue bowl by the door. She snatched their coats from the drying pegs, and backed out through the door, fumbling with her keys. She emitted a shriek when a tremendous impact shook her condominium to its foundation. Sheltering Luna with her arms, she staggered backward into the opposite wall. The keys fell from her hand to the floor. When the building stopped quivering, she reclaimed the lost keyring and bolted for the staircase, leaving her condo door ajar.

Her shoes hammered down the wooden staircase. Another concussion shook the building, closer this time. She seized hold of the handrail. Glass shattered. In the distance, a transformer blew like a cannon shot. The lights flickered and died. Diane's hand slammed into the brass bar on the exit door, and she burst from the darkened stairwell out into the bracing air of Anchorage, Alaska.

The slight foothold of civilization between looming mountains and a frigid sea had captured her heart the moment she'd first laid eyes on the city, a year before Jill was born. Those were fast times, fueled by the high-octane energy of her once youthful ambition.

Ted was moving quickly up through the company ranks. Money flowed. Their future together had never shined so brightly. Those were fun and spontaneous days, when the two newlyweds made love wherever and whenever they kissed. Diane would sometimes throw a stick into the air to determine their direction of travel, and in those days, she and Ted traveled everywhere.

Vancouver had been a weekend whim. There, they'd rented motorbikes, and they'd purred through the rolling streets of the emerald city for two days before deciding to board a ship destined for Alaska's Middle Passage. It was a voyage of lasting portents, where she'd stood alone and poised at that bow that forever plied through a slurry of floating ice as the sun crested those jagged mountains. While Ted, in his drunken stupor, filled their cabin with his snores, Diane beheld the rising sun, as Anchorage's skyline was set ablaze, as though the city had just been touched by the hand of some higher power. That moment was to impact Diane's life to a more lasting extent than the man who'd delivered her there. Two years later, she and Ted were divorced.

"Dat, Nana?"

Diane whirled in the direction of the child's finger, where thorny legs lifted higher than any mast in the harbor, vanished into the clouds, and pulverized everything in their shadows as they fell. Festooned with shredded tangles of rigging, the legs disappeared and reappeared in thunderous plunges back to earth. Whatever horror propelled those legs was one thankfully hidden above the low-hanging clouds, but its intent was discernible enough. Every devastating step carried the thing nearer to the heart of Anchorage.

A scabrous trunk fell from the sky. Diane spun from its point of trajectory. Clutching Luna to her breast, she ran through the swath of falling shadows toward the condominium's carport. The giant's foot spanned the full width of the slushy street when it landed with an impact that Diane felt in the marrow of her bones. She screamed. The jarring fusillade left her dazed and stooped in a cacophony of howling car alarms. Luna began to cry.

"It's okay. Everything's okay."

Everything was not okay. The car was not going to start. Diane knew that, even as she hurtled toward the resting spot of that rusty bucket of bolts that never failed to let her down when she needed it most. When Jill had dropped Luna off, there hadn't been time to explain to her daughter that she had a less than reliable means of transportation, limited entertainment options, next to no money, and nothing inside the condo was even toddler-proof. Jill had just shown up out of the wild blue, handed over a polka-dot suitcase, a matching diaper bag, and finally her daughter, who was still strapped into the car seat.

"The car seat!" Diane smacked her hand to her temple. She froze, midway between the condo and the carport, unsure which course of action was the less dangerous of the two, until a massive, thorny pillar dropped from the clouds to smash the entire condominium building into kindling. Jets from a fractured water main fountained in the air. Helices of mist twirled over the swelling dust, as the spiny hoof retracted back into the sky, still trailing nets and shipyard rigging. Diane hadn't even begun to turn back toward the carport before a change in air pressure assured her that it was already too late. A drop in temperature dulled the color of things, one instant before the carport, and everything parked inside it, was flattened against the pavement. A car alarm emitted a single chirp of distress before it was silenced. The pillar ascended back into the heavens.

Diane just hovered for a moment, glancing one way, and then another, as the unseen behemoth tramped toward the skyline of her beloved city. In two steps, the thing in the sky had just deprived her of everything she owned. Goodbye home. Goodbye car. Goodbye all material possessions. She held Luna close, and fought the urge to fall to her knees and cry. There was nowhere to go. Pinned between mountains and sea, there was nowhere to run.

For the last twenty years, even in the beginning, during the ugliest months of the divorce, when Jill wasn't much older than Luna, Diane had always been able to see a pretty clear course of action. While Ted lawyered-up and prepared for what he thought was going to be some epic battle, Diane relinquished everything. She gave up everything but Jill, her one precious thing, and she'd returned to her secret place ablaze in the midnight sun.

In Anchorage, she and her daughter had cobbled together something new from their ruinous past. Diane remained in survival mode, where she lived day by day, scraping her way through one week and into the next, with her love for Jill as the only fuel and inspiration she needed to keep plugging away. Somehow, that's all she'd ever needed. Through it all, she'd always managed to remain sure of herself as a mother. She found that she had a knack for finding her weaving way through life's forest of obstacles, and that had made her feel pretty proud.

However, things were different now. She felt old and desperate. With her granddaughter crying in her arms, Diane surveyed the wreckage of her world, all around her, and she had no idea know where to go.

***

Jill tapped her phone's screen to end the call. She slumped back into her seat. It wasn't like her mom to not answer. She always picked up, anytime night or day. It wasn't that she was getting nervous about her mom and daughter, per se, but the longer she had to sit aboard the Devil Ray, waiting for her flight to Anchorage to be cleared for take-off, the more time she was afforded to agonize over whether abandoning her team was the right decision.

She was a mommy. Luna was supposed to be her biggest responsibility in life. A child only gets one childhood, after all, and it's up to mommies and daddies to give it to them. There were no do-overs. As a parent, you had just one shot to be involved, and to fill those priceless years with all the magic and experiences that every child deserves. However, the longer Jill stared out the window at the captured pirate sub sitting on the side of the airstrip, the more she found herself weighing the importance of magic in Luna's childhood against some greater good for all humanity. Would her duty as Luna's protector be best fulfilled at her daughter's side, or right down there, alongside her team? She could see all four of them hovering on the periphery of the crowd, and she wondered if they could also see her. In the distance, gunships circled over the form of their slumbering giant.

"What in the heck?" she whispered, glaring back down at her phone, while her fitful right knee was chugging away. She retried her mom, and for the umpteenth time, the call went to voicemail.

She'd already left two messages. It made no sense to leave anymore. Something was wrong.

Jill slapped her phone face down on the surface of what used to be her working space, and left her seat for a window that offered a better view of the airstrip. Navy vehicles had surrounded the captured sub an hour ago, and SEAL units were sent in. The whole base was on lockdown until the sub was cleared. The search had already taken quite a while, but a few of the soldiers were starting to emerge. They were gesturing and shouting. A unit of medics pushed through the positioned ranks of vehicles, sailors, and sharpshooters. A couple of collapsible gurneys were rushed to the front lines. The medics set them up in a matter of seconds, and wheeled them right up to the submarine.

"What's going on up there?" Jill said, shouting in the direction of the cockpit. "Any word on when we're going to take off?" There came no reply through the reinforced partition. The pilot hadn't attempted to communicate with her at all since she'd boarded the aircraft, if there was even a pilot up there at all. It was possible that one hadn't yet been assigned to her discharge. Commander Bent had agreed so easily to her request for release from the Psyjack team that the initial wave of relief began to gather in the pit of her stomach like a wad of darkness. Something felt wrong.

Down on the airstrip, the two gurneys rolled away from the sub. Gunners flanked them, waving back the small crowd. There was a body strapped onto each of them. Both were covered with white sheets. By the manner in which they were enshrouded, she might've guessed that the captives were dead, if not for the urgent manner in which the armed SEALs were escorting the medics through the crowd. The sense of urgency was almost palpable. Jill watched the reactions of her former teammates as the two gurneys rolled past them to a waiting ambulance. She saw Takashi smack J.J. with a high-five. Skyler seized Collin in a celebratory embrace. As they twirled in each other's arms, Jill's smile fell.

It wasn't that she had feelings for Collin, and it wasn't that she disliked Skyler. It just felt wrong to see everyone celebrating without her. It should've been her down there slapping high-fives, embracing her teammates in a fit of joy. Skyler had only known them for a short time. Jill had been working with those three guys since their college days, back in Glasgow. Together, they'd built the program from the ground up.

Jill walked over the cockpit, and drummed her fist against the partition door. "Is anybody in there?" After a moment with no reply, she stomped back over to her phone, dropped back into her seat, and swiped the screen to bring the sleeping device back to life. With an annoyed flick of her thumb, she pulled open her favorite news app. The top drone feeds were being loaded. She could only imagine the bizarre story of a piratical sub being captured by some kind of friendly monster, who delivered it to the Allied Navy's front doorstep. With Commander Bent blocking every step of their progress, it was anybody's guess if the world would ever know the truth about what had just happened in Shanghai.

The top news headline blazed boldly before her eyes. Already shaking, as though every drop of blood sugar had just been leeched from her body, she raised the screen closer to her quavering eyes. Each piece of what she'd failed to see as being one terrible puzzle crashed at once into place. The real reason why the Navy was detaining her, and her mom's failure to answer her phone was all explained in a single image. Jill gaped in horror at the black columns of smoke billowing from a ruined skyline to the mountain peaks. Anchorage was burning in the midnight sun.

***

The hospital triage room was a riot of activity. Paramedics swarmed the covered bodies strapped to the gurneys. Medical equipment was wheeled into place. Cables were connected, power switches flipped. Overhead lights blazed to life, one by one, as they were dragged down from the ceiling on articulated armatures to illuminate the examination area in a harsh white light.

Skyler clung to Collin's arm. She was knotting the fabric of his flight suit in her grip. Despite the whirlwind of commotion, she couldn't break her stare from the tattooed arm of one of the recovered pirates. It dangled out from beneath the shroud that covered his body. She studied the tormented artwork of his tattoos, the webs of scars and burn pocks that marred his forearm and hand, and those latent terrors of her past from which she'd fought so hard to recover were ripped back open like poorly stitched wounds. Just the sight of that man's arm was enough to assure Skyler that her so-called recovery was nothing but a joke that she'd been playing on herself. Part of her remained forever crippled and cowering in that lake of blood and champagne, clutching the bag of canisters to her chest, and staring up into the face of the demon.

One of the paramedics grabbed the upper edge of the sheet, and began peeling it back. His whole body gave an involuntary jerk when the face beneath was exposed. The fabric fell from his fingertips, and he stepped back from the thing on the gurney. All activity in the triage room came to a halt. All eyes were affixed on the twisted face that leered back at them from behind a mask of taut wires.

"Good God almighty," someone whispered.

"That's him," Skyler heard herself say, in a shrill and breaking voice that she hardly recognized as being her own. She clung to Collin's jacket as though she were dangling over a cliff. "He's the one who attacked us." She pointed an accusatory finger at the demon. "He was there."

A couple of the medics eyed her, and then turned away. It took Skyler a few seconds to realize that no one in the room but Collin probably had any idea what she was talking about, and that realization made her feel more alone in her trauma than ever. She lifted her cane from the floor, and pressed the cold, titanium crook to her upper lip. It was a slender thing to try and hide behind, but apart from Collin, it was her only defense.

"They found these two trapped in one of the upper compartments," one of the medics said. "Probably the last pocket of air in the whole submarine."

"If the compartment wasn't flooded, then what exactly is the matter with them? Why are they unresponsive?"

While the medics discussed the likelihood of gases as being the reason for their patients' incoherence, they plunged an I.V. into the bend of the tattooed arm, and attached sensor pads to his chest. Military intelligence officers hovering on the outskirts reached right into the heart of the chaos to wave their phones over the sleeping pirate's face. One by one, they retracted their devices, and frowned down at their screens. Facial recognition scans weren't coming up with a match, probably due to the apparatus stretched around the pirate's head. There was some speculation over why he wore the horrible contraption, and disguising his identity seemed to be the consensus. Skyler felt like a hovering phantom trapped just outside of the moment, unable to warn these people of how dangerous this man was, unable to scream.

Officers murmured, examining each other's phones, as they sidled over to the second gurney, where the substantially larger captive still remained uncovered. Skyler couldn't stop staring at that face. It was the same face that had haunted her nightmares for two years following the attack. She could still feel the burning agony in her pulverized legs. She could hear the roar-grunts of those leashed baboons, the scrape of their claws against steel, and the ringing of their tightening chains as they lunged with flashing fangs. The demon was laughing, as though the situation struck him as being funny. He wanted to watch her being eaten.

Skyler closed her eyes, trembling, and gripped her cane until her knuckles turned white as hail stones. It made her feel all cold inside when she recalled those chain links slipping one by one through the demon's hands. He relaxed his grip with every lunge of his beasts, releasing just a little more slack each time his killer apes forced themselves nearer, ringlet by ringlet, until at last their fangs plunged into her flesh, and their shaggy heads thrashed from side to side.

"We've got an ID match."

Skyler's eyes snapped over to the second gurney. The intelligence officers had drawn back the sheet. They were examining the results of the scans on their phones. Their faces were brightening. Skyler was relieved to see that her personal demon's larger companion was not half so horrifying to look upon. Silver teeth shone from his broad Mongolian face, inset with a striking pair of emerald eyes.

"What the hell is that thing in his throat?" One officer leaned down over the body, wrinkling his nose. "Looks like a broken pen jammed in there."

"It is."

"Do you have any idea who we've got here, gentlemen?" Another officer held up his phone, allowing his question to hang dramatically in the air for several seconds before revealing the answer. "Meet Maxim Volkov, a.k.a. the Moscow Mongol. Name ring a bell to anyone? Hmm? No big deal. Just the damned leader of the Red Brotherhood."

Skyler was taken aback by the amount of credit that the Navy was already poised to snatch. It would be a wonder if Psyjack received any recognition at all, when it was they who had delivered the pirates single-handedly into military custody. However, it still felt as though the collateral damage they'd caused might be punishable, if they were ever to admit to their involvement. It didn't seem fair. The officers' faces split into wide smiles. At once, the triage room resounded with whoops and clapping hands.

"We've got vitals," a medic said, glancing at a heart monitor. "Pretty weak, but I see no reason why he wouldn't pull through. Still need to check for internal injuries."

"What about the other one? The one with the—*face*?" The officer made a clawing gesture at his own grimace.

"Vitals are strong, but he's unresponsive. Comatose." The medic straightened up, and looked around the crowded room, hands outstretched. "Alright, everybody. I appreciate you being here, but now I'm going to have to ask that all non-medical personal please clear the area. Congratulations on catching the bad guys. Please exit the triage room, stat."

The officers filed past Skyler and Collin without casting so much as a glance in their direction. They were jabbering excitedly, slapping each other's backs, already scheming about exploiting their new prize as some sort of a political bargaining chip. Regardless of how powerful and connected that man might be, Skyler's attention remained devoted to the twisted face in the web of wires. Although he did appear to be comatose, Skyler couldn't help but suspect trickery. The demon could be playing opossum, just lying in wait for an opportune moment to strike out like a viper at someone within his reach. A crop of goosebumps prickled her arms. She nearly jumped out of her own skin when her phone vibrated noisily in her pocket.

"We'd better clear out of here," Collin said, nudging her with an elbow. He removed the Mindbender Rift still strapped atop his sweaty head, and he tucked it beneath his arm. His hair was slicked against his scalp. "I'm afraid that while all these guys are celebrating, we've got a pretty long afternoon ahead, getting our butts chewed by the Mad Hatter."

She nodded, turning warily on a heel, reluctant to break her watch over the slumbering monster until her legs were in motion. Once she'd taken her first step toward the door, she felt an impulse to run screaming out of the hospital. Facing her attacker seemed like an important step toward restoring some part of her sanity, if nothing else. If there was such a thing as a complete recovery from what she'd suffered, then exposure to the source of her trauma was going to be a significant part of the process. She was grateful toward the paramedics for admitting her and Collin, and she thanked them on the way out the door. The other two guys hadn't been quite so lucky. J.J. and Takashi had lagged too far behind, and they were forced to wait outside the hospital with the dog. Skyler's phone gave another startling buzz. She withdrew the stupid thing from her pocket, tempted to pitch it right into the trash, but when she saw what was on the screen, she halted dead in her tracks.

"What?" Collin said, gazing back, when he realized that she was no longer walking beside him.

Skyler furrowed her brow. The notification had come from her iFly app. She'd almost forgotten about that search for Captain Roswell. A message was pending from RACHEL-1023, the drone she'd sent scouring the Barrier Reef base. Looked as though the search had been a success. Roswell's unmistakable visage was captured in a little thumbnail image in the upper corner of her screen. However, there was something wrong with his face.

"What is it?" Collin's arms dangled at his sides. "Something wrong?"

Medical personnel flowed around her, bumping into her shoulders. Collin approached her, and pulled her gently to the side of the hallway. Skyler tapped her thumb against the pending notification to receive the details. Roswell's image leapt upon her screen, and Skyler nearly dropped the phone. The messenger drone's feed depicted him sprawled on his office floor, just behind his desk. Dark blood streamed from a gaping hole in the center of his forehead. Captain Roswell was not coming to Shanghai to straighten everything out for his team. Captain Roswell was dead.

Skyler covered her mouth, pressing the phone against her chest to prevent anyone passing by from catching a glimpse of the horror depicted on her screen. Collin had seen it. She knew he'd seen it by his stunned expression, but he didn't appear to be any more capable than she was at verbalizing whatever emotions were flooding his head. Collin was frowning at her, chest heaving, searching her face for any sign of deceit, as if he were clinging to some inane hope that she'd somehow doctored up a photo of Roswell's murder as some sort of a prank.

"What was that?" he finally asked.

She shook her head, shooting him a wild-eyed glance.

"What do we do? Get the others?"

"Wait," Skyler replied, holding him at bay with an extended index finger. She took a few steps away from him, in order to think more clearly. She felt faint. Her heart was drumming in her ears. Someone had found a reason to murder Roswell. That much was obvious. The looming question was whether he'd been killed over something unrelated, something personal perhaps, or if he'd been assassinated because of his affiliation with the Psyjack program. If the latter turned out to be the case, then all of their lives were in grave danger.

Skyler turned back to Collin. "We need to get out of here."

"Out of the hospital?"

"No. Off of this base. Out of Shanghai. Right now." She dropped her voice to a whisper. "I think we're in serious trouble."

"Why? We were just doing our jobs."

"Collin, think about the size of military contracts for conventional weapons, and then consider the impact that Psyjack has on those contracts." Skyler gaped into his stricken eyes. "See what's happening, right now? Somebody with a whole lot of money wants us dead."

"We need to warn the others."

"Jill …" Skyler covered her mouth.

"What? What about her?"

"She's already been separated from the rest of us. She's the easiest target."

"I thought they were sending her back home."

"The Devil Ray is still sitting right out there on the tarmac."

"I'll text her." Collin withdrew his phone.

"No." Skyler grabbed his hand. "What do you think you're going to say? You can't tell her anything."

"I have to warn her."

"No!" Skyler spoke through gritted teeth. "Don't you get it? We're being watched right now. Every message. Every text. If they learn that we know what's going on, we'll be dead before we ever get off this base."

"Jill could be in trouble right now."

"Jill could be dead right now."

Collin frowned, staring past her toward the hospital doors. His expression darkened. In an instant, he'd brushed right past her, and he was marching toward the front of the building.

"What are you doing?" Skyler had to run to catch up to him. She thought perhaps she'd offended him with her attitude of self-preservation, until she saw what was standing just on the opposite side of the glass doors. It was Collin's beloved dog, Hotspot, barking maniacally outside the hospital. The animal's fur was smeared with blood.

Chapter Twelve

"Wait," Skyler said, her voice lowered to a growl. She seized Collin by the sleeve of his jacket, and reared him to an awkward halt. A few medical staff members eyed them with an aspect of unease. She could only glare imploringly into Collin's eyes. Outside, the bloody dog licked its chops, sat down on its haunches, and gazed back over its shoulder.

"I'm not leaving my dog."

"I'm not asking you to leave your dog." Skyler narrowed her eyes into slits. "I'm just asking you to talk with me for just a minute before you step outside, and go marching right out into plain sight."

She knew that Collin would never abandon Hotspot, but she was also aware that walking around the naval base with a large animal covered in blood was going to invite the same sort of unwanted attention that it looked like J.J. and Takashi might have already attracted. Skyler stared at all of the blood on the animal's fur, and she felt like she was going to vomit. The reality of the situation hit her like a cement truck falling from the sky. The worst had already happened. J.J. and Takashi might be dead. Jill might dead. She and Collin might be the only two left.

"Alright," Collin replied, as though he sensed that she was starting to come unraveled. As he glanced back at his gory dog, the dreadful realization sucked all of the color from his face. When he took her hand, his was trembling.

Their aimless walk through the hospital corridor was stiffened and strange. They didn't speak. Hand in hand, they clopped mindlessly down a crowded hall, gawping into the nothingness that seemed to be their future. They felt like a couple of dead people walking, a pair of wandering ghosts. Collin slipped into an empty room, and he pulled her after him. She followed, closing the door quietly behind them. No one in the bustling hallway appeared to notice or care.

"I've got an idea," Collin said, as he made his way over to the bed, climbed upon it, and began to draw the privacy curtain around himself.

Still stunned, Skyler could only bring herself to stare at whatever it was that he was doing. If he'd completely lost his mind, she wouldn't have held it against him. All that they'd experienced in the last twenty-four hours seemed quite enough to push a normal person right over the brink. After a moment, Collin poked his head out from behind the curtain. He'd strapped the Mindbender Rift back atop his head.

"Come in, if you want," he said.

"What the heck are you doing?" Skyler asked, as she pushed through the curtain, and took a seat beside him, on the edge of the hospital bed.

"I'm going to connect to Hotspot, and review the last hour's records."

"Records?"

"Everything Hotspot sees and hears is recorded."

For a second, Skyler felt like her eyes were about to go crossed. "Wait. The dog?"

"Yeah."

"The dog has a hidden camera?"

"Not exactly," Collin replied, dropping the Rift visor, and reclining back onto the bed. "It's just another application of the same nanobot streaming technology that we use to pilot our animal hosts. All of Hotspot's ocular and auditory nanobot data is continuously streamed to an internal drive, where it's stored in twenty-four-hour increments before it's backed-up to the cloud."

"I—didn't know that."

"How could you have?" Collin inserted the mouse-piece, and flipped the toggle on the side of his headset. He inhaled a deep breath through his nostrils, as he prepared to tap into the hard drive of his golden retriever. "Hotspot's full of surprises, but I'm the only one who can access them. Nobody hacks my dog but me."

Skyler watched his chest rise and fall. Collin was slightly built, almost fragile. His prowess was a cerebral strength, and even that was so very subtle. At times, he seemed too meek to be much of a critical thinker. In fact, he could almost seem simple. However, Skyler was beginning to understand that it was his social disconnection that made him appear out of step with the dance going on all around him. Beneath his awkward exterior, Collin was quite clever. Skyler was just beginning to appreciate how nimbly his mind raced along when he wasn't being distracted by the one species that he didn't seem to understand.

Her brow gathered when she saw his breathing quicken. His arms drew protectively up against his chest. It was almost like watching a sleeping person suffering from a nightmare, only she knew better than to touch him, or interrupt. Skyler did not envy Collin for whatever sights he was about to behold.

"It's Bent," Collin said, blurting the Mad Hatter's name around the side of the mouse-piece.

That shouldn't have surprised her, but it did. "Is he alone?"

Collin shook his head. "Got a bunch of military police with him."

"Can you see J.J. and Takashi?"

Collin nodded.

"Are they alright?"

"Yes. No. Cops are taking them."

"Taking them where?" Skyler asked, leaning closer. "Can you see where they're being taken?"

Collin began to breathe even more heavily. His fingers clenched into fists. "It's like—a garage. A mechanic's garage. I don't recognize it. It's dark inside. They're dragging them in there. Something's wrong. Dog's going nuts." Collin sucked a loud gasp, and jerked partway upright off the bed. "J.J. got away! He's running!"

"God. Are you serious?"

Collin's expression slackened. "Takashi's still fighting. They're pulling him back into that dark place." He winced. His hand rose to his face. "Stop fighting, dude. They're hitting him,

Sky! They keep hitting him with those clubs. Oh, God." Collin's hands flew up, as if to shield himself from a flurry of ghostly blows. "They're killing him!"

***

Batons rose and fell, cracking woodenly against his skull, landing with muted thumps against his ribcage. Takashi rolled underfoot on the floor of the automotive garage. Drawing his knees to his chest, he tried to cover his head. He assumed a submissive posture that would afford him some protection from their blows, but that didn't slow the officers down. Something was twisted about their motives. It seemed as though the officers had been given orders to beat him to death.

Bolts of pain shot through his forearm. His wrist dropped to a grotesque angle, leaving his hand swinging in the air. This breach in his defenses created a new opening. A police baton slashed through the gap, smashing against his temple with such force that one of his ocular implants detonated. Sparks spat from the flickering socket. The light in his left eye went out, and for a moment, everything went red. Takashi inhaled the stink of his own burning circuitry, and he threw back his head and laughed.

Takashi was no stranger to pain. He knew abuse, and he knew the vast depths to which human depravity could plunge in situations where sadists thought no one was watching. Nothing could surprise Takashi, in this regard. Not when the last sight beheld by his natural eyes was his mother's face melting onto the streets of Osaka. Beyond the doors of that bus onto which she'd thrust him, in her last act, shoving five-year-old Takashi onto the bus that saved her son's life, his mother liquefied until his eyesight was lost in the cloud of burning vapor.

Deprived of sight, his tactile senses became heightened, and he learned to feel everything with great intensity. Through the last months of the End War, Takashi felt every act inflicted by those predators whose favored hunting grounds were the squalid camps where wailing thousands of blind refugees followed ropes to musical prompts from overhead speakers. The Mickey Mouse Club theme was the call to every meal, where hapless prey were snatched from the chow lines to be dragged bleating behind those rows of regimented tents. He felt it all, every second of his suffering in that hell hole. While the free world celebrated victory in the worst war in human history, and reveled in the economic boom that followed, Takashi's personal battle had only just begun. Cancer fastened itself upon his toxified body. He fought the deadly malady while he bounced through group homes and orphanages, fighting for daily survival against stronger healthier children. By the time reparations for Japanese victims of war crimes awarded Takashi with his new set of eyes, he'd already seen too much without them, and the world had become a darker place that it perhaps might've been.

Takashi rolled over to glare up at Miles Bent through his remaining artificial eye, and he smiled. He was glad to see blood streaming from Bent's broken nose, and dripping from the lacerated flesh of his forearm, where the dog had chomped down and given him a good shaking. "You just made a huge mistake," Takashi said. "The world was watching."

Bent circled him with all the dark purpose of a shark through bloodied waters. He placed an index finger to the side of one nostril, and he blasted a reddish spray into the air. He wiped his forearm beneath his crooked nose. J.J.'s punch should have dropped Bent like a sack of potatoes, but if the blow had affected Bent in the least, he hadn't shown it. If anything, it had almost seemed to amuse him. In some twisted respect, perhaps Bent and Takashi were not unalike.

"Back on the Barrier Reef, they gave me a nickname," Bent said, as he retrieved Takashi's Mindbender Rift headset from the garage floor. "Maybe you've heard it?"

Takashi's chest rose and fell, but he did not respond. He watched every movement of Bent's fingertips as they fondled his dropped headset, and he tried his best to hide the anxiety that it caused him. It felt like he was back in an orphanage, and a bigger kid had just taken one of his few personal belongings.

"Around ten years ago, when this base was still under construction," Bent said, gesturing around him with a wave of his hand, "they were having a lot of trouble with insurgents. It's one thing to maintain your military presence offshore, but holding onto a piece of real estate is a different ball game. Turning point came one night when a wave of a thousand Jaw-long rolled right over the site, and massacred a few hundred Navy Seabees. Torture. Mutilation. All that kind of stuff." Bent smiled, and allowed a chuckle. "That's when they sent us in. That's where my military career began. We were the Shanghai street sweepers. Clearing blocks was all we did, and back then, victory was assessed by the number of daily dead. The land was already captured, see, so in order for the Navy to calculate the effectiveness of our unit's presence, it came down to corpses."

Bent turned the Mindbender Rift over in his hands, as though the headset evoked some sentiment of nostalgia. "So, I started collecting hats. Became kind of a dark joke, you know, how many hats I could carry back into field command. It was a game to me. I liked to cover the walls of our barracks with bloody hats. Bullet holes, brains and stuff all over them. Collecting hats was my thing, and that's how I earned my nickname."

Bent tossed the headset underhand to a startled police officer, who somehow managed to catch it. "They called me the 'Mad Hatter,' because whenever I decided to erase some piece of human trash from existence, I kept their hat as a souvenir. If I had your hat, you were dead. If I decided to come for your hat, you were dead. Thanks for that one, by the way," Bent said, glancing toward the captured headset with a hitch of his chin. "That's a really nice one."

Takashi didn't know what to say. Part of him refused to believe what Bent was insinuating, but something stung. The insult of being stripped of his headset hurt worse than the injuries they'd inflicted with their batons, or any veiled threats of death. Perhaps the best feature of artificial eyes was that they didn't mist over, and they never produced tears.

"Let me ask you something," Bent said. He cleared his throat, and rested his fingertips upon his chin. "Do you have any idea what's going on out there right now, beyond the walls of this base?" He stopped circling, and raised his eyebrows. "You said that the world was watching, and you're right. It is. Nothing goes unnoticed. No screw-up is ever missed, and every move you make is probably being recorded." Bent aimed a finger at Takashi, and narrowed one eye. "You and your pack of asses screwed-up big time."

"We did what we were ordered to do," Takashi replied, struggling to sit upright. He clutched his shattered forearm to his chest. "Captain Roswell of the Barrier Reef gave us orders to engage the kaiju of the Yellow Sea with our technology, and that's what we were trying to do. When Roswell gets here, and he finds out—"

Bent interrupted him with a scrape of rusty laughter. He shook his head, and turned on a heel. Military police officers stepped aside as he strode through the middle of their line. "Roswell ain't coming to Shanghai."

"What's that supposed to mean?"

Bent circled around behind the police officers. After a few tense seconds of silence, he reappeared at the far end of their line. Soon, he loomed back over Takashi, once again. "Not that you care about Chinese politics—I do. I mean, I kind of have to—but, while you were celebrating your little rampage up there on the Yangtze River, you failed to notice how your actions triggered an uprising." Bent grinned, and nodded his head. "Worst uprising in twenty years, thanks to you."

Takashi frowned.

"Oh, it's true." Bent gestured to the nearest police officer, who replied with a single nod. "It's all over the news." Bent knelt down beside Takashi, crossing his mauled arm over his knee. He picked a fleck of something out of the wound, and flicked it at Takashi's face. "China is tricky. This region has been teetering on the brink of civil war for two decades. You've got your nationalists, your patriots and freedom fighters, your cells of Jaw-long insurgents, and the corruptive influences of Russian and Mongolian crime lords, like your friends over there in ICU. China has basically been a giant powder keg ever since the End War, and all it needed was that little spark. You guys were a flamethrower."

"I don't believe you. You're just trying to hang anything you can on us."

Bent shrugged. "Doesn't much matter what you believe or don't believe, at this point. The fact is, your monster brawl took a massive death toll, and caused billions in property damage throughout those flooded lower wards."

"That wasn't our fault. That was yours. You attacked us. Your gunships and planes and rockets are exactly what—"

"Hey. Doesn't matter anymore."

"What do you mean it doesn't matter?"

"Doesn't matter. Look. Here's the thing," Bent said, pinching his nose. "Right now, several thousand Jaw-long have surrounded our base. It's alright." Bent smiled and winked. "They're just trying to pick a fight, and we're going to go ahead and give them one, but not before we let them hit us first, and we're going to let them hit us pretty hard. We kind of have to. Makes us look a little better, you know, with the whole world watching and all, because we all know how a little guy's fight with the Allied Navy is going to end—and if you don't, well, you're about one minute away from finding out."

Takashi glanced at the stony faces of the military police officers. The level of corruption throughout this facility was worse than he'd ever dared to imagine. These uniformed men were nothing more than Bent's squad of personal assassins. It was at that moment that Takashi realized that he was going to die on the floor of an automotive garage, and there was nothing that anyone could do about it.

"Why would anyone outside those walls be stupid enough to attack this base?" Takashi asked, blinking his remaining eye. He felt like a cornered dog, about to be euthanized. Any conversation he could prompt might extend what time he had left by precious seconds. The other team members were on his mind. He wondered if J.J. had managed to send a message of warning to the others. If so, Collin and Skyler might still have a chance. Jill probably had the best odds of making it out of Shanghai unscathed, since she had the foresight to turn in her resignation before the situation got out of hand. Takashi's heart tumbled in a wave of guilt. He hoped that she was safely in the air, flying home, and would soon be cradling her baby girl in her arms.

"Oh, they will. Call me clairvoyant, but I know it with one-hundred percent certainty. A Jaw-long attack on Shanghai field command is imminent." Bent flashed a grin that was just as crooked as his shattered nose. "It will be precise, devastating, and unprovoked in the eyes of the world. It's just a matter of choosing an irresistible target, and placing that target within their easy reach."

Takashi flinched as Bent rose suddenly to his feet. The Mad Hatter strode over to the nearest police officer, and extended his open hand. It seemed to take the officer a second or two before he understood, and he placed his bloodied baton into Bent's hand.

"You're not getting away with this," Takashi said, chest heaving. "They're coming back for me. They'd never leave me behind."

"Think so, do you?" Bent turned back to Takashi. He examined the polished club as though he was an appraiser, and the police baton was among the rarest of artifacts.

"I know so."

"I'll bet you—ten-ba-jillion," Bent said, pointing the baton at Takashi's face, "that you're wrong, and that they've already decided to leave you behind."

"Why?"

"Because you're a pain in the ass. You're a cripple. I don't know." Bent shrugged. "Like I said, it doesn't matter anymore, but I've seen these types of things play out, and you're not the sort of person worth saving. What does matter are those millions of prying eyes floating around out there. They need to believe that what happened up there on the Yangtze River was just a standard naval response to a kaiju threat. Doesn't need to be anything more than that. It's cleaner that way. Nothing good would come from the whole world learning that the Allied Navy was involved in some kind of a—monster puppet show." Bent spat on the concrete. He then leveled his eyes, cold and hard as a pair of polished bullets. "Sorry, little fella, but I'm afraid it's going to be a whole lot better for everyone if you never even existed, and I'm pretty sure your so-called friends would agree with me."

Chapter Thirteen

Crushed cars fell like leaf litter from the monster's spiny hoof, as the leg withdrew into the clouds. In the distance, another plunged through the mist to flatten a strip mall with a chuff of gray dust. Drones swarmed over the ruins of Anchorage like flies around a corpse. The nature of the destroyer remained a mystery. Its enormity was too vast to be discerned through the overcast sky, and it had no definite color. Those massive columns that rose and fell from the clouds were translucent and glassy, not unlike the appendages of strange forms of life that inhabit the ocean's darkest depths, where color has no meaning. Terrified crowds gawped skyward, searching the mist for a glimpse of the titan. One woman clutching an infant stumbled and fell. Jill covered her mouth and gasped, as the fallen mother and child were trampled by their own kind.

"My God."

Jill tapped back to the map of Anchorage, and swept her thumb against the screen until the seaside villas of Turnagain Arm slid into view. Her hands were shaking. She widened the screen to zoom in on her mother's neighborhood, and then highlighted the locations of all available drones in the area. There weren't many. Most had already departed the residential area, and were bee-lining toward the action at the heart of the city, where the monster appeared to be embedded. Jill had doubts about whether the few remaining drones on her mother's block were active or functional, but it was worth a shot. She whispered a little prayer as she tapped on the drone nearest the condo.

ZOE0809 leapt right up, as though eager for duty. Its e-Me character was a black cat with blinking amber eyes. As usual, the drone insisted on being "Liked" before access to its feed was granted. Jill growled as she thumped her thumb against the "Like" tab. The black cat gave a yowl, performed a backflip, and disappeared in a shower of sparkling stars.

The drone feed splashed across Jill's screen, but she couldn't tell what the heck she was looking at. What should have been a familiar setting of white condos lining the shoulders of a twisty, seaside avenue better resembled the garbage dump of some third world country. Keening gulls spiraled over hillocks of rubble. Geysers sprayed from broken water lines. Flattened vehicles shared mass graves with displaced ships and flopping fish. Splintered joists jutting from crushed condominiums were entangled in fishing nets and rigging. It looked as though a great spoon had descended from the heavens to stir the sea and the seashore all together into one terrible amalgam.

Jill dropped her phone into her lap, and stared at nothing. She'd never felt so ghostly thin in all her life. The anxiety that had frazzled her nerve endings all day had vanished, leaving her gutted and hollowed in the face of reality. Her mother's neighborhood had been annihilated, and she wasn't answering her phone. There was only one course of action, one place in the whole world where Jill needed to be, and she needed to be there immediately.

Jill stormed back up to the locked partition to the Devil Ray's cockpit. She beat her fists against the molded steel until she was sure that they could hear her down on the tarmac. The aircraft amplified her pummeling like a hollow drum. "Open this door!"

Her phone vibrated. Jill jerked it up to eye level, hoping to God she'd find a text from her mother. However, the message was not from her mom. All hope was slammed to the ground, yet again.

J.J.: R U OK?!!

"What in the hell?" Jill smacked her palm against her forehead, and gaped down at the text message, re-reading it over and over. Why wouldn't she be okay? She didn't want to believe it, but some part of her knew that bad things were happening, out there. It was the same part of her that insisted she resign from the team precisely when she did, pushing her to get out of Shanghai before the relationship between Psyjack and the SWCC turned caustic. Perhaps she hadn't seized the opportunity to leave soon enough. Being detained in Shanghai was not going to be an option. Not now. Not after what just happened in Anchorage. She had to get out of here. Nothing was going to stand between Jill and her child.

Jill: I'M STUCK IN THE DEVIL RAY!!!

J.J.: Coming now

He knew all the codes. J.J. could break into the Devil Ray from the outside. He could access his cockpit, the flight controls, and the weapons systems. Peering out over the tarmac through the nearest window, Jill watched squads of armed soldiers hustling along the base of the steel wall that separated field command from the streets of Shanghai. The men dropped into defensive formations around the perimeter, shouted into radios, and waved other squads forward. It looked as though the base was preparing to defend itself against some sort of an outside attack. Jill searched Shanghai's skyline for any sign of a Kaiju threat. Nothing but skyscrapers loomed.

A flaming bottle arched over the wall. It looped end over end like a fiery pinwheel. As it struck the tarmac, the vessel released a great lake of fire. Jill's head whipped toward the prattle of automatic weapon fire. Another burst of gunfire from beyond the wall, followed by the shouts of men. Jill shrieked and fell to her knees as a spray of bullets rattled against the Devil Ray. The shots appeared to be coming from outside the base, in the vicinity of a nearby block of derelict buildings. Denuded and scarred, the ruins were somehow still standing, probably since the last days of the End War.

Jill scrambled across the floor on her hands and knees, headed for her usual battle station. The Devil Ray was a sitting duck on the tarmac. An incoming rocket whistled over the wall. The projectile howled overhead, and struck somewhere far behind her. Mortars screamed through the air. Their explosions rattled the steel panels against the bracing. Psyjack's high-tech aircraft was left sitting alone and defenseless on the tarmac. It might as well have had a giant bull's eye painted right on it. The whole situation seemed almost too convenient.

Jill clambered into her seat. She snatched her Mindbender Rift off the wall mount, and strapped it atop her head. Thank God she'd not worn it out into the hangar, as the guys had done, or she'd likely have left her headgear back there with them. She and Skyler had been too busy assisting Collin off the aircraft to take part in the front of solidarity that the boys had staged against the Mad Hatter. She flipped the power toggle, dropped the visor, and swept her mouse-piece into her lips. Bent might've figured that she was trapped in the Devil Ray, unarmed and powerless, when in fact he'd left her armed with one of the most powerful weapons in the world.

"Mommy's coming, baby," Jill whispered. She drew deep breaths as the system loaded, ignoring the ping of bullets against the aircraft, resonant explosions that she could feel inside her skull. "Hang on. Mommy's coming."

Windows opened, one by one, displaying the feeds of available hosts within her range. She hated this. Hardware development had always come to her quite naturally, but her prowess as a computer geek had no relationship with her ability as a pilot, or lack thereof. She preferred a backstage role as the team's support system, leaving the piloting to the pilots. Sliding the tip of her tongue over the surface of the mouse-piece, she highlighted the feed belonging to Carl the Charybdis, praying that their enormous friend had somehow managed to survive its bloody engagement with the Navy fighters. It appeared to be resting on the bottom of the Yangtze.

A mortar careened unseen toward the Devil Ray. The whistle became louder with every passing second. Jill braced herself for the impact. The round detonated close enough to lift her partway out of her seat. They were dialing them in now. "Are you kidding me?" she shouted around the mouse-piece. "That is enough!" Jill tapped Carl's highlighted feed with the tip of her tongue, and prepared for the freefall.

Glittering motes of stardust began to streak by. Jill felt herself wanting to hyperventilate. Her fingernails dug into the ends of her armrests. She hated this part so much. Enveloped in whorls of spectral energy, Jill plunged into that disembodied vastness, where a soul felt as vulnerable as a newly hatched tadpole wriggling through a pond's murky abysms. These were uncharted waters where nothing was really understood, where a soul might go spinning out of orbit to become forever lost in a dynamic dreamscape between bodies.

Jill's eyes rolled back into her head. Her nails split against the armrests, and she began to convulse. It was so hard to let go. As Jill rocketed through the freefall, she felt like a trespasser in God's backyard, a place where no living human being should ever hope to be. Bolts of fire flashed through the miasma. Spoken word devolved to sound. Collective energy egressed every cell in her human body, and her cognitive one became one billion, as Jill's consciousness reentered the primeval soup as a galaxy of falling stars. All that remained was a girl's reflection on the gazing pool, if she'd ever even existed at all.

In the next instant, she was reborn. An infant on the ocean floor, she could barely lift her oversized head. Nothing felt right. Disoriented, paralyzed in the gloom, she felt all mixed-up, as though she'd been dismembered and reconstructed from scrap animal parts. Limbs squirmed beneath her hulking form like a catch of eels. Her gangly arms felt disjointed, backwards. The seemingly limitless capacity of her lungs, if they were even lungs at all, was an oddly distracting sensation. Like a flaccid balloon that begged to be inflated, she filled the empty bladders with a great rush of river water, and then released a small burst with a fluttering groan. Inhaling deeply, she filled every recess in her body with water, gathered her mess of legs beneath her, and rose.

While some estranged part of her felt the shellshock of mortars, the concussion of bullets against steel walls, and the slap of J.J.'s hand repeatedly against her cheek, she stayed committed to the Kaiju stream. Volumes of water thundered over the rim of her carapace. Brownish cascades churned the Yangtze to foam as she rose higher into the sky, until the city of Shanghai lay sprawled like a lurid garden at her feet. Unfolding her mantis forearms, she used these saw-toothed appendages to hitch her way upriver, back into view of the naval base. She could see the Devil Ray taking fire on the tarmac. The realization that her human body was down there inside that tiny vessel was the most surreal experience of her life. She had to protect that aircraft, as well as its precious cargo.

"Jill, it's J.J. Hang on. We're getting out of here, girl."

The Mindbender Rift was designed to filter the stream of sensory input to the extent that the pilot didn't feel split in two. However, Jill could hear J.J.'s shouts in her human ear. She could feel his hands on her shoulders, but she willfully distanced herself from his voice by plunging deeper into the head of the Charybdis, so as not to interrupt the stream of consciousness. She lacked the confidence that Collin and J.J. seemed to enjoy in the pilot's seat, with one foot in each world. To Jill, the experience was a tightrope. She always felt as though she might at any moment come reeling out of the stream like a dazed sleepwalker, or worse, dive too deeply, and never resurface.

She could see them now, hordes of Jaw-long insurgents spilling through a smoldering breach in the wall. The frame of a box truck engulfed in flames was still rolling across the airstrip like a shipping vehicle sent straight from Hell. While the majority of the militia engaged the soldiers in a firefight, Jill noticed a trio of fighters moving in on the Devil Ray. They had in their possession what appeared to be a rocket-propelled grenade launcher. The shooter took a knee, brought the weapon to his shoulder, and aimed it at her aircraft.

Jill thundered upon the military base, reared back, and unleashed a sonic blast that flattened every human body on the airstrip. It was too difficult to distinguish between soldiers and insurgents in the chaos of battle, so her attack was indiscriminate. Being careful to avoid hitting the Devil Ray, she swept her flattened carapace from side to side, broadcasting her sonic death blast with an intensity meant to liquefy human innards.

"Jill! Turn around!" J.J.'s shouts sounded like the warnings of some spiritual advisor reaching out to her from another dimension.

In the next instant, something slammed into Jill from behind with force enough to topple her borrowed body right into Shanghai's bustling waterfront. Jill glimpsed her otherworldly attackers as the edge of her carapace plunged through the first block of neon skyscrapers like the blade of a titanic battle axe. Buildings crumbled upon her shell. Jill gathered herself, and swiveled the natural shield of her carapace in the direction of the assault.

There were four of them. They bore down as one savage mass of muscle and rending claws. Having committed their slain cub to the eternal lull of the Yellow Sea, the pod of enraged water bears now hungered for vengeance. Jill raised her spiny claws, absorbing the brunt of their combined impact in her limbs. Collapsing beneath their weight, she watched whole sections of city lights flicker as she and her assailants took a tumble right through the heart of Shanghai's infrastructure. Transformers thundered all around them like cannon shots. Skyscrapers sloughed their skins in ghostly skeins of dust.

There were too many of them. A pebbly arm came down with a great slap atop her carapace. Stunned by the powerful blow, Jill was reawakened by the white-hot agony of claws raking furrows through her flesh, just beneath her single eye. The anguished cry that seemed to emanate from some faraway world, Jill realized, was in fact her own human scream. Jagged mouthparts like commercial blenders shredded into her flesh. Hooked claws ripped into her underbelly. They meant to tear her to pieces, and they would. The combined ferocity and power of the pack was overwhelming.

As though the water bears had all agreed that their lost cub had been avenged, the mauling came to a halt. Three of the creatures turned their attentions toward the naval base, and they thundered off in that direction. Jill was abandoned to the dark whims of the fourth monster, whose intent to devour her alive was evident as rending mouthparts ripped away great chunks of her borrowed body. Smothered beneath its thrashing bulk, every second of the agony became real. The sound of her human screams grew ever more distant, as did her connection to the other world she'd left behind. If this was all just a nightmare, she was lost within it, and couldn't wake up.

"Luna!"

That word. What was it? That little word with such huge connotations kept resonating throughout her divided mind. Jill couldn't be certain if she'd shouted it out loud, thought it, or evoked it from some fuzzy memory, but it was a word that refused to be denied. If Jill's every reason for existence was somehow threatened, that phantom face would never let her go. She would kill and die in the name of that memory, and the name of that face was Luna.

Gathering her strength, Jill dragged her mantis claw between herself and the devourer, clamping the spiked vise of her forearm around the predator's throat. Rearing back on its quivering haunches, the creature lifted her from the crater of rubble that they'd pounded into the city, but it could not pull free. Powerful as the water bear was, the grip of the Charybdis was stronger. Jill locked her opposing claw around the back of the monster's head, and pulled the alien face against her own for a deadly kiss.

Yawning her mouth, Jill unleashed what remained of the pressurized store of seawater through both barrels of her biological weapon, channeling all of the kinetic energy through the sound chamber in her throat. The conversion was a blast of galactic resonance that flattened background structures to dust, parted the Yangtze River to its exposed channel, and dispersed her attacker's head across Shanghai in a spray of deliquesced flesh.

Jill released her grip on the monster's spurting stump. The headless corpse tumbled down into the river, and dyed the swirling water with rhythmic fountains of gore. Looming over the smoldering city, Jill turned her attention to the naval base, where the remaining water bears had begun to plunder. They thrashed their heads through hangars, and shredded barracks with their claws. Navy jets roared by in tight formation, flitting lances of fire from that blew wet and ragged craters into their flesh.

From the heart of all the chaos, one aircraft arose. Sleek as the ace of spades, it tilted in the tempest, catching a flash of lightning on the blade of its wing before vanishing into the horizon with a sonic boom. The sight of the aircraft's departure brought Jill a moment of relief, because she knew that there was some sort of connection between that thing and the face named Luna.

"It's okay. You're going to be okay."

Jill blinked her eyes. A bleary visage materialized out of mist. As detail came into focus, it was apparent that the face did not belong to Luna. It was someone else.

"Autopilot is locked onto Anchorage. We're going to get you to a hospital. You just hang on. You hear me?"

"Luna." Jill gasped for breath, gaping at the man who held her head in his hands. He unfastened the buckle beneath her chin, and lifted the Mindbender Rift from her head. She somehow recognized him, but could not remember his name. His face, the setting, it all seemed so familiar, right on the tip of her tongue. The man placed her headset on the wall bracket, and smoothed her bangs away from her sweaty brow. When his hand retracted, Jill noticed that his fingertips were dripping red.

"You went too deep," he said. "I had to crash you."

Just like that, her collective memories came rushing back into her mind like a delayed download. She knew where she was, in the Devil Ray, and she knew the man hovering in front of her so well that he might as well have been her own brother.

J.J. smiled. "You did awesome back there."

"I killed people. I killed lots of people. Oh, my God."

"They were not our friends, Jill. None of them. They were going to kill us."

"What about the others?"

"I—I don't know."

"We have to go back for them!"

"It's too dangerous."

"But we can't just leave them behind!" Jill became aware of a stricken expression on J.J.'s face. She frowned, licking her lips. As though his anxiety was some contagious disease, she began to feel the same fearful reaction prickling up inside herself. Her chin dropped, and her eyes fell toward the spot on her midsection where J.J.'s gaze kept falling.

"We can't turn back, Jill. We need to get you to a hospital, right away."

Everything hurt. There were too many sources of pain around her body to be individually assessed. However, the worst agony by far practically screamed from her abdominal region, in the same general area where those water bears had ripped into the soft underbelly of the Charybdis.

"Don't," J.J. said, catching her chin on the crook of his finger. He shook his head slowly back and forth. "You don't want to look down."

***

Mr. Krupin used the giant's borrowed arms to lift the submarine hatch. He peered down through the flooded caverns of twisted metal, where the floating corpses of Red Brothers were so swollen and gray that they resembled some fallen race. It surprised him that the Allied Navy hadn't bothered to recover the dead, but judging by the commotion raging outside the submarine's walls, something of greater importance had the Navy's undivided attention. Explosions shook the vessel's steel panels against the ribbing. The staccato of automatic weapon fire punctuated the screams of dying men. Those were familiar sounds. The exhilarating cacophony of combat brought simultaneous smiles to each of Krupin's faces. The timing for this skirmish couldn't have been more perfect, affording his escape from his steel sanctuary amidst the confusion of battle.

Krupin felt the hands of medical personnel fussing over his natural body, back in the hospital. It felt like they were strapping him down to another gurney. The room was bustling with commotion, as though the medics were preparing their patients for some sort of an emergency evacuation. Trundling shockwaves reverberated through the ground. Krupin's borrowed body leapt through the portal, and plunged down into the flooded compartments amongst the bloated dead.

The surface of the water danced in response to basal concussions of such depth that their source might've been continental plates grinding together, pushing up mountain ranges, and spawning tsunamis. Droplets bounced and flitted past his face. He drew another deep breath and dove. The submarine was canted to one side, submerging portals beneath tons of water. These blocked routes of escape were signs that the Navy hadn't come in that way, decreasing the odds that his route of escape would be guarded.

Krupin seized the portal handle in Jochi's mitt of a hand, gave it a squealing crank, and pulled up with all of his might. He could hear the rush of escaping water through the broken seal, as the great weight upon the door began to lighten. Just as he feared he was about to drown, the falling water level exposed his face, and he was able to suck a huge gasp of air. Water roared through the portal in a sucking whirlpool that spun its way down to ground level. Below, daylight blazed through a large tear in the steel wall.

Krupin lowered himself to his knees, studying the aperture for any hint of a shadow cast by a guardsman positioned outside. When he discerned no evidence of a lurking sentry, he slid down through the portal, dangled by his thick fingertips, and then dropped through space until his boots struck steel with a much louder and more reverberating tone than he'd anticipated. For a few seconds, he dared not move. Fingers splayed, he was prepared to lunge and seize anyone who happened to peer through the hole, ready to crush and pop their bones into pebbles with his bare hands. However, no enemy appeared. Only the distant thump of gunfire suggested that anyone even remained to defend the base at all. A fleet of helicopters roared overhead, rotors hacking at the sky. It sounded like everyone was leaving.

Krupin stole a quick peek through the opening, and when his brain registered what he'd just beheld, he had to steal another. Where once the Pearl of the Orient lay sprawled and resplendent in lustrous neon light remained a smoldering wasteland. Drones fished through heaps of ragged metal, headlights lancing the fog of destruction, like lost souls haunting the shores of some netherworld.

"Hnn," he grunted. He stepped out through the aperture, and he cocked his head. The wastelands were not entirely uninhabited. Dark and villous forms lay strewn about the airstrip, indistinct through the haze of war, but still recognizable as corpses of the countless slain. The battle had sounded like a terrible one, but it began and ended so quickly that Krupin could hardly believe so many lives had been snuffed in such a short amount of time.

Somewhere beyond the pale reefs of dust, an unseen skyscraper crumbled. Krupin turned on a heel. Great slabs calved from the firmament with the rumble of distant thunder. A wave of dust rolled out across the airstrip, enveloping dead and living alike beneath an unfurling shroud that deprived sight, but sharpened the ears to the spattering Plum Rains. It was beautiful. No better conditions existed to facilitate an escape that would amount to a casual stroll off the military base. From there, he would vanish into the crowds of Shanghai refugees that were surely forming, and probably moving upriver. Krupin lilted his smiling face skyward, closed his eyes, and extruded his tongue to capture gritty droplets of rain. It was almost like a dark god was smiling down on him from above.

He blinked, as a shadow spilled over him.

Veils of mist parted before the descending head. Maw gaping, mouthparts chirring, the creature's jaws slammed closed over the borrowed and cowering form of Jochi. Twin screams erupted from both halves of the doubled-man, as the better half of Mr. Krupin was engulfed, and sucked headfirst into the flesh blender.

***

"We got a live one, here! Morphine!"

Mr. Krupin's eyes bulged from the sockets of his restrained skull. Medics swarmed around his stretcher. Masked against the fetid clouds that hung over the burning city, their scrubs flapped about their frames in the tempestuous airstream. Over the thumping rotors of the chopper squadron, all Krupin could hear were his screams. He couldn't bring himself to stop. Again and again, his cries pealed up from his gaping throat. Apart from the immeasurable agonies that wracked his body, it was the mental torment that he found most unbearable.

Complete psychological disintegration followed the mastication and digestion of Jochi's body. Rather than being reimbursed his halved psyche, when Jochi's brain dissolved in the monster's digestive juices, Krupin's mind felt as though half his mind had been ripped out like pages from a book, and scattered into the howling winds. Every trace of his phantom connection to his obliterated human counterpart became connections to a brand new entity that was now streaming through Krupin's mind, and it was anything but human.

"Just keep these two prisoners stabilized until we land in Japan. After that, they're not our problem anymore."

"Who are they? Some kind of VIPs?"

"Trust me. You don't want to know."

Krupin's eyes lolled over to the patient who was strapped onto the stretcher next to him. He found himself to be the focus of a hateful pair of emerald eyes that he knew all too well. Volkov mouthed words that Krupin was glad not to hear. Blood bubbled from the end of a broken pen still jammed into Volkov's throat. That struck him as being a little bit funny, but he was in too much agony to laugh. Krupin's body stiffened beneath the restraints, and he began to seize. His eyes rolled back into his skull, his lids fluttered closed, and froth came bubbling up through his gritted teeth. It felt as though his fragmented mind was comprised of a million mixed-up pixels that were just beginning to fall back into place. A new stream of consciousness was taking form, and although it was alien to the human constructs of his mind, he did not dislike the sensations of immensity and boundless power that came with it.

"Status epilepticus. Where's that morphine?"

The sensory stream flickered in and out of perception. What he began to see was the city of Shanghai, all spread out before him like a toy playset. The Pearl of the Orient had been gifted to him as a personal playground, to do with as he pleased, but already, he was imagining bigger and better things. The whole world, and every form of life upon it, would soon be at his mercy, and he didn't intend to show the world any more mercy than it had ever shown him. In fact, he'd show it less.

There was a reason for his lifelong pain and suffering. Mr. Krupin understood things better now. The world's cruelty was meant to harden him. It had all been part of a necessary process to forge him into what he'd finally become, following the last phase of metamorphosis that shed Jochi's body like a chrysalis. His transformation was complete, and his true form had emerged. Krupin glared down upon Shanghai's ruin, and he could only think of one good reason why a god would reward a monster like him with the ultimate destructive power. Filling his massive lungs with untold volumes of polluted air, he announced the beginning of the world's end with a roar that shook the planet to its mantle.

Chapter Fourteen

"Where are they going?" Skyler shouted, throwing her arms wide, at the center of the hospital rooftop. She limped over to the roof's edge, and there she stood, propped on her cane. "They just left us behind."

Collin averted his eyes from the sight of the Devil Ray roaring off toward the northeastern horizon, and he lowered his chin. He trusted his teammates. He knew that they must have had a good reason for the sudden evacuation, but that didn't make him feel any better about the hopelessness of the situation in which he and Sky had evidently been abandoned. Explosions continued to tremble the lower wards, while bursts of gunfire stitched the silence in between. Given the Kaiju threat combined with a Jawlong insurgency, being abandoned in Shanghai with affiliation to their Allied oppressor was nothing less than a death sentence, and their deaths would not likely be good ones.

He left Skyler standing at the edge of the roof, and he sat down next to a ventilation louver. Didn't seem like the rain was ever going to stop. He was so thoroughly soaked that he could've wrung a pint of water out of his underwear, and that would probably be a tastier beverage than anything he'd hope to be served in a Shanghai prison camp. Suddenly, waiting tables for a living didn't seem so bad. Hotspot plodded over to his side, and flopped down with a groan. The animal's fur was still stained with Takashi's blood. Collin couldn't bring himself to look at it, not after what he'd seen in the recording. No one could've survived a beating like that. No one. Takashi was gone.

"Aren't you freaking out a little bit, right now?"

Collin pressed his palms against his temples, and he closed his eyes. He'd seen quite enough for one day. Perhaps too much. He had to process it all. Part of being an introvert was upholding a mandatory requirement for personal time and space in order to quietly organize that clutter of mental files that got scattered all over your brain's desktop over the course of the day. If an introverted personality didn't take the time to perform those psychological grooming exercises, then the result was being overwhelmed by the next infraction upon a very fragile illusion of control over one's chaotic life.

"We're outlaws now," Skyler said, staring out over the battlefield that had so recently been an airstrip before the lives of all friendlies and foes were deprived with indiscriminate abandon by one of their teammates inside the head of the Charybdis.

Skyler was right, of course. If the Navy hadn't wanted them dead ten minutes ago, they almost certainly did now. The Charybdis lay beached and heaving on the banks of the Yangtze. After its brawl with the pack of water bears, the creature did not appear to have much life left in it. This was the end result of their collective efforts. Perhaps thousands of innocent lives had already been lost, including the life of a magnificent creature whose mind they'd pirated, and whose blood they'd looted to the very last drop. He could hardly bring himself to face the terrible truth: if they'd never come to Shanghai, if they'd never climbed aboard the Devil Ray, and had just remained in the lives they'd left behind …

"Who do you think did that?" Skyler turned away from Shanghai's bleak horizon, where the mountainous forms of the water bears lumbered beyond a hanging curtain of dust. The shrill edge to the breeze was perhaps the collective scream of an entire city. She swept back a wisp of blonde hair from her gathered brow.

Collin shrugged. He didn't see why it even mattered, at this point. They would all be held equally accountable for the destruction. The Navy was probably already assembling some team of forensic hackers to interface with nanobots and determine their networking history. If they dug deep enough, all the evidence would be there, of course. All of their fingerprints would be all over that crime scene, except for Skyler's.

"You should probably go," Collin said, glancing up at Skyler through a squinted eye.

Skyler half-laughed, and tossed up her hands. "Go where?"

"Anywhere," Collin replied, throwing his arm around the dog's neck. "But you're better off distancing yourself from me."

"That's crazy."

"Is it?" Collin cocked his head and stared at her.

"Nobody knows when and where Psyjack intervened, and if that monster was just behaving like a monster." Skyler pointed her titanium cane in the direction of the Charybdis.

"You know as well as I do that they're going to hang every bit of what happened in Shanghai on us. Captain Roswell is dead, Sky. Dead—and, Takashi ..." Collin sighed. "If that's not an indication of how the Navy plans on dealing with our program, then I don't know what is."

"We live in a zoo without cages, Collin. Every one of us. If we just stood by and did nothing, and just tried to pretend that everything was normal, then the future of humanity would be a very short and foregone conclusion. Like it or not, we are the wards of this planet."

"But, so many people have died ..."

"People are going to die. Look, I worked alongside Roswell on the Psyjack reboot for almost two years. I was practically second in command. If they killed Roswell over the work we shared, then you can bet that I'm next on the Navy's hit list. I'm no safer than you are, and I'm starting to think that Takashi was right all along."

"What do you mean by that?"

"We should've gone rogue with our program while we still had the chance. We could've done our job more effectively from a private headquarters, without tripping all over the SWCC's red tape. We never needed that leash around our necks."

"I'm starting to think that it was never a leash. It was a noose."

They shared a long moment of silence.

"What do you think we ought to do?" Collin asked.

"How much energy do you think he's got left in him?" Skyler asked, glancing back at the Charybdis.

Collin lifted his headset back atop his head, and squeezed it down over his ears. "I don't know. What are you thinking?"

Skyler strode back over to the edge of the rooftop, folded her arms, and glared into the curtain of mist. "There are Kaiju over there, right-smack in the middle of Shanghai, one of the biggest and most important seaports in the civilized world."

"Yeah."

Skyler clicked her tongue. "I don't know about you, but that's a problem for me."

"Carl might have a little bit of fight left in him."

"People are dying. Right now. Right over there." Skyler pointed toward the haze of destruction that was billowing from the heart of the city. "Who else but you, Collin, has the power to do something about that?"

"For the greater good." Collin dropped his visor, and switched on his headset toggle.

"For the greater good."

"Dropping in."

As a child, Collin dealt with a wild imagination that demanded extended delves into worlds of pretend. He could draw for hours on end without ever interacting with another human being. Great landscapes of Styrofoam and cities of cardboard were constructed for his lucky action figures, who rode in his fists through shunned creeks and hedgerows, while Collin whispered from their viewpoints like some feral madling. That was normal for him, and it was perhaps that overactive imagination that made piloting another life form feel so natural. Dropping into their minds felt to Collin like scampering down a secret woodland path to some childhood sanctuary, where the rigors of his human life disintegrated, and he experienced absolute peace. It was a blissful death.

Bit by bit, Collin was reborn. He could feel his mind and body being reassembled into something wonderfully new and inhuman. Better than any game of pretend, better than a book, a movie, or a video game, this was the ultimate escape. Visual and auditory streams began to rush through his mind's eye, as he was reintroduced to the same world he'd left behind, but through the sensations of a fantastic new form.

"Oh, God." The tactile stream hit him like a runaway bus. A deluge of agony overwhelmed his senses, and for a few intense seconds, he fought the urge to manually crash himself out of the experience. The Charybdis was dying.

"What's the matter?"

Although J.J. had survived the death of a dolphin host, he was a shallow swimmer in the stream of consciousness. His connection to the host was no more intimate than his engagement to a flight simulator. At the depths to which Collin dove, he couldn't imagine the trauma to his disembodied mind if his host died while they were coupled.

"Collin? What is it?"

Collin felt Skyler's hand on his shoulder, and he flinched away. "He's hurt. He's hurt really bad. So bad."

"His limbs can regenerate."

"It's more than just his limbs." Stabbing abdominal pains doubled him over. It felt like lava burning in his guts, as well as across that broad plane of the carapace that correlated with the side of Collin's face. The poor creature had really taken a beating. "I'm empty. All out of water."

"I don't know what you mean."

The stores of water in the creature's internal bladders were depleted. Not unlike the discomfort brought by hunger or thirst, the pangs of emptiness that Collin felt deep within his borrowed body competed even with the pain of the injuries, and it demanding correction. Some hardwired mechanism in the Charybdis was evidently in place to bolster its chances of survival by keeping the sonic weapon loaded and ready for discharge. Failure to do so resulted in an unpleasant sensation that caused the most terrible anxiety. Free will was a fleeting concept between the body's regular demands, and while those terms of enslavement almost went unnoticed in human form, they were glaring to a tourist in a borrowed body.

"Collin, look out!"

Shanghai's blurred skyline swept past with one swing of the creature's pendulous head. Neon lights smeared the sky with lurid tracers that further confused a backdrop of swirling smog and moving mountains of flesh. The water bears were upon him. Collin rose to defend himself against his attackers, but the sight before his cyclopean eye could not be reconciled by his borrowed mind. He couldn't believe what he was seeing. What the monsters were doing could not be possible.

***

Skyler knew he didn't like to be touched while streaming, but she wanted to grab hold of him. She wanted to rake her nails down the sides of her face, fall to her knees, and just scream. Without another person to cling to, she was afraid that she might just lose her mind.

It was *him*.

She didn't know how it was possible, and that's what made her feel as though she'd somehow stumbled over the cliffs of insanity. It couldn't possibly be the demonic pirate in the wire mask, but as she gaped at what appeared to be the leader of the pack of water bears, that's who she saw looming over Shanghai.

Standing upright on its hind legs, a behavior unusual in itself, the Alpha bear appeared to be controlling its pair of subordinates by lengths of bridge cables leashed around their necks. This was something beyond intelligent behavior. This was a very specific intelligence, one she remembered all too well. Clutching snarls of frayed steel in each of its clawed paws, the monster steered its harnessed beasts toward the Charybdis with much the same sick interests as she'd once beheld when she'd faced a pair of flesh-eating baboons.

Rearing back against the leashes, the Alpha bear stepped between his beasts to deliver one thunderous kick to Collin's chest, toppling the Charybdis back into the heart of the city. Skyscrapers crumbled and calved in great slabs that flickered with dying light as they tumbled to the streets. When the monster hit the ground, the shockwave was reeling.

Hotspot ran to her side, as though the animal sensed her distress. While she was grateful for the dog's company, Skyler threw an arm around the animal's neck, less for her own comfort than to ensure that it didn't approach Collin, and interfere with the streaming. The bizarre contortions of his body on the rooftop in some way corresponded to every movement of the complicated body of the Charybdis that rose to its feet in time to defend itself against the gnashing mouthparts with slashes of its mantis claws. The timing of their lunges was off, but not by much. Water bears were unaccustomed to being harnessed and controlled in such a manner. They appeared to be more distracted by the feel of the steel tethers around their throats than enraged by the proximity of their enemy. Despite their handler's rough treatment, they thrashed like leashed cats against the cordage.

Sky hated to feel helpless. She wanted to at least shout some words of encouragement, but she knew that any interference in this critical engagement would be disastrous. If they managed to escape Shanghai with their lives, and moved forward with the Psyjack program, she would demand a nanobot injection and a headset. She and Collin might make a formidable team, fighting side by side, but for now, she could only watch and pray.

Stumbling backward over one of Shanghai's writhing monorail systems, the Charybdis tipped momentarily off-balance. The Alpha bear seized the window of vulnerability. Both leashes were released from its hooked claws. The war beasts felt the slack in their tethers, and they lunged with simultaneous ferocity, slamming into the breast of the Charybdis before Collin was able to raise his arms in defense. Enmeshed, they tumbled, flattening whole wards of the city beneath their knots of rending claws and gnashing teeth.

Even standing apart from his unleashed beasts, the Alpha bear retained a horrifying likeness to Skyler's nightmarish pirate. Muzzle drawn back behind a grimacing rack of cutting plates, the monster appeared to be grinning. Skyler couldn't begin to understand how the psyche of her personal demon had managed to infect the mind of this creature, but she had no doubt that it was him, nor was there much doubt about the mechanism behind this magic trick. She feared that this was the worst-case scenario in what was already the worst possible scenario. Psyjack's technology had somehow fallen into the pirate's hands.

Entwined in cable and claws, the Charybdis rose again. This time, with their cables clamped in its pincers, Collin drew one of the beasts back against his chest by a leash twisted into a deadly garrote. Blunt paws flailed the air as the cable tightened, biting through its flesh, until a cascade of indigo blood rushed from the beast's flayed throat, spilling over its rotund belly and pouring down into Shanghai's streets. At last, the bulbous head toppled from a fountain of gore that stained whole blocks of the city a striking blue. Hopelessly entangled in cables, the remaining beast could only emit an indignant squeal as both sabers of the Charybdis' claws plunged through its nameless organs. The Alpha bear threw back its head and released a roar unintended by God or nature to be heard above the frozen crust of an ocean moon.

Skyler's head was still spinning. It was unfathomable how a comatose patient strapped to a hospital gurney had somehow managed to steal Psyjack's technology? Her first thought involved Takashi, and it was a grim one, but even if Takashi had somehow been robbed of the nanobots inside his head, there was still no account for the pirate's quick mastery of the skills required to use the technology. It seemed more likely that the security breach had to have occurred some time ago. Surely the bad guys' brand of technology was one developed separately from Psyjack's product line, and unaffiliated in any way to their program. However, as badly as she wanted to believe that to be true, it still seemed an uncanny coincidence that the same pirates involved in the attack on her research team had later plundered Psyjack's store of technology. There had to be some connection. It was beginning to feel as though that personal demon of hers was inside her head, streaming her, and spying on her from behind her own eyes.

The Alpha bear dropped to its multitudes of paws, lowered its head, and it charged. Buildings detonated to clouds of chaff before the rippling mountain of warthog hide. The power of the creature was tremendous, discernible in the effortless expansion and contraction of muscled layers that propelled the beast through reefs of skyscrapers as if the buildings weren't even there. This thing was a living wrecking ball, and the civilized world appeared to be slated for demolition.

The goal of the Psyjack program had always been to take the fight to the monsters before they ever made landfall, before they ever had an opportunity to cause damage, but the evident ease with which a terrorist could obtain the same tech and raze an entire city within a matter of seconds forced Skyler to question everything. However, it was too late to turn back. The cat was already out of the bag. There seemed to be little choice but to proceed with the program, if only to protect the world from the very threat that they'd inadvertently created.

Monsters collided with a slap of flesh that made the whole region tremble. The water bear's phantom pilot was superior to Collin in his mastery of control over the beast. Skyler awed over the fluidity of his blows, the deadly precision of every strike. It was a terrible mismatch. Even if Collin was the best dolphin pilot in the world, the fact was that he might never have been in an actual fight. The pirate, on the other hand, had probably killed more people than Collin had ever stood up against. The Charybdis could only stagger backward into Shanghai, claws raised defensively, as the pummeling continued. The water bear leapt into the air, and brought down two fists atop his broad carapace in a thunderous hammer strike that tipped the Charybdis drunkenly to one side. Savage blows drummed against the borrowed body, until the carapace cracked all the way to the cyclopean eye.

Skyler covered her mouth. It was finished. There was no fight left in the Charybdis. The Alpha bear reared on his haunches to drum two sets of fists against its chest.

Rising with the aid of her cane, Skyler limped over to where Collin lay gasping on the rooftop. Prone on his back, not unlike his broken counterpart, he pawed at the trickling blood that rolled from beneath the visor. Skyler disconnected the chinstrap, and freed him from his headset. When she saw the geometric wounds, the blotches of dot matrix all over his face, Skyler felt lightheaded and numb. The psychosomatic injuries associated with streaming could no longer be denied. Profound evidence was right before her, where Collin had just been beaten to within an inch of his life. If she hadn't removed the headset, she wondered if his life might've slipped into the hereafter hand in hand with the ghost of his borrowed body.

The Alpha bear whirled around. As though satiated with its rage against the defeated Charybdis, the thing swiveled its massive cauliflower head in the direction of the naval base, and its burning glare seemed to settle upon her. Skyler's heart chilled inside her chest. The monster was most certainly looking at her, and its pearly eyes were shimmering with recognition.

The water bear cocked its bulbous head. Contorting its throat and jagged mouthparts into unnatural positions, it looked as though it was about to regurgitate something it had recently eaten. Gobbets of slobber the size of cars dropped from that blender of a mouth, as the cutting plates shifted into a very specific position. Although the maw of this monster was designed for no greater purpose than shredding the flesh of its prey, its phantom puppeteer appeared to have another use in mind for that reeking cavern. The monster's basal voice shook the city like the condemnation of an angry god.

"You!"

Skyler shook her head in disbelief. It knew her. It recognized her as the girl who got away. She could only stand frozen like a small rodent in a raptor's shadow, as the destroyer of worlds thundered closer. In an instant, she was enveloped in the blackness of its shadow, inhaling its otherworldly stink. Whatever traces of humanity might've once resided in the heart of that man in the wire mask, they'd since been consumed by his fire of hatred.

The monster hooked an owlish claw in her direction, and emitted chuffs of air that might've been some devilish rendition of laughter. Reflections of a burning world danced on the surface of its moony eyes. "You're supposed to be dead."

Chapter Fifteen

The image of the young lady poised on the rooftop became fragmented, almost pixelated. Whole sections of the visual stream vanished, froze, and winked out of focus like poor satellite reception during a storm. The helicopter's thumping rotor blades could now be heard with disconcerting clarity. Something was wrong. Krupin emitted a growl, twisting his body beneath the straps of his gurney. The data stream from his Kaiju host was starting to break apart. He guessed that the chopper had flown too far from Shanghai's coast, and out of range of reception to his monster's signal.

"No!"

Krupin felt the hands of paramedics pressing down all over him. They were grabbing at his wrists. They were tightening straps across his chest and thighs. He could hear them reassuring him, telling him to remain calm. The stream of consciousness waned to a trickle, and then it dried up as though it had never been anything more than a bizarre dream. The ride of his life had just come to an abrupt end, before it ever had a chance to really begin.

"No-no-no-no-no!"

Krupin's eyes flicked open. A latex hand cupped his screaming mouth. That was a mistake. With a wet crunch and a snap of latex, the same hand left his face spurting red ropes of blood from the ragged stumps of missing digits. The medic's screams brought Krupin the slightest taste of satisfaction, but not the life of every person in the chopper could begin to compensate for all that he'd just lost. Krupin wrenched against his tethers, spitting fingers with a gurgling screech. Elbows crossed his face.

Needles stabbed into the bends of his arms. They tried, but they could not subdue him. Not united in all their strength and their efforts, not one or a dozen could do so. Krupin went berserk.

Snapping straps and pinging buckles could be discerned over mixed screams of rage and terror that filled the teetering aircraft. Inevitably, it was Krupin who rose from the dogpile, with two or three medics clinging to each of his sinewy limbs. The dangling feet of his handlers left the floor. One by one, he shook them loose of his arms. Medics tumbled to the floor. Needles yanked from his arms were plunged into screaming faces. Krupin sprung snarling from the gurney into their midst, and he felt those dark machinations begin to spin. Bones shattered. Faces changed shape. The sterile, white walls of the medical chopper were sprayed with fountains of vermillion chaos. Spirits departed bodies in gouts of flowing blood.

Krupin stormed past the unconscious form of Volkov, and smashed through the flimsy partition to the cockpit with a single strike of his bare foot. He was a killing machine gone haywire. The pilot died before his mind could've reckoned it possible, the queer manner in which his life had been taken. Krupin withdrew his glistening fingers from the man's brain, smeared them against his bearded cheek, popped the door, and committed the pilot's still-quivering corpse into the wild blue yonder, as he slid his own rump into the seat.

So hard to calm down from such a rush. His hands were still shaking from the desire to rip, strangle, and smash, as Krupin grunted at the assortment of weird gauges, blinking lights and switches. He'd never flown a helicopter before. The instrument panel was a very busy-looking place. Perhaps murdering the pilot had been a hasty decision, but once he started killing people, there wasn't a lot of decision making in the process. People just died, until Krupin ran out of people to kill.

He noticed a couple of pedals down on the floor. A bendy lever resembling a large joystick protruded from the lower dash. It was aimed right at his midsection, practically insisting that it be handled. These items seemed to be pretty important for flying helicopters. Krupin curled his fingers around the joystick, and slid his bare feet atop the pedals. Everything felt pretty good. His intuition suggested that the foot pedals might swing the chopper's nose one way or the other, and that the big joystick might affect the pitch and roll of the aircraft. Most intriguing was a red button hiding beneath a protective hatch atop the joystick. He liked red buttons. He guessed that it had something to do with a weapon. A bit of piddling with the controls proved his intuition to be correct. Flames spat from the chopper's nose cone, and an unseen cannon hammered beneath his feet. Krupin's eyes widened, and he emitted a shriek of delight. That would do nicely.

He banked the chopper hard to port side, amplifying the staccato of hacking blades inside the cockpit as the rotor tilted on its axis, peeling the aircraft off of its intended course toward Japan, and back into the Yellow Sea. He was nothing if not determined, and he'd never felt more passionately about anything in his entire life. Veering back in the direction from which he'd come, Krupin aimed the chopper's nose at the shelving thunderheads over Shanghai. He was going back for his monster. Once reunited, he swore that their fused minds would never be separated again.

***

It was hard for most guys to live up to their father's expectations. Seemed to be the norm amongst young men, who began to feel a little small and inadequate, maybe even lost in their old man's shadows, right about the time a guy turned nineteen. That was the age when young men were just starting to realize that maybe their fathers weren't complete idiots after all. Seemed to be the turning point there, as the childhood window slid closed, and a young and formless man stood poised before the stark reality of his future amongst the adult world. Relationships between sons and fathers came to new reckonings when boys realized their fathers would be the sounding boards for so many of their adult decisions. It was at that age when the young teenager who thought he knew everything began to question his own judgment, and started running his larval perception through a new and regular filter that suggested what his father would do, were he in his shoes. Anyway, that's how it appeared to J.J., but he could only speculate. He'd never met his father, because the man had died two weeks after J.J. was born.

All his life, he'd never been able to relate to that relationship between other boys and their fathers. It seemed as though they respected, feared, admired, and sometimes even hated their old men. The relationship between a dad and his son had always seemed to J.J. to be something larger than life, something to which you weren't capable of comprehending unless you had a father of your own. That bond, when there was a bond, appeared to be fundamentally different from a boy's bond to his mother, sister, or brother. It seemed somehow more intense than any dynamic between him and a friend or a coworker, because there was that underlying fear, admiration, and respect all melded together to form the strongest sort of emotional alloy that framed that bond, even if the bond itself was crooked. Never outright, always cloaked in humor and hobbies, the basis of that relationship was something more complex than love, something you couldn't have any other way, or with anyone else in the world.

At least, that's how J.J. liked to imagine it.

Piloting the Devil Ray over the Yellow Sea, bound for the Bering Strait, the very spot where his father's soul had departed this world, J.J. could only wonder whether he was doing the right thing by leaving his team behind in order to save Jill's life. He had to wonder what his father would've done, based on what little he thought he knew about the man, who was widely regarded as a war hero, a giant amongst men who'd earned the respect of every Allied pilot in the Bering Sea before he sacrificed his life for some greater good by turning his plane into a missile that crippled the Chinese war machine. That kamikaze run would forever be his legacy, as well as the sounding board off of which every major decision in J.J.'s life would be bounced, including this one. Which path would Dad have taken at this crossroads, knowing him only to be a man who was willing to sacrifice all he had, and everything that might've been?

"You've got to turn back," Jill said.

Slouched in the copilot's seat with a bloody towel wadded against her midsection, her voice was becoming weaker by the minute. Shallow breaths vacillated her chest. One look at the sallow complexion of her face was enough to assure him that there were no guarantees whatsoever that Jill would even to make it to Anchorage. What then? What if he gambled it all, every one of their lives, in an effort to bring Jill to safety, and his gamble failed?

J.J. had never been a religious person. He'd never seen relevance in reaching out to some unseen higher power that might or might not be available, when he'd spent his whole life trying to connect to another godlike being who actually shared his DNA, appeared in photographs, and lived in the memories of those he'd touched and affected. His missing father was the greatest mystery of the universe, so close, yet so cruelly intangible that he didn't even bother to leave behind any trace of his physical remains. The closest J.J. ever came to praying was talking out loud to his phantom dad, always alone, and probably more often than he'd care to admit.

Do you ever regret it, Dad?

J.J. needed to believe in the possibility that his father might regret his final decision if he were somehow able. He needed to believe that his dad was human, a guy like everyone else who sometimes made impulsive decisions, as well as stupid mistakes. Although there might've been no alternative course of action but the fatal one he'd chosen, J.J. had to believe that there was still room for his dad to lament all he'd forsaken when he banked into that fateful dive. He had to believe that about his dad, because if he couldn't, then there was no reason not to hate him.

What should I do, Dad?

"It comes down to a choice between one lost life, or many."

"What?" J.J. cast a glance over at Jill, who hadn't stirred from her slumped position, hadn't opened her eyes. He couldn't even be sure if she'd actually said anything at all, or if he'd just imagined it, because her voice had sounded so ethereal.

"It's the best lesson I can ever give to my child, if I'm only allowed to give once." Jill's chest rose and fell. Her face appeared to glow with a sheen of perspiration. "Give, completely, for the ones you love—if you're only allowed to give once."

J.J. sniffed at the moisture that suddenly filled his nostrils. He smeared at the corners of his eyes. Saving Jill's life at all costs was just him being selfish. He understood that, now. Reuniting her with her daughter, as important as that still seemed, would never bring his missing father back, nor would it supplement his malnourished life of forever striving to become the man that might've made an imagined father proud. Jill's plea was for something greater than the right to sacrifice her own life for the lives of her friends. It contained a deeper message, one perhaps sent to him from the outer rim of the universe in an effort to convey an important lesson that a father might've taught to his son. What J.J. heard between her words was that avoiding regret was rarely a luxury of life's bravest decisions, because not all repercussions will remain under our control—including the worst ones.

"Alright," J.J. said, clearing the tightness in his throat. "I get it."

He raised the port flaps, throttled up, and banked the Devil Ray back into the eye of the storm. Reaching across the aisle, he took Jill's hand and gave it a squeeze. There was more to his gesture than reassurance meant for the girl slumped in the copilot's seat. It was also his reply. It was his message of understanding and forgiveness, racing off to the outer rim of the universe. After a moment, the universe squeezed back.

***

The monster plunged its clawed appendages into a mountain of fire. Lifting what once were architectural marvels like an armload of burning garbage, it heaved the smoldering rubble against the base of the hospital building. If it was at all affected by the pain of molten steel that hissed and squealed against its flesh like a steak on a grill, it didn't show it, almost as though pain was a sensation that it appreciated. Considering the self-inflicted facial mutilation, the pirate's penchant for masochism should've come as no surprise, nor the fact that the only pastime a monster like him might've enjoyed more than enduring a considerable amount of pain was perhaps inflicting greater amounts onto others.

Skyler covered her face and screamed. There was no escape from the rooftop. The heat of the swelling fire was already intolerable, and another great scoop of glowing girders and debris was tumbling down into the hellish pyre that resembled a bed of coals in a cooking fire, and that's exactly what it was. What had been a rooftop sanctuary, only moments ago, had become transformed into an enormous skillet. They were being cooked alive.

For a few moments, she'd had hope. The monster had frozen, sank back to its paws, and began to exhibit normal behavior. It was almost as though the puppeteer's cords had been snipped. The man behind the curtain was gone, and then, like a sick joke, he'd returned.

"I want to feel you inside of me," the demon said, hooking a claw at its masticating mouthparts. Ropes of slobber oozed from the cutting plates, and swung like a glistening bower from its pebbled chin. Hunkering on its flabby haunches, it blew gently on the cooler spots until they blazed back to life.

It felt like her hair was moments away from combusting. She could feel the exposed skin on her cheeks beginning to blister. The demon could've added an armload of fuel right on top of them, sparing them the agony of slow roasting, but the monster seemed to know just how to fan the flames in order to bring her pain to a stinging threshold, and it knew just when to stop. It studied her suffering, as though appraising the upper limits of her agony in order to relish her torment for as long as it could possibly be extended. In the end, she knew that it was going to eat her alive.

Collin moaned and lolled his head. Blisters rose on his cracked lips. Skyler could only hope that his envelopment in a semiconscious state was by some measure insulating him from the most acute sensations. The dog clawed at the searing gravel with its forelegs, while baring its fangs at the superheated air. Mindless with pain, the poor animal was slave to its misfiring instincts.

Skyler crawled over to Collin's side. Beetling over his chest, she tried to shield his flushed and battered face from the inferno. He'd suffered enough punishment already for one day. They'd tried. God knew they'd tried, until the final second of the final play on the clock, but their fight appeared to be over. Skyler couldn't be sure if what she was doing was easing his pain much at all, but it was the best that she could do for a guy who'd done nothing to deserve such an awful death. His was a childlike soul, whose scientific passion and his love of animals had turned against him.

A double-buzz from Collin's breast pocket vibrated against Skyler's cheek. She raised her head enough to discern the rectangular shape of his phone. Clawing at the button's snap, she jerked the device loose, and read the incoming text that blazed across Collin's screen.

All of the air egressed her lungs in a single chuff. The message was from J.J. They were coming back. Without drawing the attention of the purring demon, Skyler stole a glimpse at the horizon through squinted eyes, and strained her ears for the drone of an engine. Seaward, in the same direction in which the Devil Ray had departed, she discerned the dark outline of an approaching aircraft, just beyond the billowing curtain of smoke.

"Please hang on," she whispered into Collin's ear. The rank stench of burning hair assaulted her nostrils. She couldn't tell if it was hers or his. She noticed a thin crackling sound, so close that it was distracting. Unable to determine where it was coming from, she decided that it must be the edges of her ears. Flames lapped up the walls of the hospital. Trapped pockets of gas in the building materials released in the rising temperature, emitting sharp pops. It wouldn't be long before the building collapsed.

"Being eaten," the demon said, slavering at the mandibles, "it's our oldest and deepest fear—being dragged into the night, far away from our families, where only the monster hears our cries as we're pulled apart, as our flesh rips away from our bones, as we feel its lapping tongue swishing around in our guts ... that's what nightmares are made of. That's why you're afraid of the dark, and things that go bump in the night."

The monster's titanic voice seemed to divide in two. An accompaniment in higher octave resounded from somewhere distant, somewhere in the skies above. Skyler searched the clouds for what her ears insisted she was hearing, and she heard instead the thumping rotor blades of an approaching helicopter. Hopes plunging into the darkest pits she'd ever known, she acknowledged that in fact the seaward aircraft was not the Devil Ray. It was *him*.

"That's why we're all afraid of death, Skyler Hale, because some part of us remembers those days." The demon's tandem voices bellowed from the monster's throat, as well as through a loudspeaker on the chopper. She could see that face leering down at her through the windshield. It was that nightmarish face she'd first glimpsed through an axed hole in her ship's cabin door. "You still remember it, don't you? Some part of you is still scared of being eaten alive by a monster, because you know there's no worse way to die."

The demon rose from its haunches. It stood upon its hind legs until its malformed head touched the clouds. Webs of slobber harped in the tornadic winds. The helicopter made an awkward descent, pitching and fishtailing, as though the maniac at its helm was barely capable as a pilot. Splaying its hooked claws, the looming demon reached out for her.

"Scream for us, Skyler!" As if to show her how it was done, the psychopath screamed into his microphone. His shrill screech pealed over the resonating bellow of the demon. The roar came with a blast of putrid air from the fathomless depths of its gullet. "I'm going to eat you, Skyler, and you'll be a part of me forever and ever!"

Sadistic cackles accompanied the moist huffs of air that reeked of bloated death. The demon's clawed hand cast a wicked shadow that slid across the rooftop, until that clutch of owlish talons was closing around her tiny body. It was as though her death at the hands of that man was something that was always predestined, and now, it was going to be even worse, having been delayed by two years of recovery. She'd pushed herself so hard in a single direction, only to have reached the dreaded curtain. Only now, she knew, without ever throwing the curtain back, what was in store for her behind it. For all of her work, her sacrifices, her struggle, she only mattered by the measure of her failures. Behind the curtain was nothing.

A squawk from the loudspeaker made her eyes flick open. The looming monster seemed to be off-balance, and appeared to be levitating skyward. Canting sideways, the water bear's stumpy legs paddled helplessly at the air. Its rippling body lifted higher and higher, until it thrashed over the head of the Charybdis.

The helicopter spun like a slow top on a wimpling axis. Enraged screeches from the maniac blasted over the loudspeaker.

He was losing control over both bodies, both worlds simultaneously, as separate streams of consciousness converged, and gushed over some psychological levee. Skyler grabbed Collin by his shoulders, and began dragging him out of the danger zone. That chopper was coming down.

While the whirling machine pirouetted from the sky, the mighty Charybdis turned back toward the city, still holding his rival overhead. Indigo blood spilled from the gaping crack in its carapace, where organs vacillated and throbbed. It lumbered purposefully toward the tallest skyscraper in Shanghai, a mirrored wonder of streaming neon, still gripping the squealing water bear by pinched wads of flesh. At the same instant the madman's helicopter smashed down upon the rooftop, the Charybdis slammed the body of its mortal enemy over the structure's needled point, impaling the demon upon on a neon stake.

The helicopter impact evoked a groan from the burning building. Structural elements detonated with reports like gunshots. Flames surged over the walls, trapping them inside an infernal enclosure. Still no sign of the Devil Ray.

A bare foot smashed through the downed chopper's windshield. Another couple of kicks, and the pane of glass toppled. The pirate in the wire mask came crawling out.

There stood her worst nightmare. Clutching his innards against a new hole in his belly, he lurched forward. The mask of wires had sprung from their anchor point behind his head, and they wagged from his lips like steel whiskers. For what was perhaps the first time in the monster's life, he appeared to be scared.

Gripping her cane, Skyler hitched a step forward to meet him, flanked by her growling dog. The animal seemed to sense the undiluted evil that emanating from the killer, and already, it had made up its mind. Hotspot launched from her side like a shaggy missile, teeth bared, and hurtled toward their common enemy.

The pirate cocked his head. He didn't seem the least bit alarmed by the prospect of a mauling. In fact, he seemed quite interested, as if a dog was not an animal that he'd ever seen before. In the next instant, Hotspot skidded to a halt in the gravel, midway between Skyler and the psychopath.

"Well, well," the pirate said, licking his slackened lips. "Well, well, well." He strode up to the motionless animal, who appeared so rigid that he might've recently paid a visit to a taxidermist. The pirate bent to tousle the dog's hair. He rose again, clapped the dirt off his hands, and pointed at Skyler. "Kill that bitch."

As though reactivated from its torpid state, Hotspot spun, curled back its black lips, and emitted a terrible roar unnatural to any canine breed. The hate that filled its eyes belied an emotion that was neither animal nor human. It was something else. It was something straight from Hell. Backlit by the raging inferno, the animal charged.

"Nobody hacks my dog but me."

Skyler heard Collin's voice behind her, and in the next instant, she could hear no other sound but that of the screaming pirate. Hands pressed to the sides of his head, his ruined mouth gaped wide. As though his every physical sense was being simultaneously assaulted, he fell to the rooftop to writhe, howling in the gravel. Hotspot folded at the waist, mid-charge, and tumbled end over end in a lifeless heap.

***

Something was wrong, terribly wrong. The stream of consciousness between Mr. Krupin and the dog had quite suddenly and inexplicably reversed directions. Rather than imposing his own will on the animal, he'd become the unwilling recipient of a bombardment of obscure sensory data that flooded every corridor of his mind. Senseless imagery had somehow spirited him off the burning rooftop to another world, one ruled by a dancing man with a red pompadour of hair.

While Krupin floundered in the current of the back-flowing stream, the dancing man appeared to mock his predicament. Smiling seductively, the dancer twirled, whipping his wrists from side to side. Locations changed. Costumes changed. The dancing man swapped his black jacket for a khaki trench coat in a flash, without ever breaking eye contact with Mr. Krupin. The only aspect of continuity in this bizarre realm was the background music score. String pop synthesizer chords ramped up with an unseen section of champing brass, until the dancing man parted his lips, and began to sing.

"We're no strangers to love. You know the rules, and so do I."

"Who are you?" Krupin shouted, taking a wild swing at a man he knew he couldn't touch, because this was all just some sort of an illusion. He hadn't really been transported from the rooftop. He could still feel the heat of the flames, the sharp gravel beneath his bare feet, but he could not escape the cruel trappings of what appeared to be a dated music video from some bygone era.

"Never gonna give you up, never gonna let you down, never gonna run around and desert you. Never gonna make you cry, never gonna say goodbye …"

Krupin felt the brunt of a realization that he'd just been outwitted, imprisoned in the dungeon of his own mind, where there was no chance of escape. This was the end of the road for him, bottled forever like a bug in a dirty jar. Mr. Krupin raked his nails down his face, threw back his head, and screamed.

***

The last time she'd faced him, and had managed to escape with her life, Skyler made herself a little promise. The prospect of ever being so powerless again, at the mercy of a looming madman with her life dangling by a thread, well, it was not a situation that Skyler would ever permit herself to suffer again. Not if she could help it, anyway. She valued her life too much to leave everything up to chance, and to allow herself to be defenseless ever again.

She hitched forward on her cane, hair snaking in the infernal winds. As she gazed down upon his twisted form, she almost felt pity for the pirate, who appeared to have been damned to some neurological hell. She knew all too well how it felt to be crippled, powerless before the executioner, but she couldn't afford to take any chances. Not with this one. Skyler twisted the crook of her cane a quarter-turn, and withdrew the gleaming blade that was sheathed inside of the titanium shaft. She never went anywhere without it.

"I'm sorry," she whispered, wincing in the fiery reflections that flashed off her saber's edge. She placed the point of her weapon over the demon's corrupted heart, and she pushed until the blade struck gravel.

A massive shadow spilled over the rooftop. Even the raging flames were tamped by an accompanying change in pressure, indicative of some massive presence. Skyler withdrew her saber from the slain demon's chest, but she dared not gaze up into the face of her destroyer. If this was to be her end, she preferred not to know what breed of alien abomination had come to collect the meager balance of her life. She jolted when the snarl of para-cord flopped down over her head.

"Strap into the harness and hang on tight! That building's about to come down."

The sound of J.J.'s voice blaring over the Devil Ray's loudspeaker brought her to tears. Skyler squinted up at the rotating slab of black steel, and heard a small laugh escape her throat. She smeared at the salty streams that burned her seared cheeks, and gave a nod of affirmation to the dark angel in the sky.

Chapter Sixteen

Collin opened his eyes, and blinked in the thin morning light. A draft of conditioned air wafted up through vertical blinds that shivered before the single window. A drab bird lit briefly on the sill, cocked its head, and then burst back off into the sunlight. Beyond, ranks of mirrored skyscrapers loomed. Frowning, he glanced around his cramped quarters. The room was devoid of décor. Its only furnishing was a lonely chair situated in a corner. If it weren't for the steel rails on the sides of his bed, and the needle taped into the bend of his arm, he might've been more confused. Sharp footsteps resonated down a hallway, where he heard voices chattering in a foreign tongue.

It occurred to him that his face and ears stung. His skin felt tight, as though it had shrunk two sizes while he slept. He lifted a hand, and dabbed his fingertips against cheeks and cracked lips. The moment Skyler walked into his room, looking a little flushed in the face, but beautiful as ever, it all came rushing back to him.

"Hey," Skyler said, sliding in for a quick hug, "I heard you were starting to come around, but I had to see it for myself. It's kind of hard getting straight answers around here when you don't speak Japanese."

"We're in Japan?"

"Nagasaki. This was the closest friendly hospital to Shanghai."

Collin rubbed at his tender face. "Was I really that bad?"

"It wasn't you," Skyler replied, her brow gathering. "It was Jill."

Collin sat up straight in his bed. He ran his fingers through his crazy hair, straining to recall any elusive details related to an injury that Jill might've sustained, but he couldn't remember anything, in that regard. "Is she okay?"

"She's going to be alright, but it was a close one. We almost lost her."

"I figured she'd be in Anchorage by now."

Skyler shook her head. "Anchorage got hit."

"Oh, no."

"Her family is safe, though. We just heard from Jill's mother. They're aboard a freighter full of refugees, bound for Vancouver."

"Good." Collin licked his chapped lips. "I mean, not for Anchorage, but I'm glad her family is safe."

"Yeah." Skyler sat down on the edge of his bed, and placed her hand on his knee. She stared down at the floor for a moment, as though carefully choosing the words that she was about to say.

Collin felt his heart sink. "What's the matter?"

"Listen, I've got some bad news, and I feel like I should be the one to have to tell you." She gazed into his eyes with the sort of softly pinched expression that people reserve for conversations about death. "It's about Hotspot."

Collin cleared his throat. "He's gone."

After a moment, Skyler nodded. "How much do you remember?"

"Everything."

"I'm sorry."

"Don't be. It wasn't your fault. It was mine."

Skyler frowned, adjusting her position on the edge of his bed.

"That dog recorded everything," Collin said. "Every word we ever said, every experiment we ever attempted, going all the way back to our beginnings, in Glasgow. That dog was more than just our inaugural host. He was also a living, breathing server. Everything auto-saved to his internal drive."

"But, why?" Skyler shook her head. "Why install a hard drive in a dog?"

Collin shrugged. He could feel his eyes getting moist. "Started out as kind of a joke, you know. We were still exploring, feeling out the boundaries of our science. We knew the dog was already going to be opened up on the operating table as our first test subject, so we decided to add a few extras during the surgery because, well, that's what geeks do." Collin leaned into his hands, and smeared the wetness from the corners of his eyes. "Obviously, our program continued to develop. Our store of information kept growing and growing. At some point, I realized that we couldn't risk our technology ever falling into the wrong hands. Hotspot was a potential leak source. So, I went back and programmed in a failsafe device." Collin could hardly bare to look at her. "Anyone but me ever tried to hack my dog, focused electromagnetic pulse, hard drive meltdown, instant cardiac arrest." Collin snapped his fingers. "Quick and painless."

Skyler covered her mouth.

"Yeah. I really did that." Collin raised his hand. "That was me."

Skyler shook her head. "I can't imagine how awful you must feel right now."

"Yeah. Well, better than the guy who tried to hack him. That's for sure. I made sure to add a little something special in there for him, too. Psychological torture running on a loop, powered by military-grade lithium that's good for, I don't know, probably twenty years."

Skyler closed her eyes, and appeared to rest for a moment, before opening them again. She took Collin's hand in her own. "I need to ask you something."

"Anything."

"That last fight between the Charybdis and the water bear ... that wasn't you who killed the big one. It couldn't have been you. Your helmet was off by then."

"I don't remember that, so no."

"I've already asked Jill and J.J. It wasn't either of them."

Collin guessed he could see where she was going with this train of thought. "Takashi's gone." He shook his head. "There's no way it was him. I saw them beating him into—"

"Hey-hey. It's okay. I just thought maybe ..."

"No. Not Takashi." Collin leveled his eyes with hers.

"Who, then? That's what I've been mulling over, the last few days."

"Is that how long I've been out?"

"I've been trying to eliminate all of the other possibilities, before I'd allow myself to believe that it was really him, and no, I'm not referring to Takashi."

"Who?"

"Carl."

"You mean, Carl the Charybdis? Behaving autonomously?" Skyler's eyes brightened.

"I'm not so sure that—"

"Hotspot knew. He knew that pirate was a bad guy. He sniffed out evil the very second it stepped in from of him. I don't think we give animals enough credit, you know? Especially a creature from another world that we know next to nothing about? If a dog can sense a threat and act selflessly, sacrificing itself for some greater good, then maybe a so-called 'monster' could do the same."

"Maybe so." Collin took Skyler's hand. "Maybe all along, we had one of the good ones on our side."

"That's what I'd like to believe."

Collin smiled. Her nutty love for those monsters was one of the things that he found most endearing about her. In a program like theirs, it was a pretty tall order to remain down-to-earth, but somehow, Skyler always managed to do so. "Me too," he replied.

Knuckles rapped against Collin's door. Before he had a chance to reply, Jill entered the room. She was seated in a wheelchair, and J.J. was driving. "Hey," Jill said.

"We need to get out of here," J.J. said, pushing the door closed behind him, "soon as you're able."

"Why? Where are we going?"

"Our separate ways. It's too dangerous to stay together, and we sure can't stay in Japan. Military presence is too high. People are going to come looking for us. Bad people."

"What about the team?" Skyler asked.

"There is no team. It's over. We've got no friends in the Allied Navy anymore. After what happened to Takashi—"

"Yeah, after what happened to Takashi," Collin said, interrupting J.J. "No one hated our military leash more than him. He was pushing to privateer our program from the get-go. Out of all of us, he was always the most in favor of severing ties to the

Allied Navy, going rogue, operating out of a hotel room, or the back of a van ... traveling light and fast all around the world to wherever the world needs us most. If Takashi were with us right now, he'd be so damned thrilled to be able to finally—"

"Yeah, well he's not here now, and I for one am tired of living my life according to what dead loved ones might've wanted me to do." J.J. drew a deep breath, and released it in a sigh. "My heart's just not in it anymore, guys. It's just not, and neither is hers." He dipped his head at Jill. "I've decided to see this thing through with her. Reunite her with her family in Vancouver. That's all I want on my radar right now."

"Fair enough," Collin replied, averting his eyes.

"Don't be that way," Jill said.

Collin stared out through his hospital room window at those monuments of mirrored glass. Fat clouds roamed across their sleek surfaces. "We were moving mountains, you guys."

J.J. attempted a smile, began to blink, and began backing Jill's wheelchair abruptly toward the door. "We've got a flight to catch."

"Love you guys," Jill said, lifting a weak hand, as J.J. wheeled her out of the room.

"Call us when you get there," Skyler said. "Send pics! I want to see that baby girl."

The door closed. The latch clicked. Just like that, they were gone.

Their lifetime effort that had spanned so many years, so many personal changes, suddenly seemed so small and pointless. For a moment, they were the most powerful people on the planet, sitting at the very top of the food chain, but once again, no one noticed. No one even knew that they were there.

"What now?" Skyler asked. "What about us?"

Collin searched her eyes. He guessed that he was hoping to see some sort of a sparkle in there, a glimmering hint that for the two of them, the adventure of a lifetime might not yet be over. Instead, he found himself staring into gulfs of infinite possibility, diverging and converging paths that writhed to the farthest reaches of the universe. Collin knew that if he plunged into that abyss of possibility, and explored those trails to their ends, he might eventually reach an absolute point of reckoning that would qualify every second of effort he'd spent pushing so hard in a single direction. As Skyler herself had pointed out had pointed out, whether or not a person had the courage to throw that curtain back was perhaps more important than whatever lay in store behind it.

"Well, there's just no way I can go back to waiting tables," Collin replied. "Do we have a functioning headset?"

"Theirs." Skyler smiled. "That makes two."

***

The patrolman raised his whistle. He cheeped a warning at the pair of refugees, and waved his arm back and forth in the air. It had taken nine days to quell the Jaw-long uprising, and to regain some measure of control over Shanghai's streets. The People's Liberation Army was sent in to support the overwhelmed security stations, but the presence of those regimented ranks only added to the surrealism in which their seaport was steeped. The Pearl of the Orient was yet unrecognizable as the city that it so recently had been. Even if you closed your eyes and plugged your ears, the stench of those titanic carcasses was always there, a reeking reminder that nothing was quite the same in Shanghai, and might not ever be. When the skulking duo refused to acknowledge his whistle, the patrolman racked the bolt of his rifle, and popped a couple of live rounds at their feet.

"Ribbons. Show them to me," he shouted.

The refugees froze. They lowered their satchels to the ground, and raised their bandaged hands. Enveloped in rags and blankets, much like everyone else crawling out of the wreckage, any affiliation they might have to the insurgency was obscured. Before boarding a barge to one of the camps upriver, every passenger had to be cleared. Keeping their heads in the sights of his rifle, the patrolmen clambered down the hillock of rubble. He ordered them to lift their shirts. They complied. They were not carrying any weapons.

"Where are you headed?"

The men glanced at one another, before the larger of the two finally replied. "University of Nantong," he said, in what was barely a whisper.

"Speak up!"

The man waved his hands in a strange but submissive gesture, and tapped his index finger over what appeared to be an injury to his throat. He shook his head back and forth, and croaked some unintelligible garble that prompted a fit of coughing. He appeared to be in a considerable amount of pain.

"You students?"

"No."

"Military?"

After a moment, the larger man shook his head.

"Those are Allied Navy bags." The patrolman jabbed the barrel of his rifle at the larger man's chin, which was just poking out from beneath his hood. "Where'd you get them?"

The refugee tipped his head seaward.

"What's that supposed to mean? You looters? You looting the base?"

"No."

"You Jaw-long?"

"No."

"Show some I.D."

The refugee's shoulders rose and fell. The patrolman sensed his mounting agitation. Here was a moment when a man in the wrong state of mind might decide to do something stupid, and the patrolman wasn't in the mood for any of that. The last nine days and nights had been long ones. He fired another burst of rounds right over their heads, causing both men to flinch and cover. "I.D., Now!"

Lifting his trembling fingers to the edges of his hood, the refugee peeled back his soiled headdress. Beneath, festering islands floated amidst oceanic swirls of melted flesh. Holes gaped behind his temples, where both of his ears had been burned away. He stood hairless and quavering in the humid air. "Please," he replied, revealing a flash of silver teeth. "My son and I, we've lost everything."

"That true?" The patrolman prodded the smaller man. "This guy your father?"

Lifting his chin, the smaller fellow revealed a face beaten beyond recognition. Blackened lips pursed around a few fragmented teeth. One eye was a tenantless cavity, while a faint glow through the swollen folds of the other suggested that the remaining eye was an artificial.

"What's in those bags?" The patrolman kicked one of the Allied Navy satchels with the toe of his boot. Something about the size and shape of a melon rocked back and forth.

"Just some food." The larger man slid an arm around his son's shoulders. "What little we could find."

The patrolman cleared his throat. It seemed obvious that these poor battered people posed no threat to anybody. "Alright. Go six blocks up this street to the river. Look for barges with white canvas tops. They'll take you up to Chongtai Bridge in Nantong. That's where you get off." The patrolman reached into his pocket, and produced a couple of red ribbons on strings that were issued by the Ministry of Public Security. "If you're approached by another patrolman, you show them these. Means you've already been searched and cleared. Understand?"

The larger man nodded. He eased the loop of fabric around his burned scalp, and situated the red ribbon against his chest. His young companion waited until he'd finished before following his example. Once both refugees were properly adorned with their passes, the larger man bowed respectfully, flashed the patrolman a silver smile, and gazed up at him through a pair of dragon green eyes. "Thank you," he said.

THE END

CHECK OUT OTHER GREAT
KAIJU NOVELS

KAIJU SPAWN
by David Robbins
& Eric S Brown

Wally didn't believe it was really the end of the world until he saw the Kaiju with his own eyes. The great beasts rose from the Earth's oceans, laying waste to civilization. Now Wally must fight his way across the Kaiju ravaged wasteland of modern day America in search of his daughter. He is the only hope she has left . . . and the clock is ticking.

From authors David Robbins (Endworld) and Eric S Brown (Kaiju Apocalypse), Kaiju Spawn is an action packed, horror tale of desperate determination and the battle to overcome impossible odds.

KUA MAU
by Mark Onspaugh

The Spider Islands. A mysterious ship has completed a treacherous journey to this hidden island chain. Their mission: to capture the legendary monster, Kua'Mau. Thinking they are successful, they sail back to the United States, where the terrifying creature will be displayed at a new luxury casino in Las Vegas. But the crew has made a horrible mistake - they did not trap Kua'Mau, they took her offspring. Now hot on their heels comes a living nightmare, a two hundred foot, one hundred ton tentacled horror, Kua'Mau, Kaiju Mother of Wrath, who will stop at nothing to safeguard her young. As she tears across California heading towards Vegas, she leaves a monumental body-count in her wake, and not even the U. S. military or private black ops can stop this city-crushing, havoc-wreaking monstrous mother of all Kaiju as she seeks her revenge.

CHECK OUT OTHER GREAT KAIJU NOVELS

ATOMIC REX
by Matthew Dennion

The war is over, humanity has lost, and the Kaiju rule the earth.

Three years have passed since the US government attempted to use giant mechs to fight off an incursion of kaiju. The eight most powerful kaiju have carved up North America into their respective territories and their mutant offspring also roam the continent. The remnants of humanity are gathered in a remote settlement with Steel Samurai, the last of the remaining mechs, as their only protection. The mech is piloted by Captain Chris Myers who realizes that humanity will not survive if they stay at the settlement. In order to preserve the human race, he leaves the settlement unprotected as he engages on a desperate plan to draw the eight kaiju into each other's territories. His hope is that the kaiju will destroy each other. Chris will encounter horrors including the amorphous Amebos, Tortiraus the Giant turtle , and the nuclear powered mutant dinosaur Atomic Rex!

KAIJU DEADFALL
by JE Gurley

Death from space. The first meteor landed in the Pacific Ocean near San Francisco, causing an earthquake and a tsunami. The second wiped out a small Indiana city. The third struck the deserts of Nevada. When gigantic monsters- Ishom, Girra, and Nusku- emerge from the impact craters, the world faces a threat unlike any it had ever known - Kaiju . NASA catastrophist Gate Rutherford and Special Ops Captain Aiden Walker must find a way to stop the creatures before they destroy every major city in America..

CHECK OUT OTHER GREAT
KAIJU NOVELS

MURDER WORLD | KAIJU DAWN
by Jason Cordova
& Eric S Brown

Captain Vincente Huerta and the crew of the Fancy have been hired to retrieve a valuable item from a downed research vessel at the edge of the enemy's space.
It was going to be an easy payday.
But what Captain Huerta and the men, women and alien under his command didn't know was that they were being sent to the most dangerous planet in the galaxy.
Something large, ancient and most assuredly evil resides on the planet of Gorgon IV. Something so terrifying that man could barely fathom it with his puny mind. Captain Huerta must use every trick in the book, and possibly write an entirely new one, if he wants to escape Murder World.

KAIJU ARMAGEDDON
by Eric S. Brown

The attacks began without warning. Civilian and Military vessels alike simply vanished upon the waves. Crypto-zoologist Jerry Bryson found himself swept up into the chaos as the world discovered that the legendary beasts known as Kaiju are very real. Armies of the great beasts arose from the oceans and burrowed their way free of the Earth to declare war upon mankind. Now Dr. Bryson may be the human race's last hope in stopping the Kaiju from bringing civilization to its knees.
This is not some far distant future. This is not some alien world. This is the Earth, here and now, as we know it today, faced with the greatest threat its ever known. The Kaiju Armageddon has begun.